Murder at Lac Sainte-Marine
A Muskoka Murder Mystery
Liz McGillicuddy

Northshore Noir Press

Northshore Noir Press
Toronto, Canada
www.northshorenoir.com

ISBN: 978-1-0688501-5-8
e-Book ISBN: 978-1-0688501-6-5

For more information visit: https://lizmcgillicuddy.com/

Also by Liz McGillicuddy

Murder at Sunny Lake

Contents

CHAPTER ONE

He was an ugly man everywhere but here. When he logged into La Guerre Infinitus, he was handsome, with a disarming smile that would appear suddenly when he was about to shoot someone. He would press the letters O and P on his keyboard to make the avatar smile while he walked up to the unsuspecting opponent to shoot him or her, usually her, in the head. With a light touch, the M16 would roar with a thunderous burst of rapid gunfire. Anything could happen. The head could splatter onto a nearby wall. Or the body could shimmy and shake before falling to the ground. Maybe, if the bullets hit just right, the character would collapse to their knees and beg for life.

La Guerre Infinitus was a fast-paced first-person game that featured virile avatars and vengeance. It allowed gamers to kill almost anything, including plants and birds. But there were characters who had blue eyes, and if you killed them, your character would die. You had to restart the level and if you did it five times your character died. His online name was Coeur de Lion and he would shout it out any time he shot.

He signed on with his username and password, and almost immediately, the insults flew. Don't these guys ever give it a rest? he wondered.

As Coeur de Lion, he was tall, muscular, and good-looking: the opposite of his real life. The twenty-year-old behind Coeur de Lion was the consummate loner. He had long ago given up his real life friends for his killer comrades online. The dark circles under his eyes seemed even darker in contrast to his pale skin. Like his avatar, his head would move and his mouth would open and close, but his eyes remained fixed, unblinking, empty.

In the game, he had over two hundred kills to his name. In the real world, he was just Perry Miller, just a shadow. No one noticed him, but there was no reason to. Nothing stood out. Not his ill-fitting jeans, not his scuffed up runners, not his Korean War era surplus army jacket. In the real world, he just tapped a keyboard to kill people or hurl insults at other gamers.

Miller lived in his parent's basement where he had privacy. Mostly. Sometimes his dad would come down to check his room for pornography. When Miller was fifteen, his dad found some porn. He beat Miller with a belt. He whipped his ass until it bled and shouted out biblical passages. Miller learned to only use online porn, and to lock his door every time he jerked off.

Once a month, his mom would come down and poke at his dirty laundry. She never washed it for him. She would simply berate him. If the pile got too big—Miller never knew exactly what 'too much' was—she would take his clothes out back and burn them.

But today was going to be different. Today, he had a plan, and he was ready to tell everyone. He was on the Leviticus level of La Guerre Infinitus. The new players all started in Genesis and were targets for everyone above them. That was part of the fun of the game.

Miller pressed a few buttons, strafing and shooting as Coeur de Lion. He went over to a wall and emptied his M16 into the concrete, making a swastika design out of the damage. A bullet flew in, just missing his head, and his character ran. 'You fight like a dairy farmer!' Miller screamed into the chat box. The insult did not go over well, and a hate raid ensued.

'u johnny sarlacc motherfucker' came the insult back.

'Filthy casual, yo momma a ho!' someone else screamed. A second opponent had joined the fray of insults and was shouting as loud as they could into their microphone.

'u a nigga nazi faggot' a third person shouted and shot Coeur de Lion in the head. His character was dead, and he would have to start again.

Miller's face contorted in a mix of fury and disbelief as Coeur de Lion's head splattered all over the swastika he had just created. His heart pounded in his chest, each beat resonating with a surge of hot anger that threatened to consume him. How could this happen? He had invested countless hours in to levelling up and mastering the game mechanics. Some bastard shot him, and all he could hear in his headphones was laughter.

He began sweating. The room seemed to shrink as his anger grew, his breathing becoming rapid and shallow. It felt as if a part of him had been torn away, an integral piece of his identity lost. If he shouted out, his parents would hear and berate him.

Miller's mind raced, replaying the moment of defeat over and over again. His character, once a symbol of his prowess and triumph, now lay headless against a grey concrete wall. The injustice of it all was unbearable. He had poured his heart and soul into this game, sacrificing precious time and sleep to reach the pinnacle of virtual glory. And now, it had been ripped away from him without warning.

In a fit of frustration, Miller bit his own hand to keep from screaming. He gnashed and crushed his flesh between his teeth until the pain forced him to open his mouth and release his hand. Blood flowed out from where his incisors had broken through the flesh. He wanted to cry. He wanted to scream. He wanted to scream and shout and kick and hit and piss all over everything. Instead, he shuffled to the washroom and tended to his self-inflicted injury.

He knew he was better than any of those guys, and this was the day everyone would know his name. Perry Miller would go down in history. He ripped up a dirty t-shirt, wrapped his hand, and went back to his bedroom.

It was an extremely hot July, and he had no air conditioning. He was already sweating, and a drop slipped from his cheek onto the cluttered floor. A trickle of sweat down his back made its way into the crack of his ass and he absentmindedly shoved his hand down his pants to scratch.

He looked in the mirror, admiring the rugged, macho look of the rag covering his wound. You are a raw animal, he told himself, an alpha male asserting God-given dominance. You have the power of the Lord with you.

He had taped pages from Revelations to the mirror. On them were finely written notations of the sins of the town. Grudge, grudge, bad attitude, sex desire, gossip. Miller traced his fingers along words, written and typed, paying no attention to them. He was a tightly coiled spring, ready to give way without warning.

Miller turned on his radio to Jonathan Haidt's afternoon show. The local preacher was broadcasting on CRST-FM, an all Christian station serving the Northshore region. He was a radical man with a powerful voice. Whenever he read from the Bible, Miller would stand at the mirror, speaking with him, imagining he was the preacher himself. Virile, masculine, handsome. He would imagine people before him kneeling in awe. It made him hard every time.

Miller was one of Haidt's followers. They called themselves Haidt's Heroes and would stand on street corners to preach and spread the Word. Except Miller never did that. He rarely left the basement. But he liked to think of himself as a hero.

Miller double-checked that the door to his room was locked. He locked it every time he masturbated, but he always checked, just in case. It was locked, and Haidt was on the radio. Miller stripped off his clothes, grabbed a sock off the floor, and stood in front of the mirror. He imagined being naked in Haidt's house as he continued to quote the Bible. Miller slipped the sock over his dick and rubbed, enjoying the friction and warmth it generated. His hand hurt, but it made his dick feel good. He replayed the death scene from La Guerre Infinitus while Haidt's voice filled the air. Imagining himself peeping through a crack in a door, he saw Haidt have sex with a woman. He fantasized himself being caught, being punished by the preacher, being spanked and fondled.

Miller grabbed a toy gun he had on his desk and looked at himself in the mirror. His dick was in his bandaged hand, the gun in the other. He grunted and came in the sock. He sang the lyrics of a death metal song quietly to himself and tossed the sock toward his pile of dirty laundry.

He stood in front of the mirror. He hated the orange tip on the fake gun, but he could not pull it off without breaking the whole thing. Miller held the gun down by his side, then practiced his fast-draw, pointing the gun at the mirror; from the waistband, from the side, from the front, from the back. Straight arm, arm bent at the waist; horizontal, vertical.

Pulling himself away from the mirror, he put on a white t-shirt and a dirty pair of pants. Sticking the gun in his waistband, the butt stood out menacingly in front of the white cotton t-shirt. With one last draw, he smiled. "Blam," he whispered, pretending the gun recoiled in his hand.

He headed upstairs. The toy gun got in the way, so he pulled it from his waistband and put it in his pocket. Miller looked at the clock. It was almost four in the afternoon, so he would have to be quiet or risk notifying his parents that he was finally up. He did not want to hear their recriminations.

He rummaged through the refrigerator and grabbed an opened package of microwavable bacon. The last eight pieces were wrapped in a paper towel and shoved into the microwave. It only took thirty seconds. He yanked the door open when the timer dinged. The smell of bacon filled the air.

He grabbed a couple of pieces of white bread from the bag, leaving his finger impressions in the loaf. Miller put the slices of crisp bacon on a slice, slathered it with ketchup, and squished the second slice on top. He ran his finger along the edges, scooping up the oozing ketchup and licking it up. He wrapped his food in a napkin and took one last look around.

The kitchen, weathered and worn, showed its age. Faded wallpaper peeled at the edges. Broken tiles exposed glimpses of the uneven floor beneath. The cabinets wore a layer of grime and chipped paint. Dim light flickered from the bulb, casting shadows on cracked countertops. He hated this place.

"I am going to change the world today," he said to himself with pride. He said that every single time he left his home, no matter how infrequently. He was always determined to do something, though he did not know what. And the problem was, nothing ever really came up. He never shot a criminal, there were never any drowning children to rescue, there were no bank robberies to foil. He had no chance to be a hero. There was only Jonathan Haidt. Every day for three hours, the preacher shouted about how terrible the world was. Civilization was ending. Immigrants, Jews, and queers—Haidt never used those words, but Miller knew what he meant—were destroying the world. God himself would bring His wrath and smite the sinners.

Sandwich in hand, Miller headed outside to his truck. He had bought it two weeks ago. The vehicle was close to thirty years old and did not run great, but it worked. It shimmied when he got over eighty kilometres an hour, but he did not need to go that fast. It was not like he was planning on running away from anything.

His mother watched out the window as Miller coaxed the truck engine to start and drove off. "What's he up to?" her husband asked as he stepped into the kitchen and looked over her shoulder.

"Oh, who the fuck knows," she said.

Miller turned on talk CRST radio. He sometimes preferred music, but Haidt was still talking. "As right-thinking men and women, we must support the preservation of the values and traditions that have made this Christian country great. As men, we must safeguard our faith, our children, our women and defend against threats to our morality. Sexually twisted people will be the ruin of this country," the host intoned.

"Preserve values, damn right!" Miller shouted.

"As patriotic Canadians by birth, we have a duty to keep our country clean and beautiful. Homosexual sin is a vile cancerous tumour in Northshore. Let's all do our part to protect our powerful people, our pure women, and innocent children, and maintain the natural God-fearing state of this glorious land."

Miller nodded and shouted in agreement at almost everything the radio host said. While driving, he ate his bacon sandwich and wished he had something to wash it down with.

Miller drove on, coldly staring down the highway. His hair was slicked back and his mirrored sunglasses sat nestled in the greasy mess. Sweat formed on his brow, and he wished he had had enough money to buy a truck with air conditioning.

He had no real plans, only a strong desire that today would be the day. He had the desire every day, and every day nothing would come of it. Today was different, though. Today, he actually made it outside the house.

Miller's face was pallid and drained of colour. He knew he should be happy, that this should be the best time of his life. But he was so unaccustomed to driving and even being outside that he felt terrified. He was frightened and giddy at the same time. Driving into town, a plan formed in his mind. He was driving northwest on Highway 2 when he made a sudden left turn on to 38th Town Line Road. He had to get to Kettering.

The roads twisted and turned, and to make it to the main highway, he had to drive south before heading north again. It would not take long. Miller did not live too far out of town, and despite not going out regularly, he knew its main roads. He knew where the bars and restaurants were. It took just fifteen minutes to get to Kettering, and another three to drive Franklin Street to Centre Street. Miller's entire body tingled, his eyes laser-focussed on his surroundings. He waited at the stop sign, waited for a sign.

Someone in a red Honda behind him honked. He glared into the rear-view mirror and gave the driver the finger. As his eyes swept the area, he saw it. He saw his future. A sidewalk sign read, 'Drag Show thrice nightly, 4:30, 7:30, 10:30 @ Sparkling Unicorn.' He pulled out his phone to check the time. It was 4:45p.m., the show would be on.

"Move! Look out!" a man shouted as he saw a truck barrelling down the sidewalk. The sidewalks were wide, meant for restaurant patios and slow-walking tourists, and they made a perfect roadway for Miller. Bam! He hit someone and sent him flying into traffic. Two more people scrambled out of his way, but he sped up toward a woman with her back turned. Bam! She flew against a building. Miller hit a garbage bin, sending it into a storefront, shattering the glass.

Miller laughed. This was perfect, he thought. Bam! He swiped another person. People were jumping out of his way. Cars were honking their warnings madly at pedestrians who did not know what was coming.

The Boys were sitting on the patio of the Sparkling Unicorn. Bob, Thomas, and Jens were enjoying the drag show through the open storefront of the bar. The trio had been friends for years, each having moved to Northshore as a young artist. They had been eager to set up their studios and galleries in a nearby section of highway known as Artists' Row. Parking lots connected all the galleries, so tourists and patrons could drive to many galleries without returning to the highway.

"What the fuck is this honking all about?" Thomas asked as he shook his head and plugged his ears. "Like, what the f—"

Miller hit the Sparkling Unicorn patio at full speed. Tables and chairs and people went flying. Thomas and Jens dove out of the way of the oncoming vehicle. He hit Bob. Bob, part of a table, and a large woman all ended up under his truck in one place or another. It shuddered to a halt.

"C'mon, c'mon!" Miller shouted at the truck as its wheels did not move. Something was stuck underneath his truck. He could no longer go forward, so he slammed the truck into reverse and hit the gas. Miller heard people screaming and metal grinding as he backed away and ended up on the road. Back in drive, Miller floored the truck, and it took off down the street.

A car from the opposite direction pulled into Miller's lane to block him. Instead, Miller again mounted the sidewalk. He hit four more pedestrians as he made his way to the corner. The engine roared and sputtered and smoked, and he decided it was time to flee.

He turned on to Red Road but could not resist the urge. Bearing down on people, Miller laughed and pressed the gas pedal to the floor. The truck could not go fast, but it was doing the damage he wanted to do. He steered left and right, aiming for people as they tried to scatter. Bam! "Ten points!" he shouted as he veered toward another person. He missed. Then he struck another, and another.

People were scattering. Miller hit another person and sent her tumbling in the street. People were shouting and falling and screaming and running and he revelled in the cacophony and chaos. Pedestrians were running into stores to get away from him. After a hard bounce against a wall, Miller veered onto the road again and headed out of town.

CHAPTER TWO

Detective Inspector Caitlin Murphy drove along Highway 520 toward Baker Road and the Hemmerson Cemetery in Port Hope. The sun was still high in the sky. It was a hot and sunny July day. It was late enough in the day that the usual Indigenous protesters were not blocking the road, leaving her a clear route. Murphy and the other detectives in the Homicide Unit were the only police officers invited to the burial ceremony for Cardinal Horn.

As she drove, she thought about Jose Mercado, the Sasquatch hunter whose trip into the forest yielded a femur bone. While bragging in a video call with his wife, he inadvertently drew the attention of Cornelius Price. Price overheard the story and knew his secret—the murder of his foster child Cardinal Horn fifty years ago—would be discovered if he did not act.

Price almost got away with murdering Mercado to cover up the murder of Horn. But Murphy and her team had methodically tracked down all the leads. She had so much evidence, Price had no choice but to confess.

The Tiny Flowers Reservation, where Horn was born, was long ago appropriated by the government, its people scattered across the province. Murphy had been in touch with the Indigenous Association of Central Ontario, who agreed to arrange for the burial of the girl's skeletal remains.

Murphy pulled up to the open entrance of the Hemmerson Cemetery and lowered her window. An Indigenous man in ceremonial dress was standing at the entrance with a clipboard in his hand. "Se:ko. Name please," he said as he walked up to Murphy's Trurock Brawler.

"Detective Inspector Caitlin Murphy, Northshore Municipal Police Department," she said.

He checked the list, nodded and crossed off her name. "I ask you to park just here," he said, pointing to open space at the side of the road. "And we ask that you and your colleagues stay outside the marked circle."

Murphy nodded and parked her Brawler in the grass. The gravel road served as the only way in and out of the cemetery. There were cars and vans parked further up in the small parking lot. They invited five dozen people to attend Horn's funeral, plus the four detectives.

Murphy sat inside her 4x4 while she waited for her team to arrive, and one by one, they did. Detective Staff Sergeant Adam Girard brought Detective Constable Michael Parker in his car. Detective Constable Cleo Hamilton arrived on her motorcycle. They were all similarly instructed to park at the side. They were told not to step past the marked area.

The team walked together up the road toward the cordoned off area, chatting softly amongst themselves. They stood respectfully at the edge.

The sun was high over Hemmerson Cemetery, and the invited Cree, Metis, Iroquois, Mohawk, and Algonquin peoples were ready. Chief Arthur Benoit from the nearby Chance River Indian Reserve was the appointed elder who led the others. The only person from the Tiny Flowers Reservation was Margaret Whitetail, one of the few living survivors and the only one able to make the trip.

The air was crisp with the scent of pine needles and rising summer heat. Chief Benoit chanted prayers in a soft, low voice. His voice was soon joined by Margaret's, and then others. People lit sage, sweetgrass, and cedar to purify the area. Whitetail stood clutching a bundle made of deer leather. Inside was an azurite stone, a hawk feather and, of course, a cardinal feather.

Cardinal's bones were arranged in a small white birch bark bundle and bound by thin strips of moose hide. They sat, waiting on a bed of fresh pine boughs. The attendees took turns saying their last goodbyes to Horn, placing gifts and traditional objects on her remains as a sign of respect and honour. Whitetail was the last to lay her bundle with the girl.

The men gently gathered Horn's remains and placed them, boughs and all, in a small grave they had previously dug. Chief Benoit made an offering by placing tobacco over the container. The women began to chant and sing, the sound of their voices accompanied by the gentle rustling of the leaves in the trees and the distant chatter of birds.

Chief Benoit placed the first hand-full of soil back into the hole. Others took their turns covering Cardinal with soil and fallen leaves. The elders continued to chant prayers, asking for the ancestors to guide the girl's spirit to the afterlife. They planned the ceremony to last another hour.

Murphy felt her impatience growing. She had a lot to do. The interviews for the Family and Community Liaison position were scheduled for Monday. The entire process had taken almost a month, and she was getting fed up with the delays. She knew she was part of the problem: she had not yet provided her interview questions.

As she was musing, she felt her business phone buzz. Murphy reached into her blazer pocket and pulled the phone out. At almost the same time, Hamilton reached for her phone. Then Parker and Girard.

NSPD EMERGENCY: Kettering. White older model Trurock 480 truck involved in criminal incident, driver fled the scene. Last seen heading northwest on Route 3. Multiple injuries reported.

Each of the detectives looked at each other, looked around, and then back at each other. The scene was fifty kilometres south of the cemetery and the driver was heading northwest, in their general direction. The municipality of Northshore covered over seven thousand square kilometres. With only 195 sworn members of the Northshore Municipal Police Department, the detectives knew they might be asked to assist. The message was from NSPD EMERGENCY, which meant it was sent to law enforcement only and was not common knowledge.

Murphy's phone buzzed again.

NSPD EMERGENCY: White older model truck, Trurock 480, involved in a criminal attack. Driver heading north on Highway 11, last seen near Preston. Multiple injured. 1 confirmed dead. Police and first responders en route.

The driver was now likely to pass the cemetery if he stayed on the highway. Murphy did not know if there were any other available officers, and decided to leave the ceremony.

"Cleo, you stay here. Your motorcycle makes you too vulnerable," Murphy whispered in Hamilton's ear.

"Boss, I—"

"No protest. We need a representative here, you're it," Murphy said. She motioned to Parker and Girard, and the trio headed to the parking lot. Parker had arrived with Girard and so got in his car with him. Murphy got into her Brawler and it roared to life. This beast of a 4x4 would stop the truck cold. Murphy slammed her phone into the dashboard holder and activated the speech feature.

"LouLou, call 911," she asked her device. The phone rang and rang. Murphy barrelled down the dirt road toward the highway, Girard and Parker following closely behind. Finally, the emergency operator answered.

"This is DI Murphy, badge 2231. Two unmarked vehicles in pursuit of Kettering truck. Heading south on Highway 11 from Port Hope to intercept the suspect vehicle."

"Copy that," dispatch responded. "Attention all units, two unmarked vehicles en route south to intercept from Port Hope. DI Murphy, stay on the line and report progress."

"Copy that," Murphy said. It was her personal vehicle and had no lights or sirens. She could do nothing but lay on the horn and navigate past other drivers using both the shoulder and the opposite lane. Girard's car was falling behind. He could not safely navigate the rough road shoulder. He had to slow down and speed up each time a car got in the way.

The Brawler growled as Murphy stepped on the gas. She was speeding up: sixty, seventy, eighty. Within seconds, she was at one hundred kilometres an hour and closing in on her quarry. Highway 11 was a well-used two-lane highway, and drivers in front of Murphy frustrated her. The posted speed on this stretch was sixty, a few drivers were speeding at eighty, but one saw Murphy's Brawler and sped up to one hundred to interfere.

The driver zigzagged in his lane to stop her from passing. She became furious and gave the license plate number and vehicle description to dispatch to press criminal charges against the driver. She might not get him on obstruction—the driver could claim he did not know she was law enforcement—but she could get him for speeding. Murphy pulled up close to him, horn blasting, and slipped around him on the gravel shoulder as he stepped on his brakes to brake-check her. She flew past and cursed at him as her speed went up and up.

Perry Miller looked in the rear-view mirror and saw no police vehicles in pursuit. His hands were shaking, and he was having trouble focussing. He ripped his eyes away from the rearview mirror. A vehicle was heading toward him on his side of the road. He had never seen a 4x4 like that, and whoever was driving was aiming for him. When he swerved, it swerved.

While driving directly at the truck, Murphy prayed she would survive. She had recently seen an online video of a police officer driving head-on to stop a drunk driver heading toward a parade. It was possible to survive, she thought.

"Murphy to dispatch. I am heading south toward the white truck heading north on Highway 11. No other vehicles within two hundred metres. Will physically intercept north of Wiseman Village," she said.

"Copy that. Physical interception. All units be advised suspect is heading north on Highway 11, Wiseman Village. DI Murphy, please be advised officers are on their way."

Murphy saw the truck ahead of her shimmy slightly. She glanced quickly at her speed. She had slowed to eighty. In the rearview mirror, she saw Girard's car slow down and stop across both lanes. He was blocking traffic from the north.

Seventy, sixty, fifty, forty. Murphy was confident her Brawler's safety features would keep her safe if she hit the truck at a slower speed. She needed to stop him, not kill him. Thirty, twenty. She estimated she would collide with the truck in fifteen seconds. Her heart was pounding loudly and her hands tingled.

Miller was frustrated that his truck was slow. He slammed his hands on the steering wheel. "Sixty fucking kilometres an hour! Fuck me!" On either side of the highway was a ditch and beyond that, fenced-in farmland. He knew it must be an unmarked police vehicle that was in front of him. He slowed down. Fifty. Forty. Thirty. Twenty. He glanced quickly at the toy gun on the passenger seat and decided this was the time.

Miller jammed on the brakes and swerved. Murphy swerved. He sideswiped past the Brawler. She barely felt it, but he lost control. His truck spun to the left, and he instinctively yanked the steering wheel to the right. Murphy watched as the truck veered left, then right, and off the highway. She slammed on her brakes and threw the 4x4 into reverse.

The truck drove off the road, over the ditch and carried on into a wooden fence post. It continued through wire fencing and into a field of soybeans. The truck bounced and skidded, finally slowing and then stopping. Miller sat dazed and panting.

Murphy quickly caught up and parked on the side of the road. "Suspect has stopped in a field, repeat suspect has stopped in a field. On foot pursuit," she yelled to dispatch. She grabbed a Vehicle Emergency Exit tool from the centre console and scrambled out of the Brawler. She ran across the ditch and toward the truck. The smell of gasoline was in the air, and Murphy knew the fuel tank had ruptured. She eyed the driver as he reached over to the passenger seat.

Murphy raised her right hand to her shoulder holster as she ran, never taking her eyes off him. She was breathless, laser-focussed, and tight. She might vomit. Now, just a few metres away, the driver aimed his gun at her. Murphy stopped. She withdrew her firearm in an effortless motion and brought her left hand up to steady her weapon. She saw his gun and a flash of orange. A toy? "Police! Police! Drop your weapon!" she shouted. Her eyes never left the gun in the driver's hand. There was always a chance it was not a toy. "Drop it! Drop your weapon!" she shouted.

Miller aimed his gun unevenly at Murphy. His face had hit the steering wheel when he went off the road. His nose broke and his vision was blurred. He was dazed, and his mind went blank. She was a cop. She should shoot him. He relaxed his arm, then pointed the gun at her again.

"Drop it! Drop the gun! Police!" she shouted at him. That was a toy, right? Murphy's heart was pounding. Her hands were clammy. What game was he playing at? She did not want to shoot him. If nothing else, it meant paperwork, interviews and sitting at a desk for months waiting to be cleared.

He lowered and raised the gun a few more times, but all she did was stand there shouting at him. Miller looked helplessly at Murphy. "Shoot me!" he shouted at her. He waggled the gun in the air. "For fuck's sake, shoot me!" He raised the gun to the side of his head. "Pew pew!" he said with a weak laugh. "Oh God, please, shoot me. I can't survive this. That's not how it's supposed to work."

Murphy stepped warily up to the truck. The driver was crying. He aimed his gun at her, but she could now clearly see that it was a toy. "Pew!" he bawled.

Murphy yanked open the driver's side door. "Get out! Get out of the truck!" Miller dropped the gun onto the floor and leaned forward, sobbing. Murphy quickly holstered her gun and grabbed her handcuffs and the VEE tool out of her pocket. With her left hand, she cut the seatbelt while simultaneously yanking the driver out of the truck with her right hand. His head hit the door on his way out, and he was thrown to the ground. She could see the toy gun on the floor of the truck.

"Ouch, this hurts," he whined.

Murphy dropped, with one knee on his neck and another on his arm. He provided no resistance, and she quickly cuffed him. Her heart was still pounding as she leaned heavily on his head. "You're hurting me," he mumbled. Murphy looked. She was forcing his face into the soggy ground. Sliding her knee across his face, she let it slip to the ground, allowing the suspect to breathe easier. She kept a tight grip on his hands and her weight on his back to keep him in place. She gave him a cursory search for a gun, knife, or other weapon, and found nothing.

"You are under arrest for assault with a weapon. You have the right to contact a lawyer without delay. You also have the right to apply for legal assistance through the provincial legal aid program. Do you understand?"

"Yeah," Miller said sullenly.

"You don't need to say anything. You have no hope of favours whether or not you say anything. Anything you do or say may be used as evidence. Do you understand?" Miller grunted. "Please respond yes or no. Do you understand?"

"Yes, fuck!" Miller said.

Murphy's eyes quickly darted around. She had left her phone in the Brawler. She had two choices. Stand the suspect up and head him to the Brawler, or keep him lying in the dirt until help arrived. She strained to hear sirens. They were hard to hear over her own roaring bloodstream and the blasting talk radio programme coming from the truck. She opted to stand him up.

"Okay, I'm going to stand you up. Here," she said as she grabbed the shirt collar. She eased herself off his back and shimmied around to the side. "Bend your knees," she said as she pulled on his shirt. She grabbed his arm and said, "Feet underneath. That's right, now push with your legs. Stand up." With one hand on his hands and another under his arm, Murphy helped him to his feet. She then quickly pushed him against the hood of the truck.

Murphy could still smell gasoline and decided it was best to move the suspect to her vehicle. "Let's go, this way," she said as she swung him around. In the distance, she saw the flashing lights of the arriving cruisers. Keeping hold of him, she headed toward the road. When they got to the ditch, Miller stumbled and fell to his knees. Murphy tumbled with him, her hand slipping off his shoulder and slamming against a rock. A pain shot up her arm. "Fuck, dude, stand up!" she shouted as she stood up. He staggered to his feet. She guided him to her Brawler and leaned him against the door.

"Dispatch, it's DI Murphy. Can you hear me?" she shouted into the window.

"Dispatch response, yes. DI Murphy, what is your status?"

"Suspect in custody. What's the ETA?" Before she could finish her sentence, she heard the wailing sirens coming from the south.

"NSPD responding to provide assistance, estimate one minute," the voice on the phone said. "All units be advised, suspect in custody."

"Loud and clear," Murphy responded.

"You were supposed to shoot me," Miller croaked.

Murphy pressed him harder against the hood. "I'll write that down in my diary, you little shit."

Two NSPD cruisers screeched to a halt, and the drivers scrambled out, guns drawn.

"DI Murphy, Northshore Municipal Police Department. Suspect under control," she said. They looked around quickly and holstered their guns.

Miller whined about his face. "I need a doctor," he said.

"Ma'am, I am Officer Gardener, this is Officer Hastings," he said.

"Officer Gardener, search the suspect. Give me his ID," she said. Once Hastings had control of Miller, Gardener searched Miller and handed over his wallet to Murphy.

She pulled out the driver's license and held it up, comparing the faces. "What's your name?"

"Go fuck yourself."

Officer Hastings jerked Miller hard and slammed him against the hood of the cruiser. He leaned into him, pressing his entire weight against the suspect. "Watch your mouth," he growled.

"Watch me stick my dick in it," Miller said. A kidney punch reminded him he was not playing his game anymore. He had to be careful in real life.

"Perry Lucas Miller, you are under arrest." Murphy said.

CHAPTER THREE

"Detective Inspector, are you alright?" Hastings asked, nodding his head toward her left hand. It was bloodied, and Murphy thought her wrist was broken.

"Fuck," she said as she let out a big breath of air. "Yeah, I am alright." Murphy retrieved her phone. She ended the call with dispatch as Girard and Parker pulled up.

"Officer Gardener, will you put the suspect in your cruiser please? Hold him here until I can figure out what's next."

Murphy considered her next steps. She called Suzan, the administrative assistant on the second floor at headquarters. Every Monday, Girard would bring in oat brittle handmade by his wife, Ruby. It was intended as a gift for Murphy, but she always had him put it on Suzan's desk. It would disappear within the hour and made Suzan popular. She should be willing to help.

"Suzan, it's DI Caitlin Murphy. Can I get your help? I need to transport an injured suspect to Uniondale's Medical Wing. Can you call and tell them to expect him? I need a full medical and psych eval, plus toxicology and alcohol tests. Can you arrange this for me, please?"

Suzan took all the required information and agreed to liaise with Uniondale Federal Penitentiary. Their secure medical wing would check Miller for any injuries or medical conditions and hold him until Murphy was ready for him. "I will also notify the Special Investigations Unit of the incident and injury," she said, and ended the call.

Murphy briefly recounted the capture for Girard and Parker and told them Miller's name, age, and address. "Michael, can you call the garage for a tow truck for the suspect vehicle? And collect the toy gun on the floorboard driver's side. I haven't searched the vehicle. Take a quick look, make sure it's secure. Only what is visible in plain sight. And catalogue this." She handed over the wallet.

"Yes boss," he said. He headed toward the truck.

"Watch your step!" Murphy shouted after him as he nimbly leapt over the ditch.

"Boss, you're bleeding," Girard said as he reached toward Murphy's hand.

"I fell in the ditch." Opening the passenger door of her Brawler, she reached in, flipped up the back seat, and unlocked the security box underneath. Blood dripped onto the floor. She grabbed the first aid kit and searched for something that could act as a splint for her wrist. She grabbed a wrench and slammed the lid down. With a quick twist of her good hand, she locked the security box and flipped the seat down.

"Adam, get Gardener to turn his cruiser's camera on. Read dickhead his rights, tell him he's going to Uniondale for medical attention as requested," she said.

Girard asked Officer Gardner to turn on his car cam, then opened the rear door and stuck his head in. With the cameras taping, he read Miller his rights and told him they would film him the entire trip to Uniondale. He advised that Officer Gardner would not ask him questions, but if he talked, anything he said could be used as evidence. Girard shut the door as Hamilton arrived.

"Boss, you okay?" she asked as she dismounted her motorcycle and took off her helmet.

"Broken I think. A quick hand, yeah?" she said as she handed Hamilton the first aid kit. "Ha ha, quick hand. I make myself laugh sometimes." She sat sideways on the back seat of her Brawler, facing outward, as Hamilton opened the kit and fished through it. "Wrap my arm in that towel. Use the wrench to stabilize my wrist," Murphy said.

Hamilton nodded. She wrapped Murphy's arm in the small towel from the kit and grabbed the rusty wrench Murphy had thrown on the ground. Hamilton carefully placed it under Murphy's forearm to support the wrist. She wrapped it in place with gauze, then squeezed the centre of an instant cold pack until she heard a snap. Hamilton massaged the pack and, when it felt cold, placed it gingerly on the top of Murphy's arm.

Hamilton finished wrapping Murphy's forearm and hand in gauze and secured it with tape.

"How's that, boss?" she asked.

"Hurts like hell. Thanks," Murphy replied with a smile. "What's the update on the scene?" Murphy could hear the grinding engine of a heavy wheel-lift tow truck as it arrived.

"Boss, it's a nightmare. Seems he drove down a few streets, hitting pedestrians. Lots of damage. At least seven injured; four serious and three critical. One dead. Paramedics, fire and law enforcement on scene. It's chaos, but they're getting it under control." Hamilton knew Murphy well enough to know that if it was not under control, she would want to go to the scene to help.

"One dead, okay. What are you all doing?"

"I've checked with the Forensic Unit. Dr. Chen said it was all hands on deck. What the hell was this guy doing?" Girard asked as he joined Murphy and Hamilton.

"I don't know," Murphy said. "The vehicle went off the road. He is heading to Uniondale Medical Wing. He seems alright to me."

"This guy kills someone with his truck and he is the one who is alright," Girard said with disgust.

"Tell me about it. The SIU will look into it since there was an injury to the skull. Miller's nose was bleeding. Okay, Adam, you go with the uniforms to Uniondale, get him booked and to the doctor. Suzan called ahead. Michael?" she asked as he joined them, toy gun in hand.

"Just this boss. I saw nothing else."

"Okay, travel with the truck back to the garage. Cleo, can—"

"I can come to the hospital with you," she said.

"No, I can get there. It's just a small thing. Summary: I arrested a man named Perry Miller on suspicion of vehicular assault. Driver's license says he lives at 17 White Pine Cone Road, Harrisburg. I think that is just outside Northshore municipal lines. Who wants to liaise with the OPP?" When no one responded, she assigned Parker.

"Michael, call and tell them we will execute a search warrant in their jurisdiction. Adam, prepare ITOs and get search warrants for his home and truck to begin with. Before we go, I want to know about this guy. Cleo, find out who he is. Get his socials, any previous arrests, all the vehicles he owns, all the properties, everything you can as quickly as you can. Let Adam know if you find any other property or vehicles that he has. Adam, include that in the search warrants."

"Yes, boss," Girard said.

"Okay, Michael, Cleo, when you are done here, I want you to head to the office, process information. Once Adam... no, Michael, you do it. You get the warrant for the truck. Once you have it, you head over to the garage and hover until they check it. Cleo, that leaves you to concentrate on creating the initial case file. Get his financials and phone too. Try to sweet talk the companies, but if that fails, you get the production orders. I will call once I get my arm looked at, and we will head to the scene. Are we good?"

"We are," Girard said as he looked at Parker and Hamilton. "Are you?" he said to Murphy.

"Yeah, I just need a splint or something. I am going to head to the hospital and get it looked at. Probably change clothes since I ended up in a freaking ditch. Everyone keep each other updated."

Murphy grabbed her phone out of her 4x4 and dialled the Chief of Police. "It's DI Murphy sir. I have a suspect under arrest." She told Chief Valencia about how the arrest went down. "He'll be going to Uniondale for medical attention since he crashed his truck."

"Excellent work DI Murphy. This is a mess. I am going to oversee the case directly. Superintendent Shevchenko is coordinating the teams and the Forensic Unit. Email him the details directly, suspect name, address. He will get search warrants and arrange for execution."

Murphy was taken aback. The Chief had never taken over a case and while she knew this was big, she disliked the idea of Shevchenko's involvement, too. "Yes sir, I'll have my team get in touch with the Superintendent," she said and hung up. "Cleo, guys, come here," she said, motioning her team over to the Brawler.

"The Chief is taking over the investigation and bringing in his own teams. We're part of it, but only part. We are not leading the investigation. Supt. Shevchenko will work under Valencia. Oh c'mon guys, no grim faces, we still have a job to do. It just isn't the way we are used to doing it. Adam, you liaise with Supt. Shevchenko. Let him get all the warrants, decide who goes where. Both of you work on building a case file, but stick to the office until either Shevchenko or I say otherwise. What a shitstorm."

Thirty minutes after she left the scene, Murphy was parking her Brawler at the Kettering Hospital. Her hand was throbbing. She had blood on her shirt and pants and it was splattered around the driver's side area. Murphy struggled to extend her hand to reach out of the window and get the parking ticket. She finally grabbed it and tucked it into the dashboard. The flat fee was thirty dollars, whether you were there for an hour or the day. Highway robbery, she thought to herself.

She parked and trotted over to the emergency bay. Inside, the chaos was palpable. This was where all the people injured in the attack sat with others who needed medical help. More than a dozen people sat in chairs that were separated by half-height plexiglass partitions. It was an upgrade implemented after COVID had struck. The chairs were all occupied, so other people leaned against walls, waiting for their turn. Everyone had been triaged and given a number. Just like an old butcher shop, Murphy thought as she headed over to the registration desk.

She wondered if she could jump the queue: she had a lot to do. Numbers were called out by ER staff and people discussed issues with nurses through shatter-proof glass. Police wearing NSPD uniforms accompanied a man with a head injury, an elderly person with an arm injury, and a young woman with a leg wound who appeared terrified. These were the minor injuries that could wait.

"Did y'all register yet?" a woman asked. Murphy turned to see a Black nurse looking at her. She spoke with a warm, charming accent.

"Where are you from?" Murphy asked.

"Georgia, why?"

"I meant, are you from the Registration Desk?" Murphy said. She smiled, and the woman gave a bright smile back. Was she flirting? "I haven't registered yet. Detective Inspector Caitlin Murphy." She fished out her OHIP card, flashing the badge on her hip and the gun in her shoulder holster.

"Y'all come this way," she said as she headed towards the treatment area. Quickly scanning her employee badge, she opened the glass doors that separated the emergency room from the rest of the hospital. "That is some Hollywood movie scene right there with all you police," she said, joking about the emergency room waiting area. "Are you part of the truck accident?"

"Not an accident," Murphy said darkly.

"Mmm," was all the nurse said. She led Murphy down the hall quickly. In the treatment rooms, the scene was even more chaotic. Patients were shouting and crying out in pain, begging for doctors or drugs. "Here," she said as she pulled back the curtains to a small area. The room comprised curtains for walls, a bed, and a smattering of equipment.

Murphy's cell phone rang, and she apologized to the nurse for taking it. "No worries," she said. "I have to enter y'all into the system, anyway."

"Thanks. Uh, what's your name?"

"Jasmine. Nurse practitioner. I'll enter you in, y'all sit down," she said as she stepped to a computer and began typing.

Murphy spoke with Shevchenko and provided as quiet an update as she could. She told the Superintendent she was in a public area of the hospital waiting for treatment, and that she would be back at the office as soon as she could. They chatted a few more minutes. She directed him to Girard and hung up.

"Now then," Jasmine said to Murphy, "what about y'all?"

"What about me?"

Jasmine cocked her head and smiled slightly. She waited a few seconds before responding, "Y'all are wearing a dirty wrench."

"Oh, yes!" Murphy laughed. "Hurt my hand apprehending the suspect. I think it's broken. But I have an ice pack on it."

Jasmine cocked her head the other way. "How long has the ice pack been on? A long while? Sit." She gestured toward the bed, but Murphy did not move. Jasmine cleared her throat and gestured toward the bed again. Murphy sat on the corner of the bed while Jasmine rolled a small table to her. "Put your arm down on the table. On a scale of one to ten, what's your pain level?"

"Four or five. Maybe six," Murphy said.

"Tell me exactly what happened," Jasmine said as she cut the gauze off Murphy's arm.

"I had hold of my suspect and he slipped in a ditch. We both fell, and I put my hand out. Hit a rock or something."

Jasmine nodded as she slowly lifted the cool ice pack from Murphy's wrist. The area was heavily bruised, and there was a round, shallow puncture in her palm. She put pressure on the open wound to stem the bleeding, careful not to hurt the wrist. "Mmm, maybe fractured," she said as she slipped the rusty wrench from under Murphy's hand. "You had nothing cleaner to stabilize the joint?" she asked.

"Not really. I don't carry splints around in my Brawler."

"A Brawler? What's that?" Jasmine asked.

"It's a really big 4x4," Murphy said.

"So, is it big enough to store some splints?" Jasmine asked as she cleaned Murphy's hand. Murphy liked Jasmine's sarcastic humour.

"Yeah, I—" Murphy stopped speaking when she saw a figure in the hall. It was Ellen Longboat. Ellen was a local Mohawk activist who had cut her chops during the Oka Crisis and was now living in Northshore. She was a well-known and respected figure. She stood at road blockades, attended crime scenes to provide elder support for families, and was an all-around intimidating woman. Ellen hated Murphy.

"Detective."

"Ellen."

Ellen walked into the room and watched as Jasmine tended to Murphy's wrist. "You have him?" she asked.

"This is going to feel cool," Jasmine said, carefully squirting saline solution from a bottle onto the open cut. She cleaned it and put gauze on it.

"There are no outstanding suspects," Murphy said.

"Why did he do this?" Ellen asked. Murphy saw Jasmine raise an eyebrow, but she kept her head down, focussing on her work.

"I have not interviewed him."

"Detective," Ellen said as she stepped closer. "The community is terrified and they want answers."

"I don't think it's been two hours. We have no answers. How did you get back here? Were you injured?"

Ellen smiled. "I lied to the nurse, said my nephew Charlie was back here. He is always getting into some kind of shit. Where is the guy who did it?"

Jasmine stood up. "You keep pressure on this," she said to Murphy, gesturing at the hand. "You, out you go. Out, now, please." Her formidable size took Ellen aback for a moment, but she stood her ground. "Into the waiting room. You have no business back here. It's too busy, you are in the way. Out now, go. Please." Ellen reluctantly nodded and left the room. Jasmine watched as she headed through the doors into the emergency room. "She a friend of y'all's?"

"Oh, no, absolutely not. Nice enough person, but definitely not my friend," Murphy said. Murphy's phone rang again.

"You go ahead and answer. I am getting the portable x-ray machine for your wrist. Keep the pressure on the gauze," Jasmine said. She pulled the curtain across and walked away.

Murphy curled her fingers into her palm as best she could and answered the ringing phone. The call was from Parker. He was at the office. "Boss, we have the name of the deceased. Kitty Meyers, she was fifty-seven years old. She's with Dr. Chen now. And you should know, there is a crowd gathering outside HQ. Nobody is really doing anything. They are just standing around, but security is thinking of shutting down the parking lot," he said.

Murphy sighed. Nothing like this had ever happened in Northshore, and people did not know how to react. It did not surprise her that people would head to the police headquarters for information, to feel secure.

Murphy had experienced terroristic attacks before, but this still unnerved her. She grew up in Ireland, coming to Canada with her family when she was a teenager. During The Troubles, she had seen sectarian violence up close and had lost a childhood friend and an uncle to the fighting.

"Here we go," Jasmine said as she yanked back the curtain. She wheeled in a large x-ray machine and positioned it near the bed.

"Michael, I have to go. Thanks for the update," she said as she hung up.

"I didn't know nurses could do x-rays," Murphy said.

"Well, I'm a nurse practitioner. I can do most anything except surgery," Jasmine said with a smile. She grabbed one of the lead vests that was hanging on the back of the machine and slipped it over her head. She strapped the sides and reached for the second vest. "You get one t—Don't move your hand! Just leave it there. I will put this on you. Don't move."

Obediently, Murphy sat still as Jasmine slipped the vest over her head and secured it around her body. She moved the machine right up to the bed and gingerly put Murphy's left arm on to the metal plate. "Any chance y'all could be pregnant?"

Murphy scoffed. "No, no way."

"Okay, Caitlin, sit still." Jasmine pulled the screen down and tapped a few buttons. Red lasers shone down onto Murphy's arm, and Jasmine adjusted the plate to match the grid. "Don't move for thirty seconds." Jasmine stepped behind the machine and pressed a button. The x-ray buzzed for a few seconds and shut off. "I lied," Jasmine said. "It doesn't take thirty seconds." She smiled warmly at Murphy. "Now, just sit here. The x-ray will be ready in a few minutes."

Jasmine removed and stored the vests and rolled the machine back to its storage spot. Murphy was alone for a moment for what felt like the first time all day. No people, no ringing telephone, no insistent text pings. She listened to the hush of people in the hallway. Murphy thought she heard Ellen's voice again, far away yet distinct. She was suddenly exhausted, and she closed her eyes for a moment.

"Hey," Jasmine whispered. Murphy opened her eyes and smiled. "How y'all doing? How's your pain level now?" Jasmine wheeled in a cart and pulled the curtain.

"Six, seven."

"Okay. Well, you have a distal radius fracture. It won't require surgery, but you will need a cast for four to six weeks."

"How long does it take to get a cast? I really have to get going," Murphy said.

Jasmine laughed. "Typical cop. My daddy was a street cop down in Atlanta. He broke his foot one morning and worked the whole day through, didn't tell nobody. The cast will take twenty minutes. Thirty if you fuss. Sit still. Your shirt is tight on the arms. I'm going to roll—No! Don't move y'all's arm! I said I will do it. Let me be the one to move you."

Murphy nodded and tried to follow directions. She was not good at letting other people control her. Jasmine pulled over a cart of supplies and gently rolled the shirt up Murphy's arm. Murphy shivered slightly. That felt oddly sexy, Murphy thought to herself.

She watched Jasmine's eyes as she worked. Jasmine made sure Murphy understood why she was getting a cast and how to care for her arm and hand. She removed the gauze from the open wound, replaced it, and placed a stockinette on Murphy's arm. She wrapped the wrist in layer upon layer of padding and casting material. Water trickled down her arm and a couple of drops fell onto Murphy's pant leg.

"I'd say sorry about the water, but I think your pants have their own thing going on." Murphy looked down at her pants. She was soaked in ditch water and her pants were covered in blood, dirt, and leaves. She also realized her white shirt was covered in brown water stains and blood drops.

Jasmine ran her palms back and forth to smooth out the cast. Murphy really wanted to make a joke about getting a hand job, but she stayed silent. "Sit still for fifteen minutes. Don't move the wrist," she said as she inspected her work. "Y'all okay Caitlin?" Murphy nodded. She laid a linen-saver pad on Murphy to catch any part of the plaster that might leak. Murphy clenched a little at the sight of the nurse's hands on her lap.

Twenty minutes later, Jasmine walked back into Murphy's room. "Okay, time for y'all to go," she said in a cheerful voice. She tapped the cast and was satisfied it was dry. "We need the room for sick people. Have your doctor check the dressing on the palm on Monday. It will need replacing. Here is your prescription. Out you go Caitlin." She set Murphy up with a sling around her neck and shoulder and positioned her arm carefully. "You keep this elevated, okay? Don't have it resting down around your waist. Keep it high." Murphy gathered her things, thanked Jasmine, and headed out to her Brawler.

The cast was awkward. It ran over her knuckles, around her thumb and halfway up her forearm. Although she had been injured before—by exploding glass, a high-pressure firehose, a knife and a gun—she had never had a cast. Murphy rested her left hand in the sling, awkwardly reached for the seatbelt, accidentally hitting the cast on the door, and buckled herself in. Headquarters was just a couple of kilometres away, and it took her less than one kd lang song before she arrived. Parker had been right: more than a dozen people gathered on the sidewalk after having been moved out of the parking lot.

Murphy rolled down her window. Birds sang in the nearby trees and traffic hummed around her. She flashed her badge and security let her pass. She parked the Brawler and got out. Murphy could hear Jasmine's warm Southern voice tell her to keep the arm elevated, so she readjusted the sling around her neck and made her way to the atelier.

CHAPTER FOUR

I t had been three hours since the truck attack. Media gathered outside the front steps of police headquarters, waiting for a statement from the Chief. Murphy knew she would have to see Shevchenko before she did anything else. Murphy entered through the rear door. Scanning her employee ID card, she opened the secure metal door. She had to walk through Admin Human Resources and had hoped to go unnoticed.

"DI Murphy!"

Murphy rolled her eyes, smiled and turned toward the voice. Mary Newman was the Human Resources representative, and an ex-lover. She was organizing the hiring of the Family and Community Liaison for the Homicide Unit. The candidate interviews were scheduled for Monday.

"Hi Mary," Murphy said. "We can't do the interviews Monday. You might have heard that we have a major case."

"Caitlin, I'm sorry, but we have to. Two of the three candidates will travel to get here. One from B.C. It would be unprofessional to reschedule," Mary said.

Murphy shook her head. "Would you like to explain to Chief Valencia that I cannot work on this truck attack? I will tell you what. You speak to the Chief and have him tell me to attend the job interviews. How about that?"

Mary huffed. "Why are you so angry? I'm not the bad guy here. I've been working on this for a month and a half. Do you have your questions written out? You haven't given them to me yet and I need them and the answers plus the scoring. You have twenty-five points to account for."

"No, Mary. I will take orders from Chief Valencia, not you. Why are you here on a Saturday?"

"I am working on your goddamn interviews!" Mary shouted. "If you want to put them off, you tell the candidates!"

"That is one hundred percent not my job, Mary. In fact, it is over one hundred percent yours. Cancel the interviews. The Liaison interviews will have to wait."

"You are trying to make me look bad, aren't you? You are literally trying to ruin my career. You're trying to get back at me for breaking up with you," Mary blustered.

"I am really not, Mary. If I tried to get back at every woman who dumped me, I would have no time to breathe. You aren't even the last girlfriend to do that. Send me everyone's emails and I will contact the candidates. Okay? And I'll let the Chief know you think we should not delay. How is that?" Murphy asked.

Mary nodded. "Good. Yes, please be nice in the email, though. You can be a little unceremonious sometimes."

That caused Murphy to burst out laughing. "You are absolutely right. I will try to be nice." With that, she headed up one flight of stairs to the Homicide Unit.

In the atelier, Girard, Hamilton and Parker were staring solemnly at Parker's computer. He was live-streaming the CBC's news program, marvelling at the footage. "Hey boss," Hamilton said when Murphy joined them.

"Hey, what's this?"

"News coverage of the attack. Linda said Supt. Shevchenko needs—" Parker stopped speaking as soon as he saw the cast. "Is your arm okay?"

"No worries. Not even broken. You okay? Everyone okay?" She did not wait for an answer. "Dr. Saunders is available for counselling if anyone needs it," she said. The Northshore Municipal Police Department had their own psychologist available to staff. That he was so burned out he was next to useless was beside the point.

Most police avoided going while the civilian staff loved to see Dr. Saunders. Law enforcement personnel risked demotion for going too frequently: at least that was the rumour.

"I have to see Supt. Shevchenko. Where are we?" Murphy said, turning to the white link board that held all the information on the case.

"Perry Lucas Miller, born February 2nd, 2003. Lives at 17 White Pine Cone Road in Harrisburg, with both parents, Clifford and Mable. Clifford owns the house. Perry is twenty years old, has a driver's license with no infractions. No police record. Owns a 2009 Chevrolet Aveo and a 1991 Trurock 480, which we have in the police garage." Parker pointed out the Trurock truck had only been owned by Miller for two weeks.

"So, possibly planning the attack, but also possibly not. Okay, Cleo?"

"He has some social media: a FamCo page and a ChaTrend page. Nothing there suggesting any kind of attack, nothing radical. He hasn't posted to FamCo in a few months. He posted on ChaTrend a week ago. A comment on the Jays."

"Okay, thanks. Where are we on financials and phone?"

"He had no phone on him, and I am tracking down his banks," Hamilton said.

"Get on that, Cleo."

"Yes, boss," she said, "but it's a Saturday. There are skeleton staff in the banks and they are having a hard time getting their authorization."

"Dr. Chen has the deceased and will do his postmortem tomorrow. Uniondale has not sent any medical information yet," Parker said.

"Okay, stay on that. I have to change before seeing Supt. Shevchenko. Anything else I should know before talking to him?"

"No, boss," Hamilton said.

"Right. I have to talk to the Superintendent and Chief, get to the scene, hit Harrisburg, then get to Uniondale once the suspect is cleared to be interviewed. Sweet Jesus, what a mess."

Murphy walked into her office and opened the wooden closet door. She had two pairs of black pants and two crisp white shirts hanging in the narrow storage area. Having the hangers run parallel to the wall meant the closet was wider than deep, and she could easily have multiple outfits available at a moment's notice. Behind the shirts was a black blazer, and she pulled it out, along with a shirt and pants. Perfect to wear when meeting with the Superintendent. She took everything into the women's washroom and changed.

Back in her office, Murphy saw the blinking red light on her phone, showing a voice message. It was Shevchenko.

"Bring your team up to three. I've taken over the large conference room. I want the teams to meet," Shevchenko's message said.

"Well, I have to hand it to Supt. Shevchenko. He was quick. Says he has teams already, teams plural. He has the third floor conference room. We are to go up and meet. Now," Murphy told her detectives.

"Boss, are we giving up the case?" Parker asked.

"Yeah, we haven't even started," Hamilton added.

"No, no, the upper mucks just want to get involved. We'll go, come on," Murphy said. "Go, now," she said, channelling her inner Jasmine.

The team walked up the stairs to the third floor and into the conference room. A large industrial table sat in the centre of the room with a dozen chairs around it. Another, smaller table was pushed up against a wall. It held a pitcher of water and some glasses on a plastic cafeteria tray. On the far wall was a white board and nearby an overhead projector.

"I haven't seen one of those since I was a kid," Murphy said as she sat down.

"What is it?" Parker asked, as he poured himself a glass of water. They met his question with groans and guffaws until he admitted he was just joking. He took a sip of water. "Ugh, stale water. Why is it that water tastes so bad when it's been left out?" While the team discussed their own theories on stale water, Murphy wrote a quick email on her phone.

Subject: Job Cancellation—Community and Family Liaison Position

Hello. Just wanted to drop a quick note to let you know that we're cancelling the hiring process for the Community and Family Liaison position with the Northshore Municipal Police Department. A major incident has occurred, and we can't proceed with the recruitment right now. No reschedule date in sight, sorry.

Thanks for showing interest and going through the motions, though. We'll keep your application on file in case we decide to revisit this position in the future.

Best of luck elsewhere,

DI Caitlin Murphy.

By the time Murphy looked up, two more people had entered the conference room. Parker was warning them about the water.

Shevchenko walked into the office with a large group in tow. The woman caught Murphy's attention immediately. Fucking gorgeous, Murphy thought. She was tall and muscled and very butch.

"Everyone, please sit. I am Supt. Shevchenko. I am overseeing the investigation on behalf of Chief Valencia. I have pulled together this team to conduct the initial inquiries and provide support to our Homicide Unit. Detective Inspector Murphy, please introduce your team."

Murphy gave the name and rank of each of her detectives and said no more. Nothing more was requested of her.

"What's happened to your arm?" a man to her left asked.

She held up her left hand. "Fractured my wrist while apprehending our suspect." Shevchenko asked her to describe the case. Murphy informed them she had not visited the crime scene, the suspect's house, or questioned the suspect.

"This style of attack seems to be on the rise. There were attacks in Ottawa, Winnipeg and Vancouver last year. Now here. I never would have expected it," Neal said. "I'm Sergeant Jeremiah Neal, Accident Reconstruction Team. My team and I will look at the scene. Reconstruction, scene forensics. We will document everything that happened on Centre Street and Red Road. Up Decarie Boulevard to Highway 3. We have approval to work the weekend. We will photograph and catalogue everything, and provide a wireframe rendering of the attack. We should have it within two weeks if the scene is not contaminated, if witnesses cooperate, and if the weather holds."

"I am Sergeant Clayton Bradshaw, Forensics Unit. I am heading up the forensics at the suspect's home and his truck. This is Constables Caleb Weiss and Nikolas Conley. We are happy to provide support for your team as required, Supt. Shevchenko."

"And I am Michelle Tremblay. Call me Mitch. I am an IT Specialist," the last person said with a smile. "I will handle any computers, phones, electronics, digital storage. It's just me." Murphy liked the sound of her voice.

"Thank you," Shevchenko said. "Neal and Bradshaw, your teams will work here. Tremblay, you are on your own office in the basement. Here is how it will go. We will meet regularly in this room for updates. Thorough and transparent updates. Everything gets fed to Homicide. Murphy, you and your team will collate the information, construct the profile, identify and fill any gaps. You have the authority to give direction to other team members. Got it? She is reporting to me, and is my representative. Now, where is our suspect?"

"The suspect may have been injured in the apprehension. His truck went off-road, hit a ditch, a fence and a fencepost. He was bleeding from the face when I arrested him. He is being evaluated at Uniondale. We will interview him as soon as he is cleared by doctors," she said. "SIU has been notified."

"Any ideas why he did this?"

"We have nothing on that front, sir. He had a toy gun, which he used to provoke me to shoot him."

"You didn't, did you?" Tremblay asked.

"No. The gun still had the orange plastic piece on the front of it. To my knowledge, the suspect was only slightly injured, but SIU will look at the arrest. Uniondale is also performing a psych evaluation and toxicology."

"What was going on in our parking lot? Why are those people there?" Shevchenko asked. No one knew.

"Murphy, you interview Miller. Find out why the hell he did this. I will be there with you. I need information for the Chief who needs it for the mayor. Okay, I will have media relations give an update saying nothing for now. You all know your next steps? Good, no sleep until it's done," Shevchenko said.

"I'll get back to you as soon as I can," Murphy said as she rose from the table. Everyone stood up, but only the Homicide team left the room.

"Make me look good," Shevchenko said to Murphy as she walked past. She nodded and walked out, heading back to her office with her detectives.

Back in the atelier, the team sat around the couch to discuss the meeting. The help had been unexpected; they were all grateful.

"I've never worked with multiple teams before," Parker said. "This is kind of awesome. They do the grunt work, and we get the glory."

"I just hope they do the grunt work right," Murphy said. "It means we have to nitpick everything they tell us. We have to guess at what might be missing. Ah, it will be fine," she said, unconvinced. "Okay, all information flows through me. Like a river."

"Like a broken dam," Girard said with a smile. His computer dinged, and he turned to read a new email.

Murphy grinned back. She thought it was vital to the team to keep a lighthearted view of the very tragic events. Murphy spent her entire life skimming the surface of emotions and credited it with keeping her sane. It was certainly a struggle sometimes. "Give me whatever timeline you have—" Murphy's phone buzzed. It was in her right jacket pocket and she struggled so long with her left hand to get it, she missed the call. Del had called her personal cell phone. She put it on the table. "Okay, sorry, timeline."

"Sorry boss, update. This is much worse than we thought. The hospital reports seventeen vehicle ramming victims. I have to call and find out if that is the final number," Girard said as he picked up the phone.

"Okay, everyone, thirty minutes. Gather your information, Parker, get a case number. Let's get our paperwork started."

Team members turned to their desks while Murphy returned to her office. She shut the door, put her phones on the desk, made an instant coffee, and sat down. Murphy always carried one phone for police business and one for personal matters. Both phones showed she had received messages.

Murphy unlocked her police phone first and browsed the text messages and emails. Shevchenko's assistant gave names and contacts for the team and said the project was called Project White Horse. She forwarded that to her team members. The next message was from Sarah Coleman, one of the interview candidates. Murphy ignored her.

Her personal phone dinged again. A text message from Del read, 'Bob injured. Call me ASAP.' Murphy hit the call return button, and the phone rang. Maria answered in a breathy, tearful voice. She had been Del's personal support worker for years and was close to her and her friends.

"Oh Caitlin. It's Bob Olsen, Del's friend. He was at the bar. They were all at the bar when the truck came." Maria explained that Thomas, Jens, and Bob had all been at the Sparkling Unicorn for the 4:30 drag show when the truck hit. Thomas and Jens got out of the way, but Bob was badly injured. He was in the hospital. No visitors were allowed, so the men had come to the house. "It's terrible. He's terribly hurt. What happened? Why did he do this?" Maria asked. Her voice was shaking, and she was on the verge of tears.

The Boys were good friends of Del. The men had befriended and supported Del when she moved to Northshore after her car accident. They had helped Del find a wheelchair accessible building to purchase with her insurance settlement money. Since they were all artists, they helped her set up her studio and gallery when she became a full-time artist. They had been instrumental in helping her settle and make a new life for herself after her old one had been ripped away from her.

Murphy hung her head and let out a soft moan. "Is Del there? Can I speak with her?" For a moment, Murphy heard sobbing, and Maria got back on the phone.

"She can't talk right now. Can you come home?"

Murphy sat back in her chair. "No. I'm investigating the incident. Can you put me on video?"

"Yes, just a minute. Okay, yes. Hi."

Maria sat on a chair and held her phone at arm's length to get everyone in the frame. As she turned and angled the phone to get all four of them, Murphy spoke.

"Del, Thomas, Jens, Maria. I don't know what to say. This is going to be really hard. I have already arrested the suspect—"

"I hope you shot the fucker," Thomas spat.

"No, not shot. He's in prison. Listen, they have brought in more people to help me with the investigation," Murphy said.

"I thought you caught him," Jens said. A second call came through on her phone, but she ignored it.

Murphy nodded. "I arrested him. But we still have to investigate. We still need evidence to prosecute him. I am going to be working full out on this. You know that. But it means, it means I can't be with you right now. I am sorry. I love you all so much, but I need to be here. Can you... you can all stay at the house. Be together, yeah? I... I... shit. I am so sorry this happened." Murphy knew others felt the loss deeper than she did, and that her presence at the house would not be helpful.

"Did he plan on killing people?" Thomas asked. Murphy paused a little too long without answering. "Did he attack us because he hates gays?" he asked.

"We don't have a reason for the attack, but he travelled the length of the street. Many people were injured, all kinds of people."

"So you're saying Bob is just one of a bunch of people? Got it," Del said between sobs.

"I'm not saying that. C'mon, it's Bob. It's Bob and you can't go see him. Listen, maybe I can, okay? I'll try to go see him, they will let me in if he's okay to talk." Murphy immediately regretted making the offer. She had a million things to do rather than go see Del's drinking buddy. But she felt like she had to do something.

"Please, please let him know we are thinking of him. We will be in to see him as soon as they let us. Please," Del said. "We've got each other. He needs someone, too." Murphy wondered if they knew how important the investigation was. Murphy's phone buzzed, showing someone left a voicemail.

"Caitlin, thank you. Give Bob our love. You make sure this wicked man stays in jail," Maria said. With that, Murphy hung up and listened to her voicemail. It was Sun, and she was hysterical. Murphy looked at the clock. She had ten minutes before she was to meet the team in the atelier.

Murphy wanted to ignore the call until she remembered that her store, Sun Flowers was on Centre Street, just south of the Sparkling Unicorn. She called her lover back. "Hey babe, what's—"

"Caitlin! Oh my God, Caitlin! He was right here, outside my store. I was working and suddenly this garbage can just, just comes through my window. I—"

"Comes through your window? What do you mean?"

"I don't know. I... He... Oh..." she cried uncontrollably.

"Where are you? Were you in the shop? Are you in the hospital?"

"Hello?" a man's voice came over the phone.

"What's going on? Where is the woman I was talking to?"

"Sorry, she's right here. She's really upset, so I thought I would help. I'm Fred."

"Okay Fred, where are you? Where is she?" Murphy asked, shaking her head. Fred explained they were on a bus at the scene of the truck attack. The police had arranged for everyone to have a seat while waiting to be interviewed. He assured her the police were taking care of them all, offering water and sandwiches to anyone who was waiting.

"Can you tell her I will be there in a few minutes, Fred?"

"Oh sure. She's pretty shaken up. But I don't know if they'll let you in," he said.

"I will figure it out. Thanks for your help Fred." Murphy hung up and walked into the atelier. "Hey, everyone. What have we got?"

Girard outlined the case, pointing to the relevant photos on the link board. It was still very early in the case, and none of the other teams had reported back.

"Okay, I have found out a friend was hit. He's in the hospital. And someone else. She had a shop on Centre Street. I have to go to the scene and the hospital. It's getting late and everyone else is working. Let's do this: finish up tonight, get as much done as you can. Then go home and stay home. Take Sunday off—"

"No way, there's so much more to do," Girard said.

"That's for other people right now. I'll be working. I have to interview Miller. If I need you, I will call you. But I won't need you. I won't call you. Take Sunday off, be prepared to go full speed on Monday. Lots to do, but that's Monday. Day off tomorrow. Have a life. See you Monday."

CHAPTER FIVE

R ed Road, the north end of the scene, was just over one kilometre from headquarters. As Murphy walked to the scene, she called Neal to advise she was on her way, then called Shevchenko to advise the same. She let Shevchenko know about her personal connections to the incident.

Murphy met up with Neal on Red Road, and he walked her through the scene. His large Accident Reconstruction Team roamed everywhere. "We are going in reverse. He drove Red Road last, hitting four pedestrians, there, there, there and there." He pointed out large orange cones on the sidewalk. "Two are in hospital, two treated at the scene. At one point, it looks like he hit this wall here." Shopping bags and shoes lay scattered in the street: clear signs of people running for their lives.

"He exited up Blue Road, sorry, Blue Street to the highway. He came from Centre Street." Neal and Murphy turned the corner. "It is just 585 metres from where he started, at Franklin, and here. We believe he hit fourteen people on Centre. We are still verifying exact locations," Neal said.

Murphy stared down Centre Street. It was empty of civilians, but running rampant with clutter. In the fading sun, everything looked duller than it ought to. A bright pink plastic chair was no longer bright, but was now stained with the tragedy of the day. Miller had knocked the mailbox from its concrete base and it now lay on its side. A parking sign leaned casually across the sidewalk. Cars were left in a disorderly hodgepodge on the street. Murphy notice a lot of shoes laying about after people ran out of them.

Murphy and Neal walked down the roadway, where the truck had not been. "He stayed on the east side of the street," Neal said, as if to explain why one side of the street was almost pristine while the other was encrusted with madness. Upended tables and chairs ringed by police tape marked the patios where people had been enjoying a late afternoon respite.

"These poor people went through hell," Murphy said as they continued down the street. She stood in front of the Sparkling Unicorn and stared at a drying pool of blood. "I had friends here, watching a show," she said. A glittering size ten high heel shoe sat all by itself at the curb.

"Is your friend in the hospital?" Neal asked.

"There, I guess," Murphy said as she pointed to the orange cone closest to the blood pool. It stood in for Bob who, just hours ago, was laughing and drinking with friends. Glass crackled under their feet as they walked.

"I'm sorry about your friend," Neal said. Murphy nodded and looked up at the darkening sky. She wondered at how Bob's life had become so thoroughly shattered.

As they walked further on, Neal's team began setting up floodlights. It chased away the shadows, and it left the remnants of lives with nowhere to hide. She looked at Sun Flowers. The truck had scraped along the brick and left a trail of white. The remains of the plate-glass window hung like swords of Damocles, precarious and deadly. A large metal garbage can sat on the sill amid dirt and broken pottery. Crushed flower petals were scattered about.

"Who was this?" Murphy asked, pointing at an orange cone on the street.

"Brenda Kelsey, 43. Multiple lacerations, in serious condition in hospital. She was victim number two. The first was here," Neal said. He pointed to an orange cone that sat in the street. "Hank Filson, 18, critical condition." Murphy turned and looked behind her at the west side of the street. Undamaged. She looked up Centre Street. It would forever be damaged in her memories and nightmares.

Murphy took a deep breath and slowly released it. Freeze up, she told her heart, this is no time to get emotional. "Where are the busses for the witnesses?" she asked.

"Most people are gone now, interviewed and released," Neal said as he took Murphy outside the police perimeter to a single bus provided by Blue Moose Bus Line. Only three people were on the bus, and none of them was Sun. She looked up Centre Street. The once familiar road was now uncharted territory. She would have to create a whole new emotional map to find her way in the heart of town.

Murphy thanked Neal and walked back to headquarters. Outside the perimeter, life continued as it normally would. Cars buzzed past, people floated in and out of stores, dogs tied to poles sniffed at every passerby. Murphy called Sun.

"Hey, I got here, but you already left," she said.

"You said you would meet me an hour ago. Where were you?" Sun asked. She was furious.

"I was walking the scene with Sgt. Neal. That was—"

"Walking the scene? Walking the... You said you were coming to me. I really needed you, I asked you, and you walked the scene? It couldn't wait, eh? You couldn't come to see me first and instead you put the street ahead of me. A street!"

"Hey, don't get angry at me. I mean, I get your upset, but I did nothing wrong."

"No, you did nothing at all. I was at the counter when this metal thing comes flying in. Flying in! There is glass and it almost got me and there was so much noise and you weren't there!"

"Oh come on," Murphy said. "How could I be there when it happened?" She was feeling defensive.

"You weren't there afterwards, when you said you would be. You weren't there at all," Sun hissed. Her hands shook as she gripped the phone tighter.

"Look, I'm sorry—"

"Sorry you had to walk the scene before coming to see your lover? Sorry you didn't call to tell me you weren't coming? Sorry you just left me there? Well, I'm sorry too. Sorry I didn't stick around while you strolled down the street. Sorry I called my son to come and get me. Sorry he took only ten minutes to come. Sorry I don't want to talk to you. I don't want to talk to you right now," Sun said. Murphy heard the soft click of the call disconnecting.

She stopped in the street, staring at her phone. *Jesus, I don't have time for this,* she thought. Murphy hurried back to the Brawler, still parked at headquarters. There were several people standing on the sidewalk, praying. She stood, crossed herself, and whispered, "Oh Divine embodiment of boundless benevolence, cast your compassionate gaze upon those who have been injured today, grant them solace, strength, and health in their time of need. Amen." She crossed herself again, touched the gold cross around her neck, and proceeded to her vehicle.

Murphy looked at her Brawler. Not much damage had been sustained. The grill guard had taken the brunt of Miller's truck and was barely scratched. Miller had sideswiped her passenger side: the side-view mirror was hanging by its wires, and a white streak ran a portion of its body with only minor damage. She knew she could not get it fixed until the Forensics Unit had documented it, but she could still drive it. Murphy climbed in and headed to the hospital to see Bob.

She called Bradshaw, who was heading up the forensic investigation and asked if he had anyone at the hospital. She was told Constable Caleb Weiss was on scene wrapping up interviews.

Murphy walked through the doors, past the waiting room, and asked at the information desk where Robert Olsen was. After proving she was a police officer, the staff person told her he was in critical care on the fourth floor. Murphy took the elevator up and looked at the sign. Critical Care, green line. Murphy followed the green line on the floor and was soon at another reception desk. "Detective Inspector Caitlin Murphy, Northshore Municipal Police Department. I'm looking for Robert Olsen. He was brought in this afternoon." She held out her warrant card for the woman to see.

"Sure, he's out of surgery. Room five. He isn't able to talk right now, though," she said.

Murphy nodded and walked down the hallway. A melody of soft voices and rhythmic machines filled the air. Murphy stood outside the glass door for room five. A curtain was drawn across to give Bob privacy. Murphy hesitated. She called Weiss to let him know she was on the floor in a personal capacity. He told her they could not yet interview Bob. She thanked the Constable and hung up. Murphy cleared her throat, ran a hand through her hair, and walked in.

She stood in the doorway and stared at him for a moment, then looked at her shoes. He did not look like Bob: he looked like an old man on his deathbed. The old man's eyes were closed, whereas if it was Bob, his eyes would be open and bright. There would be a grin on his lips, a joke on his tongue, a lightness in his step because Bob loved life. This man, grey and still and hooked to machines to stay alive, this was not her Bob. She had been kidding herself about his importance to her, as she often did. She cared for him dearly.

A nurse came into the room behind her. "Are you a friend of Mr. Olsen?" she asked.

Murphy held up her badge. "Police. But also a friend, yes. Is the doctor available to give me an update?"

"Yes, I'll go get him," she said, leaving the room. Bob was still lying with his eyes closed, an oxygen mask on his face, intravenous lines going into both arms. A crisp white flannel blanket lay over him, the blue stripes tucked under his chin. Beside his bed, lights on the patient monitor displayed their pulsing lines of green, yellow and blue. The machine was quiet, but the numbers spoke volumes.

"Hi, I'm Dr. Rae." He and the same nurse walked into the room.

"Hi, Caitlin Murphy. Can you give me an update on Bob?"

"Sure, how much do you know already? Katrina tells me you're a police officer," Dr. Rae said.

"Yes, I am," she said, pulling her jacket back to show the badge on her belt. "I know he was on a patio when he was hit by that truck."

"Yes. Okay. I will be more blunt with you than I would with a family member. He suffered significant injuries. His legs are so damaged, he will probably lose them both. It looks like the tires ground the flesh, and there isn't much left to save. He has broken ribs, his left kidney and spleen were so badly damaged we have removed them, and we repaired some damage to his stomach. We have stabilized him, and we will transfer him via ORNGE to Toronto General. He should leave within the hour. We don't know who his next of kin is. Do you?"

Murphy shook her head. "I know close friends, but not any family. I'll try to find out later tonight and have someone contact the hospital. So he has lost his legs?"

"Lost the use of them. Toronto General is expecting to conduct an amputation. He has crush injuries," Dr. Rae said.

"What are his chances? If he makes it through tonight and gets to Toronto, what are his chances of survival?"

"Of survival? Fifty fifty. He will have paraplegia, perhaps incomplete quadriplegia depending on spinal damage. There is a lot of swelling, and we were having a hard time imaging. He has a long road ahead of him."

Murphy nodded and sighed. "Okay, thank you. I will try to locate family members. Do you have a card?" Murphy and the doctor exchanged contact information, and the doctor left her with Bob and her thoughts.

Murphy leaned over the bed and placed her hand on Bob's heart. She could barely feel the pulse. "Oh Divine embodiment of boundless benevolence, cast your compassionate gaze upon this humble man who endures various injuries and wounds, granting him solace in his time of need. Reach out with your curative touch and shield of guardianship upon him, ensuring his restoration and well-being. Amen." She crossed herself and kissed Bob's forehead. "Del, Thomas, Jens, and Maria send their love." It was time for her to go home.

At this time of night, creatures abounded in Northshore. On the drive, Murphy rolled down the window, rested her left arm on the door, and kept the radio off. The sound of the travel was purely mechanical as the Brawler's engine growled and the tires rolled on the roads. The air was still hot from the day, but the wind felt cool as it whirled through the 4x4. Twice on the forty kilometre drive, she slowed for a deer crossing the road. She avoided three racoons, two skunks and one toad. In the glare of her headlights, she could see the glowing eyes of a fox in the brush at the side of the road.

She slowed and turned left into the parking lot of her home. She could see a few cars parked there: visitors joining together for Bob. Murphy parked the Brawler at the side of the building, rolled up the window, and turned off the engine. Gathering her things—her bag, her files, her dirty clothes—took her a minute. By the time she locked the vehicle, she had an audience. When people in the house heard her 4x4 pull in, they came wandering outside and stood near the building, waiting for her.

Murphy nodded and said, "Let's go inside," as she walked up to them. "We will talk in there." Telling people bad news about loved ones was familiar to Murphy. She could be good at it, great, even. It did not matter whether the family was of the victim or the suspect, the same tone and manner of speaking worked with both. The only variable was the reactions of the family and friends.

"Let's all meet in the living room, okay? Not in the kitchen. It isn't big enough for us to be together," Murphy said. She disliked having people in her home. Del's living area was a combination of living and sleeping quarters. While Murphy had her own space upstairs, she was not about to head up and get changed or put her gun away. By keeping her gun in the holster and the badge on her belt, she conveyed an authority that she knew would work to her favour. Many people disliked crying in front of authority. A leftover childhood trauma, Murphy guessed.

"Please, everyone sit," Murphy said as she stood with her bag over her shoulder and the files in her hand. "I don't think I know all of you," she said to the dozen people crammed into the space. "My name is Caitlin Murphy. I'm Delaney's wife, and I am a police detective. I have been able to go see Bob at the hospital." Murphy decided that keeping it formal was the way to go. "Bob was badly injured in today's truck ramming incident," she said.

"How is he?" Jens interrupted.

"He is in critical care. Bob is on a breathing tube and has already had some surgery to remove damaged organs. His left kidney and spleen are gone. He has some broken ribs. They are flying him tonight by air ambulance to Toronto General Hospital." Murphy paused and surveyed the room. So far, so good. "His legs suffered devastating injury."

Del burst into tears: she feared what was coming.

"He has lost the use of his legs. He won't get them back. It is possible they will amputate one or both of his legs. There may be some spinal damage," Murphy said. Del wailed when she heard, and Murphy walked over to her and crouched down in front of her. "He's going to be in expert hands," she said, stroking Del's shoulder.

"What are his chances?" someone asked. He was a shabby young man, an artist, Murphy thought, when she saw his paint-covered pants.

Murphy stood up and continued to address the room. "I asked the doctor what his chances of survival are, if he gets to Toronto General Hospital tonight. The doctor said he has a fifty fifty chance." Murphy put emphasis on the 'doctor' part of the statement, letting him bear the weight of the estimate. She explained Bob was not awake when she arrived at his hospital room and had not spoken with him.

"Can I call the hospital?" Jens asked.

"Yes, but Bob is likely in the air on his way to Toronto, so the hospital will only be able to tell you they have transferred him," she said.

"Can I call Toronto General?"

"Yes, but he hasn't arrived yet. Your best bet is to call late tomorrow morning," Murphy said as she glanced at the clock on the wall. It was almost midnight. "The doctors will need time to assess and care for Bob."

"What about the guy who did this? Where is he?" a woman asked.

"He is in police custody. This is going to be a very long process. It will take a long time for Bob to recover, and the trial will take a long time."

"But police caught him, like, right after, right?" the shabby man asked.

"Yes, but it still takes time. The most important thing to focus on is Bob. He is going to need a lot of support from everyone," Murphy said.

"I can fly down there, see how he's doing," Del said as she blew her nose.

"Call ahead. Make sure you can visit. The only reason I could see Bob was because I am the police. They were only allowing family members in. Does anyone know Bob's next of kin?" Everyone around her insisted they were all family and should all have the right to see him. Murphy tried hard to keep her face neutral. "Hang on, hang on. Hospitals have policies, and the policy is, only his legal next of kin can visit until he is well enough for other visitors. That's all. You can see him, but not right now. It's just a phone call to check before you spend hours travelling to Toronto."

"Will they take video calls?" Thomas asked.

"I don't know, but you can call and find out." Murphy answered a few more questions before the side conversations took over and she was freed from being the centre of attention. Everyone was now sitting in small groups, drinking and chatting. Calculating the right time to step out, Murphy headed up the stairs to her living quarters. It had been just hours, and she was exhausted. Sunday would not be a day of rest for her, but it was a day of being less busy than normal. She hoped.

She laid her hand on the biometric reader of her gun safe, and the door clicked open. She carefully placed her weapon, badge, and warrant card on the shelf and locked the door. The last thing she needed was a distraught friend to get hold of her gun and begin their own rampage. Absentmindedly, she scratched at her cast, trying to ease the tickle underneath. She had heard that a hair dryer, set to cool, could blow air between the arm and the cast to help with the itching. She did not have a hair dryer.

Murphy stripped, tossed all of her clothing into the laundry basket, and slipped into pajama bottoms and a white tank top. As she did every night she was alone. She knelt at the side of her bed and said a prayer for the people whose homicides she had investigated. "In your hands, O Lord, are humbly entrusted our brothers and sisters. Welcome them into Your paradise, free of pain and worry. Grant these souls eternal rest. Paula Gilray,

Hugh Wyatt, Rose Barker, Yusef Ingram, Frank Addison. Amen." She cracked the window to let the warm air in and crawled into bed.

The crisp cotton sheets felt cool against her skin as she fell into a deep sleep. She dreamt of exploding flowers with orange smoke, legless men crawling toward her screaming for help, white trucks transforming into winged demons, and a figure sitting in a tree on a hill.

CHAPTER SIX

In the wee hours of Sunday morning, Murphy sat in the Uniondale Federal Penitentiary parking lot in the Brawler. She was on a group call with Neal from the Accident Reconstruction Team, Bradshaw from the Forensic Team, and Tremblay, the technology expert. They were talking about Perry Miller. She watched as Shevchenko pulled into the parking lot and parked near her. She waved him over and rolled down the window so he could hear the conversation.

"Sgt. Bradshaw provided me with Miller's cell phone. It has a passcode, but I am in," Tremblay said. "His service is with Phone-Etics. They have sent over his data, but he called only a half dozen numbers in the last month. His parents, Füd Fül and Go-Fred, which are two local food delivery services, and a pizza place. He called Phone-Etics customer service once, and there are two calls to a local pot shop, Potassium," she said.

"He has one bank account, with a balance of $21.56. My guy looked at the last three years, and there is almost no activity aside from about two weeks ago," Bradshaw said. "He seemed to put in $20 occasionally, and take out small amounts, make debit transactions for small amounts. Once it got past $1500, he withdrew that amount. That was thirteen days ago. We spoke with his parents. They were hostile to questioning, but I got that they paid for almost everything. Internet, phone, food, gas. They weren't sure how he paid for the truck."

"Tell me about the truck," Murphy said just as her phone beeped. "No, hang on." She checked the message. Uniondale was ready. "Okay, I have to go. They are ready for us. Email me the truck information ASAP, but I have to leave my phone behind so I won't be available. Thank you, everyone."

"Wait, before you go! He had pages from the Bible taped to a mirror, with writing on it. Revelations, it looked like," Bradshaw said.

"Okay, great to know. Thank you." She hung up and turned to her boss. "Sir, how are you this morning?"

"Not bad, Murphy. How's the arm?"

"Not bad, sir, not bad. Shall we go?"

It had been a few years since Shevchenko sat in on an interview, but he felt he had to attend. He wanted to see this man for himself. Murphy had a strong reputation for being a skilled interrogator, and he wanted to watch her in action. Talking to your run-of-the-mill killer—an angry husband or pissed off drug dealer—was one thing, but this suspect, well, he was going to be something else.

They walked in through the glass doors and up to the reception. Handing over their identification, Shevchenko asked for the Correctional Manager.

"Superintendent Shevchenko, hello. I'm Valentin Huber," he said as he walked into the reception area. Huber was a stubby Austrian who managed the prison with a firm hand. His presence loomed large despite his height, and his voice echoed through the halls.

"Hi, Detective Inspector Murphy," Murphy said as she shook his meaty hand. "I appreciate your helping us out with this."

"Door!" he shouted. The lock buzzed and released the door. "No problem. Dr. Jenner has cleared Perry Miller for an interview." He took the pair to a secondary reception area. "Weapons and hard objects, including your phone, in the locker. Choose your own lock code," Huber said, gesturing to a grey row of lockers. Murphy put her sidearm, badge, and two cell phones into the locker and closed the door. She tapped a five digit random code into the digital lock. Shevchenko did the same with his badge and phone. He was not carrying a sidearm.

"If you forget that number, you're screwed," Huber said with a laugh. "Here is his paperwork, his booking photograph and the medical clearance letter from Dr. Jenner. I have you in Interview Room Yellow. There is a table and three chairs, a motion-activated cold water tap and some paper cups. They will bring in Miller when you're ready. The tape will begin as soon as you say you are ready."

"Thank you. Start the tape. We will go in once he's secured in the room," Murphy said with a glance at Shevchenko. She wondered if he was going to talk during the interview, or leave it to her. It was not clear.

"Oh yeah, he's already been in a fight. Got into it with another inmate in the medical ward. Talked crap to a Black guy in the next bed. Like I said, he's cleared, but he got a black eye from a fight with another inmate in the medical ward. He seemed pretty happy about it."

"Happy? Why would he be happy about it?" Shevchenko asked.

"He seems to think it's some kind of manly thing. Word of warning, he talked just fine with the doctor, but any time a guard or another prisoner talks to him, he is really offensive."

"Offensive?" Shevchenko asked.

"Names and swear words. He is disrespectful. You can hear it for your-selves. If he was actually an inmate and not on temporary hold for you, he would have been written up a dozen times."

While waiting for Miller to be sent to the room, Shevchenko whispered to Murphy she should lead the interview. Once Miller was sitting in Inter-view Room Yellow, they walked in.

They sat down opposite the suspect. The room was small and smelled like urine. There was dirty white soundproof tiling on the walls, but other people had ripped away chunks of it. Two cameras sat in corners of the room, nestled high against the ceiling. They aimed one at the suspect and the other at Shevchenko and Murphy.

"Hi, hello. This is Superintendent Shevchenko. I am Detective Inspector Caitlin Murphy. Homicide. Northshore Municipal Police Department. For the record, can you please say and then spell your name for us?" Murphy smiled and waited politely.

"Fuck you," Miller said.

"Respect, young man," Shevchenko said.

"Fuck. You. Asshole."

"Okay, this is being recorded, so for the tape, today is Sunday, the sixteenth of July. It is 8:57a.m. I am speaking with first name Perry, P-E-R-R-Y, middle name Lucas, L-U-C-A-S and last name Miller, M-I-L-L-E-R," she said. "Date of birth is 02-02-2003. Correct? Yes."

"Yeah."

"Yesterday, I advised you of your rights. And another detective, Detective Staff Sergeant Girard, advised you of your rights. If you would like to call a lawyer, you can use the phone outside the door. There are phone numbers of Legal-Aid lawyers there."

"I already fucking called, douche bag," Miller said. "Who is he? Is he the bad cop?" he asked, pointing at Shevchenko. "Is this good cop, bad cop? Fuck that shit."

"No, he's my boss, actually. Superintendent. Above my rank. Even though I am not in a uniform, I am a law enforcement officer, a cop. Now, I am a bit of a different type of cop than you might see on the street. I'm a detective. But I still do investigations, arrest people."

Miller eyed them again. "You should have shot me."

"That is the coward's way out," Murphy said.

"I don't see what's so bad about being shot by a hot chick cop. I'd fuck you, cunt," Miller said.

"Since I arrested you, I guess I am the one who fucked you," Murphy said with a slight smile.

"Can you say that to me?" Miller asked.

"I can say anything I want."

Miller rolled his eyes, then looked away and around the room. He looked at the tight walls, the concrete floor, the florescent lights in their own cages hanging from the ceiling. He started humming.

"Do you have anything to say, Perry? Do you want to talk about yesterday?" Murphy asked. Her quarry stopped humming and just shrugged. "Okay, no problem. What was that song you were humming?"

Miller shrugged again. "'My Devil Soul' by Midsummer Killers."

It was Murphy's turn to shrug. "I don't know it," she said as she wrote it down.

"You're too old. An old fucking hag," Miller sneered.

Murphy looked up from her notepad. "You just said you would fuck me, so that's a lie. I am a homicide detective. Do you really think calling me names is going to hurt my feelings?"

Miller frowned. "Faggot."

"Ooh ouch, so hurtful," Murphy said.

"I was talking to him," Miller said as he nodded his head toward Shevchenko. In response, Shevchenko rested his head on his hand and feigned a yawn. Murphy saw a flicker of disappointment on Miller's face.

"Do your friends call you a faggot? I mean, if you have friends, do they call you names?" Murphy asked.

"I hate this fucking shithole. I hate Kettering, and I fucking hate Northshore. Did you talk to my shit bag parents yet? Did they tell you why we moved to this piece of shit place in the middle of nowhere?"

Murphy knew he would talk if she kept him agitated. "Maybe I did and maybe not. Maybe I heard a few things. They don't, uh, do not..." She was delighted when he took the bait.

"They don't fucking do anything! He's the reason we moved! He is, not me. He's always blaming me, saying I am the one doing that fucking shit. But he's a fucking liar. Fucking stupid piece of shit!" Miller shouted.

"He told us a few things, a few reasons," Murphy said. She was guessing Miller was talking about his father, and it seemed to be a sore spot she could tap into.

"I don't want to talk about him. He's a piece of shit."

"No worries. Your dad has had enough to say for both of you."

"He is to blame. He is the fucking perv, not me," he said.

"No love and affection there, eh?" Murphy asked. Miller slammed his hand on the table and began to tear up, but remained silent. "Not from your mom, either." She made it a statement, not a question. Miller fought his emotions and turned his head. His chin quivered. "So you bought yourself a truck?"

Miller stared straight ahead, trying not to listen.

"Was it because you wanted to get away from your parents? Get away? Get away from your life and this shithole?" When Miller said nothing, Murphy continued. "Or were you running toward something? Toward your destiny, maybe? Toward freedom?"

Miller was silent. He crossed his arms and sat back as he gathered himself. Murphy was losing him. *Why would a little nobody like Perry Miller do this?* she wondered. Then she remembered the Revelations scripture taped to his mirror, and the preacher on the radio. It was at odds with the music he said he was humming. Of course, Murphy thought. It was not about his conflicting religious beliefs, not his parents, nor Northshore.

"Notoriety."

"Do you think this little shit is notorious?" Shevchenko said. He had been so quiet it startled the others.

"I am going to be known around the world. You are going to die in some fucking old folks' home shitting in your diapers!" Miller shouted.

"I won't. I'm the fucking hero. No one will ever be able to talk about what you did without talking about me," Murphy said. She smiled. "Thanks."

"Fuck you, cunt! They will write books about me!"

"And the books will always always always end with me busting your ass."

Miller held his breath and turned red. "Fuck you! No! I did this! I'm famous! I am fucking famous! Not you!"

"I am going to be the one who gets to be interviewed by reporters. I am the one who will appear on television. I am the one who will be paid a shit ton of money for interviews, maybe even book rights. You can't keep any money you earn talking about what you did. Not you. Me," Murphy said. She was happy to have him angry again.

"No! No! It's about me. Maybe they will talk about you, but you are only famous because of me. You are nothing without me," Miller sputtered.

"I am the one who solved Cardinal Horn's murder. Journalists and writers are already writing books about it. And I caught you. And I will catch the next killer and the next killer. You are only famous because of me. Because I caught you and I did not kill you and now, you can talk to writers and journalists. If I had shot you, you'd have nothing. Nothing without me," Murphy said. She leaned back in her chair and crossed her long legs, a slight smile on her face. "I won. You lost."

Miller was overwrought. "I did not lose! I did not. I could kill you, then I could be more famous. I could be really famous all on my own."

Murphy shook her head. "We may not release your name. We will only refer to you in the press as P.M. You know how the government feels about giving people like you attention."

Miller lunged violently at Murphy across the table, his hands clawing at her face. Instinctively, she bolted backward and raised her arms, hitting Miller in the face with the cast.

"Oh fuck! My nose! You hit my nose, you fucking cunt!" Miller screamed as guards rushed in to restrain him. Murphy and Shevchenko both retreated to the back wall while two burly, uniformed guards got Miller under control.

"Missed me," Murphy said. Shevchenko laughed. The guards hand-cuffed Miller to a bar on the table, and chained his ankle to a bar on the floor.

"Do you want a spit hood?" one guard asked.

Murphy looked at Miller. "Do I need to put a spit hood on you? No, no. I get it. Thanks guys, I appreciate the help." Murphy waited until the men left and then sat down. Shevchenko pulled his chair to the back wall and sat down. "I get it now. I do. You attacked another prisoner in here earlier, and I bet you were pissed he only hit you. I bet you thought attacking me might get you killed."

"No."

Shevchenko, who had been on the edge, settled into his chair. It was fascinating to watch Murphy work. For a woman known for being no nonsense, she was exhibiting a great deal of tolerance with Miller. She seemed more like a patient kindergarten teacher trying to understand why a student peed on the floor.

Murphy shook her head. "You want to die."

"Leave me alone."

"No. I don't have to. I won't leave until I find out why you did this. But I think I am seeing what is going on. You hate your insignificant life, living in your parents' home, doing nothing and going nowhere. You want to do something big and then die before it shrinks down and becomes nothing too."

"That's not why."

"Yes, it is. You can't stand being nothing."

Miller was breathing heavily, fighting tears. "I just get so fucking mad that no one likes me." He turned away from Murphy, looking more like a child than a murderer.

"You think no one likes you?" Murphy affirmed.

"I know no one does. I don't know why not. I'm a nice guy but if I try to talk to a girl, like at the grocery store, I always get these looks. Like I am a rapist. I'm not a rapist, but not one girl will look at me. It makes me so angry. I... I play La Guerre Infinitus, in it I am nice to anyone. Sometimes I won't kill a noob, just giving them a chance to live. They call me faggot and loser. Then they fucking tea bag me and fucking kill me. I am nice and they turn on me. I give my fucking loot to chicks, and then it turns out to be some guy using a femme filter, and he takes all my shit. I end up losing all my gold and they just, they just destroy Coeur de Lion. I have had to rebuild him so many times." Snot ran down Miller's face and he licked at it when it reached his lips.

"No one respects you," Murphy said with a faux tenderness in her voice. Miller sobbed. "You just want a little respect, you want people to stop dumping on you."

Miller nodded. "I'm an alpha male. I don't get why no one respects me," Miller whined.

"Alpha male. Above others. How did... Why did you do this?"

Miller looked at his fingernails and bent down to nibble on a nail.

"Why did you do it?"

"Run people over?"

"Yeah. Run people over."

"I had to get away from my parents. I had to get away from my life. I needed to become an alpha male. Then no one can fuck with me," Miller said.

"So you bought a truck?" Murphy asked. Miller nodded. "And that was a couple of weeks ago?" Miller nodded again. "So you came up with a plan. Why now?"

"I don't know. I was going to do it last week, but then it was getting late so I just drove around pretending. You know, just thinking about it. Bam, bam," he said as he moved his hands from side to side, mimicking steering.

"Why this time?"

Miller shrugged and then smiled. "I saw a sign, and I thought, that's it. I'll get them."

"Get who?" Murphy asked.

"Nobody likes queers anyway. I thought, if I kill fags and drag queens and trannies and groomers, then I will get respect," Miller sighed. "And I will. I will get respect as soon as the truth comes out."

"The truth?"

"That I was targeting fucking queers. I'll be the hero."

"Because you hate gay people." This was not the first, nor would it be the last time, Murphy heard the vitriol of a homophobe.

"They should all die. Be exterminated."

"Why did you hit everyone else? People who weren't gay?" Murphy asked. She held her breath, waiting for the answer.

"They were in the way," he said.

"You hate gays so much it was okay if other people got hurt, if you could get the queers?"

"Yeah. It just builds up, you know. Assholes calling you faggot and shit. I just cleaned up the world a bit. I did my part," Miller said.

"You were aiming for gays? You didn't kill any gays, though." Murphy wanted Miller to talk about his hatred, his targeting of queers. It was proof his hate motivated his crime, and that could increase his sentence after being found guilty.

"Maybe next time," Miller said.

After another twenty minutes, Murphy ended the interview. Shevchenko stood up and opened the door. "Okay, Miller, we are done. Back to your hole," Murphy said as dismissively as she could.

They left without another word and made their way to the glass security doors, passing through to the room with the lockers. *Fuck,* Murphy thought, *what was my locker number?* She looked quickly at Shevchenko, who was tapping his number in. She turned to the guard at the desk and asked, "What happens if I forgot my locker password?"

He smiled and tapped a few keystrokes into the computer. The locker buzzed, and the door swung open. "It happens all the time."

Murphy grabbed her possessions and together, she and Shevchenko navigated their way outside. "Excellent job Murphy. You have him admitting to planning the attack a week ahead. You had him say he was targeting people."

"He targeted gays, so it's a hate crime," she said with a sneer. "We have to check his online chat activity for hate speech or pre-planning. And look into where the family came from and why they are here. He said something about not being a pervert and being looked at as a rapist. We might find incidents of sexual assaults or harassment at past schools or jobs. We will have to check out his parents a lot closer, too. I don't think for a second he has told us everything. I am not sure he has even been all that honest, but it's a good start."

"Don't underestimate yourself. It's a great start. I'll speak with Chief Valencia and give him an update. It's a Sunday, take the rest of the day off," Shevchenko said as a joke. With the suspect interviewed and behind bars, there was no pressing need to continue working.

CHAPTER SEVEN

While Murphy and Shevchenko worked, the other detectives were treating the Sunday as a well-deserved day off. Girard was asleep when his wife, Ruby, knocked on the door. "Adam, wakey wakey," she said, pushing the bedroom door open. "The boys made you breakfast," she said as they walked in, carrying a bed tray between them. After the Great Spillage of December, the boys could only bring him dry food in closed containers. Adam smiled and sat up, scooching over and piling pillows up behind his back. Steven, six, and Allan, four, carefully walked around the side of the bed and brought the tray toward Girard.

"Breakfast!" Steven shouted as Girard took the tray from them.

"Brakfast!" Allan screamed louder before clambering up on the bed beside his dad. The tray tipped as Steven, only slightly more coordinated than Allan, climbed onto the bed and hit the tray with his foot. Girard righted the tray and put his arms out around his boys. He pulled them in closer and kissed each on their heads.

"Make room for the ladies," Girard said with a smile. He and his wife had treated themselves to a king-sized bed after the last mattress was soaked in cold milk and room temperature coffee. Ruby, who had been carrying two-year-old Ruthie on her hip and a reusable shopping bag over her shoulder, put the child on the bed, then climbed in on the edge. The first thing Ruthie did was bounce a dozen times, shouting with glee as the food containers bounced with her.

Once the kids were settled in, Girard opened all the containers. "I did that," Steven said when one container revealed dry, sweet cereal.

"That's mine," Allan said, pointing at the cookies he had broken to fit into the container.

"Me! Me!" Ruthie shouted when Girard opened a container to reveal grapes she had kindly bitten in half.

"And me," Ruby said as she dug into her bag, handing juice boxes to everyone. She pulled out hard-boiled eggs—already peeled and wrapped in a large paper napkin—tangerines and packaged breakfast pastries. "So what's up for the day, handsome?" she asked.

"Staying home, playing with the kids. We can join mama, mimaw and poppa. How does that sound, guys?" All the kids shouted excitedly, even though Girard's mother and grandparents just lived feet away in a granny flat in the backyard.

***

It took an hour and a half for Hamilton to ride to North Bay. She usually attended the Sunday Black Looks Book Club virtually, and was psyched to attend in person today. When she arrived at Angela's home, she parked her motorcycle on the street and walked toward the front door. Laughter from the back yard led her to the gate in the fence.

She found the book club members gathered in a shaded circle on the grass. She smiled and her heart felt a little lighter when the half dozen Black faces looked up and greeted her. Their voices scattered and flowed in the heavy summer air like the songs of birds. It felt so different, so special, to be among other Black people.

"Cleo! There you are. So nice to see you in person," Nathan said as he beamed. Hamilton felt a rush of familiarity, of connection.

"Nathan, nice to see you," Hamilton said, as she gave him a friendly hug. She greeted everyone by name with a friendly hello before sinking into a lawn chair. Across from her, Gabrielle leaned forward and handed her a glass of sweet tea. Everyone was laughing and making jokes and it felt good in her soul.

Conversation turned from the weather, to the drive up, to the truck attack. "Yes, it really was terrible," Hamilton said. She tried hard to keep her voice steady as she recounted the event. She kept it high-level and instead turned the conversation to procedures. "We are only just starting the investigation," she said.

"I thought the guy had been arrested already," Tara said. "What's left to investigate?"

Hamilton laughed a little. "We need to get the same kind of evidence against him as if we didn't know who he was, as if he hadn't been caught. We still have to prove it was him. And we need to know if it was impulse or planned, if it—"

"Why does that matter? He killed someone, isn't that a murder?"

"Well, it's homicide. But we need to know if it was culpable and intentional, not intentional, or not culpable. It makes a big difference."

"How so?" Nathan asked.

"First degree murder is an automatic life sentence with no chance of parole for twenty-five years. If it is unintentional manslaughter, there actually is no minimum. He could get almost no prison time," Hamilton explained.

"Well, that's an excellent segue to our book, Eye of the Hurricane. Shall we begin?" Nathan asked.

***

Parker loved to run; he had been with running clubs since he was seven years old. Over those twenty-seven years, he ran every day. In winter, he ran through gently falling snow and sleet with winds so cold it felt like his lungs were being ripped apart. In summer, he ran through soft warm mornings and blistering afternoons, risking heatstroke and mad dog bites.

He checked his club's Sunday Funday web page and was excited to see it was a dinosaur fight. They paired each runner with another runner to draw a dinosaur on his or her route. Parker selected a route and downloaded the directions. He went to his starting point, checked his watch and turned on the app that would track his run. He was up against Garry, an excellent runner. Both men had to start at the tail and follow the directions. They would end up face to face on a street corner, but whoever completed the run fastest was the winner.

The app dinged and Parker took off. It was a hot July afternoon, and he was well-prepared with a CamelBak on his back, giving him instant access to water whenever he needed it. He ran past beautiful houses and sleepy parks, through some woods and past the water tower. Grain silos stood tall in the background as he passed fields and farms, creating the distinctive shape of the stegosaurus. The first hour passed easily.

He kicked up a light dust trail as he ran along the dry dirt road. Parker glanced at his watch: he was over two hours into the marathon distance and had another hour to go. Sweat poured down his face as he took a corner onto a paved road. His legs were tightening, his heart pounding, his lungs burning. He wanted to take a break, but this was a competition and he would not lose. At the Farmer's Market, he began the zigzags for the teeth. Almost done, he thought.

Parker was running in the small circle for the nostril when he spotted Garry across the street. He quickly judged that Garry was on the teeth and therefore a little behind him. His legs felt like cement as he ran up the street toward where the eye would go. Parker screamed out loud as he approached where the last eye went.

"Yeah! Suck it, Garry! Wooooo!" he shouted as the app beeped, showing he had completed his stegosaurus drawing. He quickly stopped his watch and laid down on someone's front lawn, gasping for air. Moments later, Garry dramatically laid down beside him. The two exhausted men clumsily high-fived each other.

"Michael, dude, you are an absolute monster," Garry gasped.

"I know, I know. Monster Michael. Ugh. You owe me a beer."

***

Murphy was bone tired after the interview. She needed gas and a coffee and pulled into the nearest gas station. She filled up the Brawler first, then herself, grabbing a large black coffee, and a packaged sandwich. Leaning against her Brawler, she put the coffee on the hood of the 4x4 and used her teeth and her good hand to open the sandwich. She sniffed at it and turned it around, looking for any green mould. It passed inspection and she bit into it. The turkey and spinach were melded between two slices of dry white bread. It was terrible, and maybe that bit of spinach was, in fact, mould, but Murphy was glad for the food. She took a big gulp of searing hot coffee to wash it down.

She tossed her garbage into a receptacle, got into the 4x4 and drove home. It was just past two o'clock when she pulled into the gravel parking lot. A large 'Closed' sign stood outside the gallery door.

When she walked in, she could hear a murmur of soft voices coming from the living room. Murphy walked into the room. Del scooted her wheelchair around the coffee table and invited her to sit down. Maria, hunched over and exhausted, got up. "Coffee?" she asked.

"No, no, Maria, please, sit down. Let me get coffee for everyone. Real coffee, I promise." Her lighthearted joke about real and not instant coffee was ignored. "I'll just be a minute," she said.

In the kitchen, she put a fresh filter and ground coffee in the basket and slipped it into the coffee machine. She turned on the switch and rummaged around for coffee mugs. She gathered five mismatched mugs. Two were handmade by local artists and had a slightly askew look. One was a tourist mug from Ottawa, another was a plain blue mug. The last one, her favourite, was a find at a local thrift shop. It simply read, GTFO.

Murphy walked upstairs, put her gun and badge away, splashed cold water on her face, changed into jeans and a t-shirt, and headed back down-stairs.

The aroma of coffee filled the air as water trickled through the grounds and into the glass carafe below. She watched as the stream of dark brown flowed, the machine hissing slightly. Murphy grabbed the carafe a little too early, and coffee dripped onto the heated element below. Murphy stuffed her GTFO cup underneath to catch the last drops and poured the coffee. Filling her own, she put the carafe back and brought the cups out, one at a time.

Maria was teary-eyed as she held Del's hand. She took a cup and put it down on the table. When Murphy returned with another cup, she did the same thing. Neither Thomas nor Jens tried theirs. Only Murphy drank, and she did not even like drip coffee. She looked at everyone carefully.

Murphy did not like seeing other people's emotions, though as a homicide detective, she saw them all the time. From the rage that led to a murder to the sorrow of a mother whose child had been killed, everyone's emotions were on full display for Murphy. After her own childhood trauma, she did everything she could to keep her own emotions in check. She was good at it, too. Murphy expressed her anger through art, her happiness through sex and her pride through arresting murder suspects. Fear had long disappeared, and she was no longer surprised by anything human beings did.

She waited for a while, sipping her coffee, listening to the others reminisce about Bob as if he were dead. For her, he was a flamboyant queer she saw once or twice a month at the local bar. For the others, he was a staple of daily living. Bob had provided humour when there was tragedy, and kindness when the world was cruel. Now the world had taken its revenge for his defiance.

Murphy's head jerked, and she realized she needed to sleep. She silently nodded to no one in particular and left the room. She poured the last of her coffee out, set the mug on the counter, and went upstairs.

Unsettled, she looked around her room and grabbed a colouring book and pencil crayons. Murphy sat at the table and added some shading to a kitten's face. She loved the simplicity of kids' colouring books, but it was difficult to colour with the cast on. She took everything over to the bed, laid down on her stomach, and started again on the shading.

"Caitlin, dinner is ready. Caitlin?" Maria tiptoed into the bedroom. "Caitlin?" Murphy stirred, grunted, and stretched. She had fallen asleep for a few hours and, although she was still tired, she was also hungry.

"Okay, thanks. Coming down in a second." She quickly washed her face with cold water and descended the stairs, joining everyone at the kitchen table. It was tight.

Maria put steaming paella in front of Murphy. A symphony of aromas wafted from its golden surface. The tang of the sea mingled with the sweetness of the shellfish, an olfactory dance that stirred thoughts of the Mediterranean coast she had never been to. The rice was infused with saffron, a burst of colour and flavour that elevated the dish to new heights.

"Maria, this smells amazing," Thomas said.

"Fantastic, as always," Murphy agreed. Succulent prawns, tender squid, and plump mussels filled each bite. The flavours of briny seafood and smoky chorizo blended together. It was a feast for the senses, a reminder of the rich bounty that the ocean provides and the artistry of those who know how to harness it. Maria's expert hand was like Picasso's.

"What happens next?" Del asked as she refilled her glass of wine. "Like, what happens with Bob?"

Murphy took a sip of the light-bodied Verdejo, enjoying the crisp citrus flavour of the wine, and shook her head. "I do not know. Has anyone called? No? Then I would say, call Toronto General, find out what's going on. If they won't tell you, I have the number for the doctor here. He can probably help."

Murphy spent the rest of the evening with the foursome, chatting while watching a movie on television. Throughout the show, Murphy tried texting Sun, but all the texts went unanswered.

"Let her decide when she's going to answer. Stop harassing her," Del sniped. "You don't have to be a jerk."

Murphy was taken aback. There was venom in her voice. She knew it wasn't about her at all—it was about the fear of losing Bob—but Murphy did not care for it.

As the movie credits rolled, Murphy said her goodnights and headed up to her own room. She changed into pyjamas, kneeled at the side of her bed, and put her hands together.

She said her prayer and added tonight's names: Jenna Renley, Bradley Presley, Jodi Matthews, Len Ainsley, Joe Hancock, Arthur Benoit. Each night, she said the names of a few of the over fifty murder victims. They were cases she had over the years, and would say other names in the next prayer on the next night.

She crawled into bed, turned off the lamp on the side table, and fell into a restless sleep. Nightmares of vicious anthropomorphic cars disturbed her sleep. She woke up twice in the night and each time she returned to sleep; the cars returned.

In the early morning, Murphy awoke to the rising sun and the chirping of birds. She knew some by sound: the cardinal and the red-winged black-bird were the easiest. These birds were neither of those, but their songs were still a pleasant sound to wake up to.

Murphy showered. After drying herself off, she gingerly took off the plastic she had wrapped around her cast and checked it, making sure it was still dry. There was a bit of Miller's dried blood on it. "Asshole," she mumbled. She wondered briefly whether the cast would get in the way of sex. But since her lover wasn't speaking to her, it might not be tested.

She crept quietly downstairs to make herself an instant coffee. Grabbing fruit and a yogurt from the fridge, she headed back upstairs. In her sitting room was a small nook where she had set up an office. She sat down at the small desk and booted up her police-issued laptop. Murphy went to the secure police login page and typed in her username and password, then waited for the next prompt. She stared at the small screen on the Titanium Identity Security token and when it switched to a new seven digit number; she typed that in to the prompt. After a moment, she was logged into the Northshore Municipal Police Department network. She would use her early Monday morning to catch up on emails. Today, there were almost none. None of the team had updated her on their Sunday work. Fair enough, Murphy thought. I told them not to work. She logged out and drove to the office.

CHAPTER EIGHT

Murphy was already sitting in the third floor meeting room when Shevchenko arrived. "Murphy, I hope you had a good rest after your Sunday interview."

"Yes sir, thank you," she lied. She spent it hanging out with crying people while her lover ignored her. Not great at all. "And you?" When he said he had gone to a barbeque at his neighbours, Murphy realized she needed a different downtime. Barbeques and beers with the neighbours sounded great.

Over the next twenty minutes, the rest of the Homicide Unit arrived. Mitch walked in. Murphy decided she may be a bodybuilder or boxer. Members of the Forensic Team and the Accident Reconstruction Team arrived. Shevchenko introduced a new attendee, RCMP Counter Terrorism expert, Saul Goldstein, who advised he was there as a consultant only.

Shevchenko gave the first update, presenting the high-level postmortem information on the only fatality. Kitty Myers died from blunt force trauma received in the attack. Murphy gave her update next, talking about the suspect interview and the hate crime overtones of the attack. "This tracks with what we found in his home," Bradshaw said as he handed printed copies of his Evidence Collection report. There were ten sections documenting the forensic evidence collected in Miller's home, truck, and a second car. "Section Two, starting at page two-one. There were pages ripped out of a bible, with writing on them. Lots of homophobic slurs, name calling, lists of bad things people have done."

Murphy flipped to the specified page. It was a photograph of pages from Revelations and Genesis taped to a mirror. The next page was a typed list of all the words Miller had written on the pages, and the number of times the word appeared. Another five pages of photography showed the pages close up. There were photos of dirty laundry, mostly empty takeout food containers scattered around the floor, the packaging from the toy gun, and a computer. Only the computer desk was clear of clutter and filth. "The computer was turned over to Mitch." More photograph showed the rest of the house, and the property outside.

Bradshaw continued with his summary. "Section Three. This is the truck. A white 1991 Trurok 480. Purchased by the suspect on June twenty-first." Murphy turned the page to find a photograph of the provincial registration, then Miller's driver's license. "A cell phone was found under the driver's side seat, turned over to Mitch." Bradshaw pointed to the photo of an empty chocolate milk carton and a napkin. "It was covered in bacon grease and ketchup," he said. He said the truck radio was tuned to CRST-FM, a Christian radio station broadcasting from Ravensburg. The rest of the physical evidence from the truck was outlined. "Sections Five through Ten are forensics on the exterior and interior of the truck, as far as we have gotten. We have identified twenty-three different DNA samples. Some clearly from the attack. We have not yet matched all of them. There was no evidence of anyone else being in the truck with him."

The next five sections covered forensic evidence obtained at the scene. Bradshaw was clear that these photos had to be considered along with Neal's reconstruction. There were photos of streaks of white paint on brickwork, poles, chairs and a mailbox where the truck bounced from hard object to hard object. There were pages and pages of images of everyday items left behind by people fleeing for their lives. A single flip-flop, a spilled shopping bag, a pair of glasses. Dozens of objects. Murphy paused at the photograph of Sun Flowers. The smashed store front. A splatter of dried blood outside. The fractured flowers scattered on the ground, with glass shards glinting like diamonds.

"We have logged all the evidence with NSPD, the complete catalogue of items is the last section," Bradshaw said. He then yielded the floor to Neal.

Neal pulled down a white screen and started up his laptop and projector. Reconstruction Team member Xavier Solis handed out their team's report. "We have what we believe is an excellent reconstruction of the ramming attack," Neal said. "We have collected video from five different store cameras and have put together both an edited video for the timeline and a wireframe."

He played the recorded video first, showing the truck driving down the sidewalk. Murphy watched intently, seeing if there were any inconsistencies or areas of interest. The truck bounced and veered down the street, and the path looked more random than chosen. And then it was over.

"How long was that?"

"The truck turned on to Centre Street at 16:45. The truck turned north on to Blue Street, at 16:47. It was one minute, forty-one seconds, travelling seven hundred and sixty-two metres at thirty kilometres an hour, on average. Right here," Neal said, pointing to the patio of the Sparkling Unicorn, "he reversed and then accelerated forward again. Based on the wounds of the two victims at this location and the video, the driver could not get past a table, and so reversed."

Murphy quickly looked down at her hands to hide her eyes from the others. Miller had hit Bob, hit Kitty, then reversed over Bob. Eighteen injured and one dead in a minute and forty-one seconds. She cleared her throat. "Is it possible he chose which people to target?"

A five-minute debate ensued. Neal thought it was not possible. Bradshaw said no. Shevchenko agreed with Murphy because he had heard the interview. Then Mitch spoke up. "When I was reviewing his computer, I saw he had a game called La Guerre Infinitus. It's a first person game where users kill other players. Typical fps. I checked online reviews and videos. It is really fast, players have to make quick decisions about whom to kill and whom to spare. If he's been playing long enough, he would be well-versed in fast decision making based on visuals."

Mitch explained she had located the account name and requested the user's login times, chats, and saved videos from the gaming company. "It will take up to a month," she said.

"Okay, so Miller only went once down the street. He never scoped it out first, right? Yes, so he drove at a speed of about thirty, down a wide sidewalk, hitting some people but not others. And you're suggesting his gaming habits might explain how he could decide quickly about whom to hit," Murphy said. "Okay, another opinion then, please. Based on what we have covered so far, the religious material, that he said he saw a sign, the area he drove, what little we know about his personality. Was this a Hate-Motivated crime? Does it rise to the level of a Hate-Motivated or Bias-Motivated crime?"

Another heated argument ensued, with most members saying it did not, and the Homicide detectives and Mitch saying it did. After hearing different takes on the issue, Murphy held up her hands. "Okay, okay, okay. Thank you. It's something we will consider when we turn the file over to the Crown Attorney's Office. Thank you."

The meeting lasted another hour, wrapping up just before noon. Saul Goldstein walked out of the room to discuss the case in private with Shevchenko, while Murphy and her team walked out. "That was kind of amazing, " Murphy said to her team. "All of that work in two days, a day and a half. Amazing."

As the team walked down to Homicide, they passed by a large window that overlooked the street in front of the building. A sizeable group of people had gathered. Some people carried religious signs that read 'Love the sinner/hate the sin' and 'Redemption through Christ'.

"Lots of religious signs. After what we heard this morning, is there a connection?" Hamilton asked as she watched them slowly circle.

Parker shook his head. "I don't know. Where did they get those signs so quickly? Has this been planned, or..."

"Signs are probably easy to come by. But, I don't know. Look at who is carrying them. See? Lots of white people, middle-aged white people. And look at the Confederate flag. What is that about? When was the last time you saw a Confederate Flag in Northshore? And when do middle-aged white people protest anything around here?" Hamilton asked.

"We do not get a lot of protesters here, but I've seen them on TV. They are usually, I don't know, anti-vaccination, anti-choice protesters, these days," Girard replied.

"So why here and why now?" Murphy asked. The question went unanswered.

"By the pricking of my thumbs, something wicked this way comes," Hamilton said.

"By the what?"

"Pricking of my thumbs. Intuition. Like, a tingling feeling you get in your hands when something is wrong."

Parker nodded and said, "Like right now, with the hair on the back of my neck standing up?"

"Yes, exactly that," Hamilton replied. The detectives stared out the window for another few minutes before heading back to the office. They began checking out Perry Miller's former jobs and schools, finding out if he has been in trouble. Bullying, harassing, cheating, vandalism, everything.

"I'm looking through the report from the Forensics Unit on the house. There is no sign that the neighbours were interviewed," Girard said.

"We still have a lot of work to do. Have you seen anything from the Reconstruction Team checking for door-cam footage near his home, or on the way to Kettering?" Murphy asked.

"No, nothing," Girard said, looking through the report's table of contents. "They focussed on Centre Street. Itchy?"

Murphy had been absentmindedly scratching at her arm. "Oh yeah, incredibly. Plus, I am supposed to get to the doctor to change the dressing for the wound on my palm. Maybe I'll just hit the ER later. Listen, feel like taking a drive?"

She and Girard took the Brawler to Franklin Street, going westbound, just as Miller had done. Nothing was out of place on the street, but as the large 4x4 drove slowly past, pedestrians eyed it warily. One woman stepped into a doorway, waiting for it to pass. "People are scared," Girard said as he watched another woman run across the street from them.

"I think they will be for a while," Murphy said. "Can you see anything that might have triggered him? Any, I don't know, any porn shops or massage parlours? Anything gay here? Rainbows? He said something about a sign. Did anything on this street trigger him?"

Girard looked from one side of the street to the next. He shook his head. "No, not even a lingerie shop. There was a sign back there for a drag show, but—"

Murphy hit the brakes. "A sign? A drag show? Where?" Girard pointed it out, and Murphy insisted he get out and take a photograph. "Hurry, I'm blocking traffic," she said. Maybe Miller was literal, not figurative, about seeing a sign, Murphy thought. Girard scrambled out and took a photo.

A car behind Murphy began honking, getting more insistent with every passing second. By the time Girard had taken the photo and was jogging back to the Brawler, the horn was one continuous blast.

Just as Girard reached the car door, Murphy put the Brawler into park and got out. The driver of the car behind her also got out and came aggressively toward her, yelling. She held her badge out in front of her at eye height and made sure her gun holster flashed. "Get in your car. Now!" she commanded. "Move it! And lay off the damned horn." Unhappy but feeling helpless, the driver got back in his car and slammed the door. He pouted while Murphy glared at him before finally walking back to the 4x4.

"I love being able to stop yahoos like that," she said to Girard. "If he was just patient for ten more seconds. Geez." Murphy turned up Centre Street and drove up the street slowly. Everything looked almost normal, except for the plywood covering the missing windows and an absence of trash cans. The patios were open, people were enjoying beers and burgers in the sun. Even the Sparkling Unicorn patio was open, three drag queens and a drag king standing at all four corners like honour guards for the bar's queer patrons.

Murphy turned east on Red Road, just as Miller had. "What do you think, Adam? We went slowly, that was about twenty kilometres an hour. Could you see what people were eating? What they looked like?"

"Easy. You could pick and choose." Girard was right. At slow speed, seeing what people were doing was easy. She pulled into a laneway and turned around, driving the route in the opposite direction. It was vital for a homicide detective to turn around one last time and look at the scene before they left. Floral memorials, teddy bears, crosses and candles sat in groups on the street, honouring the injured and dead.

On Highway 2, Murphy rolled down the windows. Highway 2 was part of a provincial highway system, snaking its way from Lancaster to Windsor. Without provincial funding, the section that cut through Northshore was badly neglected. The road was cracked and pitted with gut-dropping potholes.

Trees pressed in on both sides anywhere they had not been cut down for a house or store. The air was cool and fragrant, the scent of pine needles and dry earth filling Murphy's nose. Ahead, the road climbed and dipped, following the contours of the land. The occasional small waterfall or creek provided a refreshing break. It was a short drive, and the only sounds were the engine's roar and Girard telling Murphy about his Sunday off work. The sky was a brilliant shade of blue. It was a nice day.

The WeeSee GPS app told Murphy that White Pine Cone Road was coming up on the right. She said "Weezy, end my trip." Obediently, WeeSee ended the trip and went to sleep.

Seventeen White Pine Cone sat ominously on the side of the road, its poorly maintained exterior exposed a sense of unease. Junked cars lined the land beside the driveway. The walls of the house were a sombre shade of grey. A single weathered Canadian flag hung limply from a post, casting a foreboding shadow on the otherwise barren yard. A narrow gravel driveway led up to the house, cutting sharply through the acre of land that surrounded the property. The land was devoid of life, a wasteland of dying weeds and dead trees. A gnarled oak stood sentinel in the centre of the yard, its branches twisted and bare. The windows of the house were streaked with grime. A few wilted flowers sat on the windowsills, their petals brown and withered. The scent of neglect hung in the air. It was a place of dark secrets.

"Boss, what is that smell?" Girard asked as they got close to the house. Murphy's nose wrinkled, and she rolled up the windows. It smelled of rotten onions, vomit, and raw sewage.

Murphy parked, and the detectives got out of the vehicle. They had not taken five steps before a man appeared in the house's doorway, shouting at them. "You get the fuck off my property!"

"We are with the Northshore Municipal Police Department," Girard said, reaching for his badge. The man burst out of the door and charged the detectives. "Whoa whoa whoa!"

"Get off my fucking land! Unless you have another fucking warrant, you get the fuck off my property!" he screamed.

"You bastards arrested my Perry," a woman said, stepping onto the stair. "He's innocent! He's a good kid, a God fearing boy! You bastards got it wrong!" she yelled. When she gave Murphy and Girard the finger, Murphy almost laughed.

"Okay, we're leaving," Murphy said as they headed back to the 4x4. Perry's father kicked gravel at the Brawler as it pulled away from the house.

"Wow," Girard said. "How can they defend that monster?"

"Well, it makes me wonder if they encouraged him. Or maybe you don't even have to go that far. Maybe they knew their son was troubled, that he was capable of this, and did nothing. We still haven't checked his school and work history. You saw the photos of the inside of the house, that was a pigsty. It smelled worse than a pigsty." Murphy turned into the next driveway, hoping for a better greeting. Girard wrote in his notepad that the Millers were hostile and refused to be interviewed.

A man appeared from the side of the house before she turned off the engine. "We are from the Northshore Municipal Police Department," Murphy said as she rolled down the window.

He shook his head. "You have a warrant?"

Murphy turned off the Brawler. "No sir, I'd just like to ask you some questions about your neighbour, Perry Miller." She undid her seatbelt and opened the door.

"You stay in that thing unless you have a warrant. This is private property. And I'm not talking to you."

"What the hell?" Girard whispered under his breath. Murphy made a calming gesture with her hand.

"It's about your neighbour Perry Miller. He was arrested for—"

"I'm not talking."

Murphy nodded, rolled up the window, and started the Brawler. "Sometimes they just hate us," Murphy said. "Sometimes it is justified. And sometimes they are the assholes." The Northshore Municipal Police Department had a significant number of complaints against them, but the complaints review team was part of the NSPD and, not surprisingly, rarely substantiated any complaints. When they did, the consequences for the officers were minor.

Only one neighbour, three kilometres away, agreed to talk to the detectives, but did not know the Millers and had nothing relevant to say. Murphy and Girard went back to the office.

Parking the Brawler at the rear of the building, they walked around to the front and looked at the crowd that had gathered. A tall man with a megaphone was talking to the crowd.

"Unleash the righteous fury! He is truly blessed who does not follow the evil advice of sinners." The charismatic preacher was donned in impeccable attire and commanded attention when he spoke. "But mark my words, for I bring forth a thunderous proclamation: repentance is not a mere suggestion, it is an absolute mandate! Cast off the shackles of your transgressions, strip yourself of the rot that festers within! Turn away from every vile indulgence that poisons your very being!"

Murphy walked up to a uniformed officer who was part of the line of police keeping the crowd away from the cars. "Who is he?" she asked. She thought she recognized the voice.

"Jonathan Haidt. He has a radio show on CRST-FM." Murphy nodded and walked back to Girard, suggesting that they should go into the office. She let Girard know this was who Miller had been listening to.

"Did he know Miller was listening? Or is this coincidence?" Girard asked.

"You know I don't believe in coincidences."

"I demand a complete and uncompromising abandonment, not only of lust and drinking and pot smoking, but of every loathsome vice that stains your existence! Your sinfulness must be purged without exception!"

"Hey boss," Parker said as they walked into the atelier.

"Michael, Cleo." She settled onto the couch and put her feet on the coffee table. Girard sat down beside her and grabbed a mint from the candy dish. Only the crinkling of the wrapper could be heard.

"That preacher is troubling. Miller was listening to him during the attack: well, at least when I arrested him. It won't be long before Haidt spouts hate speech. They all do. But he's doing it with a megaphone in front of police headquarters." Murphy said. She got up to get herself a cup of instant coffee.

"What was he saying?" Hamilton asked. "Is there a connection?"

Murphy considered for a moment as she stirred her coffee. "Yeah, somewhere. Maybe. But correlation isn't causation. Do we think the preacher is a conspirator?" She returned to her seat and took a sip of coffee. Hamilton hesitated. Murphy could see her discomfort. "What is it? Cleo?"

"Off the record?" Hamilton asked.

"Never. But I'd like to hear what you have to say."

Hamilton nodded and took a deep breath. "We know Miller was listening to Haidt. The Chief released Miller's name to the media this morning, but not a word about religion or Haidt. That never left our meeting. But the exact guy shows up using religious language, inflammatory language.

How did he know? How did he know to show up here? Did someone tell him? Did he tell Miller to attack?" Hamilton spoke quickly. Murphy could see the anxiety in her eyes.

"I don't think for a second that one of us spoke to the guy," Parker said.

"But what if he was told? And that's why he's here?" Girard added.

"Fuuuuck," Murphy groaned. "The guys were opposed to considering the truck ramming a hate motivated crime. I said I was probably going to try for it. Now we have this guy on the street saying inflammatory shit."

"What has that got to do with Miller's hate motivation charges?" Parker asked.

"If Haidt isn't charged with hate motivated speech for saying hateful stuff or promoting violence, then Miller's actions night not be considered hate motivated either. I would want the longest sentence possible for this guy. Proving this is a hate crime will increase his sentence. I really want the longest time in prison we can get."

"You always do. There is no way he won't be going to prison for the max," Girard said. "You're catastrophizing."

"Is that even an actual word? Look, we've all agreed the truck ramming was a hate crime. And Supt. Shevchenko saw it. He agreed. If Miller says hateful stuff but is not held accountable specifically for that hate, it emboldens others."

Murphy tried to recall the training she had received after the Ottawa debacle of 2022. A convoy of vehicles with anti-vaxxers, white supremacists, and those wanting to overthrow the government obstructed the city. Ottawa is the capital of the country, the seat of the federal government, and a target for the action. The police failed on many fronts and it became an embarrassment to law enforcement. Chief Valencia had ordered mandatory training for all personnel, from riot control training to spotting hate motivation. The sudden appearance of Haidt concerned her. "I will speak to Supt. Shevchenko about this. Maybe one of the other team members released the information," Murphy said.

"Or maybe the Superintendent himself."

"Okay, update the board with what we have. Find out who Jonathan Haidt is and if he is tied to any previous protests," Murphy sighed. "Miller talked about La Guerre Infinitus when I interviewed him. Some kind of online game. Find out if it's linked to any protests or radicalization, please. Talk to Mitch. And someone talk to the man who sold Miller the truck. If there is an inclination that he knew or was involved, I want him in for a formal interview."

Murphy walked into her office and sat down quietly. She would let the record show she did something about her Haidt concerns. Dialling the phone, Murphy cleared her throat and thought about what she had to say. Superintendent Shevchenko was her immediate superior, and she had to report Hamilton's suspicions to him. He was an old school cop, and on more than one occasion, he had chastised Murphy for reporting directly to Chief Valencia, skipping reporting levels.

"Superintendent Shevchenko," the heavy voice said.

Murphy launched into concerns about the protesters, the street preacher, and the possibility of a leak within his chosen team. He grunted a few times while she was talking, unsettling her. Finally, he told her to put it in writing, said he would raise it if appropriate. It was the best she could do. It worked as she had intended: it was now something she had told him about immediately and was going to put in writing.

Murphy turned her mind back to the matter at hand and flipped through the reports. Miller was a loner with no real life friends they could find, and neighbours refused to talk. He had no job record after dropping out of school at sixteen. He had no political literature, no flags or memorabilia, nothing to show he was radicalized by any group. But he had the bible and CRST radio, and they could be radical enough. Plus, the RCMP Anti-terrorism unit was involved with the investigation.

Parker had spoken with the food delivery services: he was a regular, but unpopular because of his poor tipping and body odour.

Hamilton had spoken with his high school and grade school: he did poorly academically. Throughout grade school, he was suspended seven times for disrupting the class, talking back to teachers and once for cheating. Nothing about sexual harassment. In highschool, he was expelled for bullying in grade nine, and for fighting in grade ten. He never returned.

Murphy went to see Dr. Chen, to get details of the cause of death for Kitty Meyers.

CHAPTER NINE

"Detective Inspector Murphy, so nice of you to come and see me," Dr. Chen said. "Did you know house cats share almost ninety-six percent of their genetic makeup with tigers? Tigers."

"No doctor, I did not know," she said. Occasionally, Chen would provide completely irrelevant facts, and this was one of those occasions. "I am here about Kitty Mey—" Murphy just caught the cat fact connection. "Kitty Meyers, doctor."

"Yes, of course. She has been waiting here for you for a while," he said as he walked over to the small bank of cold lockers. "The Forensic Team came, but I know you like to see with your own eyes." Chen had been the pathologist and coroner for Northshore for twelve years. His unusual habits—spouting random facts and repeating words—made him the butt of jokes within law enforcement. He must have known, Murphy thought, he just did not care.

Chen opened the door to locker four and pulled out a large, shrouded body. "I should warn you, she suffered significant head and face trauma. Warn." Murphy girded herself and nodded. Chen pulled back the cloth from the upper body. Kitty Meyers looked only somewhat human now. "Crush trauma to the head. Tire impressions on the skin, which I have catalogued for the Forensics Unit. Here, the hair and scalp were torn off," he said as he pointed his gloved finger at a mess of flesh. Murphy made a mental note to check that the forensic report included findings of hair and flesh on the truck tires. "Fortunately, some of her teeth are still intact in the skull. We used her dental chart for official identification. Teeth."

"Closed casket for sure," Murphy said. "Were there any mitigating factors? Her heart or…?"

"No. Though it wasn't the best. There was pericardial fat. She was a large woman, as you can see. One hundred and eight point three kilograms, and just one hundred and sixty centimetres. Two hundred and thirty-nine pounds. I know you prefer imperial. Five foot three."

"Thank you, Dr. Chen."

"It was the vehicle impact that killed her. Extensive physical internal damage to the lungs, heart, kidney, intestines. Her spine was broken in four places. Spine. There was significant damage to the skin and flesh, as it appears the truck spun its wheels while she was underneath."

Murphy would have to correlate the findings of the reports to get a clear picture of Kitty's death. "Doctor, if he had continued forward. If the driver had not stopped and reversed, could Kitty have survived?"

"There is no way to tell," Chen said. "The cause of death was massive blunt trauma to the head, crushing the skull, as you can see. I cannot tell you if that happened on the first impact, or the second. It would likely have been a brief interval between the two contact events. Contact," Chen said. "The full list of injuries is in my report," he said as he covered Kitty's body and pushed her back into the cold locker.

"The family has asked for her remains to be collected," he said. "I have no reason not to release her."

"Toxicology is here too?" Murphy asked. She envisioned a defence attorney blaming Kitty for being too drunk or stoned to get out of the way of the truck. Blaming the victim was just one way to mitigate the responsibility of the killer.

"Of course. She had three or four margaritas, or glasses of wine, before the event. Her BAC was point zero seven. But she was not driving, was she?"

Murphy shook her head. "No, I'd have to check where she was, but probably on a restaurant patio. At least, I hope she was on a patio, having a drink and a laugh with friends."

"Laugh with friends. A good time to go," Chen said.

Murphy thanked the doctor and headed back to the office. When she arrived, everyone else had gone home for the evening. With the suspect in custody, there was no need for overtime. Murphy scanned the reports and walked up to a clean board, grabbed a marker, and wrote.

'Kitty Meyers, 57. 7/15. Crush injuries. Reversed over. Black House patio.' When she wrote the location, she grabbed a red marker and circled the restaurant on the map. It was next to the Sparkling Unicorn. She realized that Bob's injuries were like Kitty's, and it was possible that they were both hit at almost the same time. Both trapped under the truck tires. Murphy blinked rapidly to cast the image from her mind's eye. '3-4 drinks. Verify DNA on tires/undercarriage', she wrote. It would probably take months for all the DNA tests to come back.

She then began allocating survivor interviews to her team by email. She gave Parker the first six survivors, Hamilton the next, and Girard the last six. Eighteen people in all. The Accident Reconstruction Team had already interviewed everyone they could. Many had received only minor injuries and were treated at the scene, then held in the busses with Sun and other uninjured witnesses. But a few days had passed, and the initial shock would have worn off. She wanted the witnesses to get to meet Homicide detectives and to ask additional questions. Did they hear the driver say anything? Had they noticed anyone hanging around the location in the days previous to the attack? Did they know Perry Miller?

Murphy's phone rang. It was Sun. "Hi. I saw the flower shop. You got some plywood up."

"Yes, Chris helped me out. He picked up the wood and put it up late Saturday night. He's a wonderful son," Sun said. "I would like to apologize to you for the last time we talked."

Sun often apologized for getting upset, and although Murphy was not one for emotional outbursts, she did not mind too much when Sun had a blowup. It usually meant great apology sex.

"Are you interested in dinner tonight?" Sun asked.

"Yes, absolutely. When and where?"

Murphy had forty-five minutes to get to the restaurant. Sun had chosen Un Bassin Versant, the Watershed, a high-end restaurant with amazing vegetarian options. At least, that was what Sun said: Murphy would not know the difference between a great vegetarian meal and a terrible one, except that both were missing meat.

Murphy headed down to the showers at HQ. The best she could manage was a lukewarm wipe down with a face cloth. Looking in the cracked mirror, she smiled at herself. She was forty-eight years old and somehow was loving a life no one would ever have been able to predict. She was a leader of a great homicide team, married to a great friend, developing feelings for her new girlfriend, and was selling her art. "Don't get too happy, Cait," she said to her reflection. "You know your luck." She smiled and blew herself a kiss.

Getting dressed and putting a trigger lock on her gun, Murphy threw everything, including her badge, into her bag. She was planning to leave the hotel room tomorrow and go directly back to work. This would be the eighth official date with Sun. Sun had no problem—not anymore—with Murphy's marriage and seemed to be okay with her walking out at a moment's notice. She gets it, Murphy thought.

Murphy called home to check on Del. Jens answered the phone. "It's about time you called," he chastised." When are you coming home?"

"Tomorrow," Murphy said.

"You are one cold-hearted bitch," Jens spat into the phone. He hung up, forcing Murphy to call again. This time, Del answered.

"Hey, was that you before?" Del asked.

"Yep. Is it okay I don't come home tonight? Or do you need me?"

"No, you don't have to come home," Del said. "I have Thomas and Jens. And Maria is here too. The four of us are making a quick trip to Toronto tomorrow to see Bob."

"Oh, that's great," Murphy said. "Okay, I'll get an update from you tomorrow. Bye." Murphy hung up and headed to the Brawler. She put her bag in the lockbox under the back seat and got in. The engine roared to life, as eager to get going as she was. She tapped the address into her WeeSee GPS system and pulled out onto the street. Protesters were still on the streets, although the preacher was long gone. She headed to Un Bassin Versant up 11, across 3 and over to 60.

"Turn left at Muddy Shoe Road," WeeSee said. Murphy hit the indicator and turned left. She wondered briefly how this road got its name. As the Brawler bumped and bucked along the pitted road, she decided it was one of the older roads in the area, probably once a cattle path. Likely it had no name for most of its life and when it came time, some municipal employee simply looked at their feet and filled in the paperwork.

"Your destination is on the right."

"Thanks Weezy," Murphy said as she pulled into the parking lot. "Wish me luck." Of course, the app said nothing, and Murphy was not expecting it to. The lot was mostly full, and once inside, Murphy was glad Sun had made reservations. They would not have been seated otherwise. Murphy gave Sun's name at the door and was escorted to an empty table for two at the back.

The vegetarian restaurant felt like it belonged nestled in the heart of Paris. It was a beacon of refinement and taste. Its elegant decor, a fusion of classic and modern styles, set the stage for a romantic dinner for the two women. The ambiance was lively yet intimate, with soft classical music adding to the romantic atmosphere.

"Sorry I'm late," Sun said as she kissed Murphy on the cheek and sat in the chair opposite. "There was a traffic slowdown on 11. Kind of weird."

"But you're here now," Murphy said with a smile.

"I'm here now."

The waiter came and went, bringing water, explaining menu items, taking orders, providing drinks and finally, bringing food. "Filigree of Wildflowers for the lady," he said, putting the appetizer in front of Sun, "and Mellowed Fabaceae for the other lady. Enjoy."

A single pod lay in the centre of Sun's plate, surrounded with wildflowers. "Look at this milkweed pod pickle. Have you ever had one?" Sun asked.

Murphy smiled and shook her head. "Milkweed? No, never." She leaned forward, eager to hear what Sun had to say about it. Murphy did not care too much about what she ate, but she enjoyed listening to Sun describe the tastes and smells of anything botanical. The woman had a love of flowers that she had translated into a very successful flower shop in Kettering.

Sun pricked the pod with her fork and lifted it up to her nose. "They pickled it in apple cider vinegar, pickling spices and..." She inhaled deeply, "And garlic. Look, it's a soft pickle." She held it up for Murphy to see. "Milkweed is good for Monarch butterflies, so it must be good for me." She bit the pod and flavour burst into her mouth. "Uhnn, oh, mmm, so good," she said, the sounds spilling sloppily from her lips. She held out a bite for Murphy, then gobbled it when Murphy declined.

Sun raved about the raw Canada lily and high mallow petals. Neither was strong tasting on their own, but together offered a unique lamella for the aniseed herb extract that was drizzled on. "The violets are sweet, slightly salty. There is no drizzle on them. They are, they are cool," Sun said as she smacked her lips.

Murphy ate her Mellowed Fabaceae with little ado. The carrots had been lightly candied with maple syrup and the puffed fabaceae—peas and green beans—added both crunchy and chewy textures to the salad.

Conversation passed easily between the women, with the events of the previous day covered and left behind. The waiter brought the mains, and Sun enthused over her pommes boulangère aux poireaux with peppergrass coulis. Murphy wondered why her crunchy tofu with strawberry-blite and honeyed quinoa did not taste at all like strawberries.

"Chenopodium capitatum. You are right, it does not taste like strawberries. They must grow their own here. Trying to find it in the wild is pretty hit and miss. Mostly miss. It can take a year or more. May I try a bite?" Sun asked. She parted her lips as Murphy plucked one flower from her plate and fed it to Sun. "Mmm, oh, that's delicious." She moaned a little louder, licked her lips, and winked at Murphy.

With dinner finished and paid for, the women kissed and headed to their respective vehicles.

The promise of a night of passion at the Serene Inn was just five kilometres away from the restaurant. Murphy and Sun were inside their room quickly.

Between the women was an atmospheric, flawless desire. It flowed from one to the other without effort, without interruption. Sun looked up and kissed her. It was, at first, slow and soft. But Murphy's response grew and her hand was pushing aside the straps of Sun's dress, sending them over her shoulders and down her arms.

Sun felt the zipper of her dress come down, felt the cool firmness of Murphy's hand on her back. It was familiar and new at the same time. "Let me," Sun whispered hoarsely as she caught the dress slipping off her body. A flash of green and blue hit the floor, and she stepped lightly out of it. Murphy undid her bra with one hand and it, too, fell to the floor. Sun's arm brushed against the hardness of the arm cast, and she once again said, "Let me."

Sun stepped in close and unfastened the buttons on Murphy's shirt one by one, slowly, purposefully. Her mouth remembered, and she kissed the dry skin of Murphy's breasts, her neck, her shoulders. Pushing the white shirt away, pulling the red bra off, she saw and kissed the scars on Murphy's back. She easily undid Murphy's pants and let them drop to the floor, the black mingling with the green and blue and red and white already there. Expressionist art in a vivid moment.

She slowly kissed Murphy onto the bed, shedding the remnants of clothing like the last strokes of a master artist. She slipped on top, one arm extended to hold her left hand still. "Don't move," she murmured. "Don't. Move." Murphy obediently let her injured left hand lay unmoving on the bed. Sun's mouth and hands continued their journey, touching and tasting flesh and hair and salt and sweetness, thick and sultry. She wanted to awaken every part of Murphy's body, to arouse love and desire and lust and devotion.

As soon as Murphy's body began to tremble and shudder in response to her climax, Sun moved up, her fingers rhythmic, her breathing paired. She was overwhelmingly moved, connected, as she hovered her mouth over Murphy's. She took in each breath, each moan, each pleasure until, at last, as the orgasm ebbed and flowed, it rippled to an end. Murphy was panting. Sun smiled, her body saturated with love. This, she thought to herself, was how you created love, how you birthed love into the world. This, she thought, is how you made love.

Murphy lay nude on her front on the bed, Sun squatting on her back, giving her a massage. She ran her fingers firmly over the scarred flesh, pondering the faded white lines. They were scattered across her back in all directions. She bent over and kissed each of them gently.

"How did you get these?" Sun asked, rousing Murphy from her blissful drowsiness.

"I work out," Murphy said, flexing her back muscles slightly.

Sun laughed and tousled Murphy's short hair. "I meant the scars."

"Hmm," Murphy said sleepily. "A wild childhood. Plate-glass window."

Sun kissed Murphy's neck. "Are you in to rough sex? Are they leftover marks?" She ran her finger down one of the longer scars.

"Not into it, not from sex. Just a wild childhood." Murphy was a little annoyed. She already gave an honest if incomplete answer, and she did not like being accused of lying. She did not feel like talking about this with Sun.

"Hey, your back just tensed up. Take it easy. I'm just asking where the scars came from. No need to get testy about it."

Murphy grunted. She had to get up to pee, and Sun slipped off her back. Murphy got up and walked into the bathroom, shutting the door behind her. Flipping the toilet lid up, she sat down to sulk. They had been dating for a few months and while it had its fair share of turmoil already, the sex was great. Poking her toe at the fuzzy bath mat, she sighed. She had not had a girlfriend for this long for years, since before she became a detective. She did not know when the 'let's talk about childhood trauma' talk was supposed to happen. But it wasn't now.

Sun knocked softly at the door. "You alright?"

"Yep, almost finished," she said. Murphy counted to twenty, flushed the toilet, and got up to wash her face. She ran her fingers through her hair, made a face at herself in the mirror, and walked back into the motel bedroom.

Murphy propped up some pillows and sat up in bed, pulling the covers up a little. She put out her arm and gestured for Sun to come to her. Sun tucked herself under Murphy's right arm and began tenderly drawing circles around her nipple and up and down her breast.

Murphy wanted to change the subject without it being too obvious. "What about you? What is this scar on your leg?"

Sun laughed. "I was just thinking about that. I told you I was born in Pondicherry. Do you know anything about it? No? Well, it's very low, sea level, really. When I was six years old, the government constructed a two kilometre long seawall where there used to be a beautiful beach. It was stunning. But there was too much erosion from the sea, and they just covered it up."

Sun sat up as she replayed the images in her mind. "It's like it was yesterday. My sister Lakshmi and I were forbidden to go, because it is just large pieces of granite piled up and a child could easily slip and break a leg or an arm. But Lakshmi loved to collect sea shells—"

"Lakshmi's seashells by the seashore?" Murphy said with a grin.

Sun laughed. "Oh stop, you. It was no joke. We went to get some sea shells and while we were climbing over the boulders to get to the beach, I slipped between two rocks and cut my leg so bad! I did! I did! Stop, ha ha ha, stop laughing. I, ha ha, I ran home with Lakshmi behind me, but on the way, all the other kids joined us. My leg was streaming blood and there was this train of little children running down the street to my house. Oh, my mother was so mad at me. But when my father saw us, all these kids in this little parade, he laughed."

"He laughed at you being hurt?"

"No, no, laughing at this line of shouting, screaming kids. He was a nice man. He picked me up and carried me to the local doctor. Not really a doctor, but we called him that. So now, it's me and my father heading up this line of children who were running after us screeching. Oh! Everyone was staring. As an adult, I can objectively say it was hilarious. The doctor cleaned the wound and bandaged it, and that was it. Done. The excitement was over. All the other children went on their way, and we left. On the way home, we stopped at a little shop and he bought ice cream. It was just him and me. We sat for hours and watched the sunset, the two of us."

Sun paused, tearing up. Murphy pulled her in closer and stroked her long hair. "That was one of the best days of my life. I miss him. I miss them both, you know? Are your parents alive?"

"Yes, they live in Ottawa. It sounds like it was a great day for you."

"It was. My leg hurt so bad, but that ice cream with my dad was worth it."

CHAPTER TEN

M urphy and Sun were both up early the next morning and grabbed a quick breakfast at a nearby coffee shop. "How much are all these hotel rooms costing you?" Sun asked as she sipped from her steaming tea.

"Way too much. I'm broke. Listen, I'll need some flowers from you later today," Murphy said.

"A bouquet for that man who died?"

"It was a woman. Kitty Meyers. Yes, for her. Is your store open for business?"

"No, we are going to clean up today. I'm not even going to the warehouse for new flowers. I cannot give you a bouquet. We have to check everything for glass shards. I can't sell teddy bears that will cut you," Sun said.

"Not to children, but there might be a market on the internet," Murphy said with a laugh.

Sun laughed, but abruptly stopped. "I am a terrible person for laughing," she said.

"No, laughing is fine. Laughter brings light to the darkness."

"Very philosophical," Sun said. "Nietzsche?"

"Murphy," she said with a grin.

Murphy took a bite of her bagel. "I'll find something." Murphy always brought a bouquet to the scenes of each murder, after the Forensics Unit cleared it. It was a visual statement to the deceased that they would not be forgotten. She suspected no one would ever forget this.

"Sure. Just to change the subject back again, is there some other place we can meet?" Sun said. "It just seems really expensive to keep getting hotel rooms."

"Well, we can't go to my place, for obvious reasons. I mean, Del is cool and everything, but I don't even have a bedroom door. And you said no to your place," Murphy said.

Sun shook her head. "With my son's family there, no way. There's no privacy at all. It's almost as bad as having no door with those kids."

Murphy took one last gulp of coffee and shrugged. "We don't meet often enough to justify getting a little love nest of our own," Murphy said with a smile. "A love nest, that's funny. But rent around here is probably pretty high, eh? I mean, I haven't looked, but..."

"It's high. My flower shop is almost three thousand a month, all in. I've heard that the rent for the two-bedroom apartment above the store is over two thousand. It's, you're right. Way too expensive. Hotel rooms are cheaper unless we meet more often. It would be nice, though, to have a little place of our own," Sun said. She had a distant, wistful look in her eyes.

"And while it would mean a lot more sex, I don't have that kind of money. I mean, look at all the flowers I buy." Murphy smiled. "Gotta go," she said, standing up. She bent down to kiss Sun, but Sun pulled back and looked around furtively. "Okay, see you later," Murphy said and walked out the door, shaking her head slightly. She is a grown ass woman, Murphy thought. She was okay sometimes with kissing in public, but not at other times. Murphy could not tell why.

As she walked up to the Brawler, Murphy ran her finger through the dirt on the side of the 4x4, then looked at her dirty finger. *That was stupid.* She brushed her finger off and climbed into her vehicle. The engine roared to life, then purred softly as she drove away. It was a short drive into town. Waiting in the street, ready to turn left into the parking lot, Murphy marvelled at the number of protesters on the sidewalk. They were blocking the parking lot entrance by meandering past it to the end of the street and then coming back. Murphy sighed and drummed her fingers on the steering wheel.

There were people of all ages and types in the protest, although it was not clear to Murphy what they were protesting. Or supporting. She looked for Ellen Longboat, but did not see her. Murphy finally saw two uniformed officers and, rolling down her window, gestured to one of them to come to speak with her. He looked away. Incensed, Murphy laid on the horn and, when the officers looked again, she waved them over. Neither responded. *What the hell is this?* she thought to herself. She turned the 4x4 off, got out, and retrieved her bag from the locked storage box under the rear seat. Slinging it over her shoulder, she left the Brawler parked in the road and crossed the street to speak with the officers.

"Ma'am, move your vehicle now," one officer said. She reached into her bag and showed him her badge. He repeated himself. "Ma'am, you can't block traffic. Move your vehicle."

Murphy's face hardened as she held out her badge and stepped closer to the officer. "That's Detective Inspector to you. Stop the protesters and let me into the parking lot. Now." The officer just looked at her. "Where is your badge?" she said, noting it was not on his uniform.

"I must have lost it. Look lady—"

"Don't you give me this shit. Name and rank. Now." He remained silent.

"Sorry ma'am, Detective Inspector, we'll block the protesters so you can drive through," the other officer said. Murphy looked at him. Badge number 724. She nodded and headed back to the Brawler. By the time she had the engine started, the entrance was clear, and she drove into the parking lot.

Although she parked around the back, she came in through the front entrance. At the reception desk, she asked the officer on duty who was overseeing the police presence for the protesters. It was Inspector Foster's detail. Swiping in with her employee card, she headed to Foster's office, knocked on his office door and waited to be waved in.

"I'm Detective Inspector Murphy, Homicide," she said as she put out her hand. She rarely needed an introduction, but always gave one.

"Inspector Foster. How can I help you, Detective Inspector?" he said, rising from his chair and shaking Murphy's hand.

"Your men are the ones outside on entrance security?" she asked. "One of them was insubordinate. I identified myself, showed my badge, and he refused a direct order to clear the entrance. There were two officers. Badge 724 obeyed orders, the other did not. He has removed his badge from his uniform, and he refused my direct order."

"That little shit. I am sorry, DI Murphy, I'll take care of it."

"Thank you, inspector, I appreciate that." With that, Murphy walked out of the office and up a flight of stairs to the Homicide Unit. She was the first one in.

Murphy walked into her office and put her bag down. Fishing out her badge again, she snapped it to her belt. She put her shoulder holster on and unlocked her gun, secured the firearm in her holster and shook her head. She had never seen that kind of behaviour from an officer on duty. Sure, they could be stubborn, but refusing a direct order was a huge deal. She made an instant coffee and sat down at her desk.

There was an email from Mary suggesting another round of interviews, and advised her a candidate complained. "Ohhhh," Murphy said as she leaned back in her chair. *No way am I going to hire a whiner,* she said to herself. She typed a quick response to Mary, saying she would contact the candidate in question. She really just wanted the person's name so she could strike them off the list.

A kilometre and a half away from headquarters, Haidt gathered his followers on Centre Street. Parker, whose running route to work today took him up the street, ran on the road. It was easier to pass oncoming cars than loitering pedestrians on the sidewalk. He slowed to a walk as he approached the preacher.

"Their hearts, consumed by the flames of arrogance and defiance, have become a breeding ground for darkness. Their souls, tainted by the poison of immorality, bear witness to their transgressions with every beat!" he yelled to the crowd through his megaphone. People gathered on both sides of the street. "Oh, the depths to which the sinners have descended! Their insatiable lusts and insidious desires have ensnared their souls in a web of spiritual decay. They have forsaken the path of righteousness and chosen to embrace the path of eternal damnation."

The crowd shouted back at him in support with "Amen" and "Praise be the word" peppered throughout. Parker stopped to listen. He had taken to heart everything the team talked about. He would spend a moment here, listening for hate speech. He felt like he was undercover.

Haidt continued. "Sinners, I extend to you a lifeline amidst the tempest of your wretchedness. Repent, I implore you, for the gates of redemption remain open. Cast aside your sinful inclinations, for salvation awaits those who turn away from their wickedness. Let the light of divine grace wash over you, cleansing your tarnished souls. Embrace the burning power of repentance, for only then shall you find solace in the embrace of the Almighty. Only through the flames of God's love with there be salvation!" He held up his hands in prayer, and the group across the street shouted in response.

Parker strained to see what was happening and started to cross the street. An older man grabbed him by the arm. "Leave it, son. God's will." Parker huffed and looked across the street again. Much of the crowd had dispersed, leaving behind only three people dressed in white. He had not seen them before, but now they stood out. They all were wearing white painter coveralls. He tried to shake off the grip, but the old man grabbed his other arm and held him tightly. "It's not safe," he said. Parker could feel the old man's hands trembling.

"The reckoning is at hand!" Haidt shouted. A cheer went up and a person in coveralls pulled a petrol bomb out of a grocery bag. The second person lit the rag that hung out of the bottle. The last person grabbed the bottle and hurled it at the Sparkling Unicorn.

Liquid fire flooded the outside of the building. The three people in coveralls fled up the street as Parker ripped himself away. He grabbed his cell phone and called 911 as he stopped in the middle of the street. The fire spread to the flags that hung over the building before the emergency operator answered. Black smoke curled skyward before Parker could give the address. Glass shattered from the heat before the emergency operator could reassure Parker that help was on the way.

He wanted desperately to run to the fire and fight the flames, but he had no way to battle raging gasoline. Settling for running madly to work, he passed emergency vehicles racing to the scene. He called Murphy, his speech breaking with each thudding step. "Boss, that Haidt preacher! His followers set the gay bar on fire!" he shouted. "The place is on fire!"

Murphy kept her work phone to her ear, talking to Parker, while she used her land line to call Sun. "The Sparkling Unicorn is on fire. Get out, now!" she said.

"The what? Sparkling Unicorn? That's nowhere near me," Sun said. Her store was almost five hundred metres away. She could hear the sirens blasting past her, but she could not see out: the window was still boarded up. Instead, she stepped out of the door, phone in hand, and looked. Thick smoke streamed along the Sparkling Unicorn's eves and coated the shop next door. Flames shot up and out as the fire found an additional source of energy. "Oh my God, Caitlin, it's really burning up!"

Inside the bar, things were easily catching fire. The wooden chairs, the alcohol-soaked carpet, the cheap plastic decorations that covered the walls. The glass bottles of alcohol on the shelves cracked and exploded in the heat. The old sprinklers were no match for the fire.

"Fucking Paki!" someone shouted at Sun before slapping her across the face. Her phone tumbled to the ground.

"Sun! Sun! What was that? Hello? Are you okay?" Murphy yelled as she bolted from her desk. She ran into Parker as he arrived at the atelier.

"Boss! There is a huge crowd—"

Murphy gathered herself and ran back to her desk. She grabbed the phone receiver she had dropped in her panic. "Sun?"

"Yes! Caitlin I'm okay. I'm back in my store, but what—"

"What happened? What the hell is going on?" Murphy waved Parker into her office. "Michael?"

Their words tumbled together, jumping over each other, tripping in front of each other. There was a crowd. Slapped my face. Grabbed me by the arms. Called me. God's will. Paki. Walking by. Fire bomb.

"Stop stop stop!" Murphy said. She held a finger up to silence Michael. "Sun. Get out. Quick. If you have a back door, take it. Go home. You aren't safe."

"Caitlin, I'm shaking, I don't—"

"Leave. Out now. I'll call later. Can you leave? Yes? Go now, please. Call me when you are home." Murphy hung up the phone, then listened to Parker explain everything he had seen.

"Boss, that old man knew something was up. He warned me. He knew it was going to happen."

"You said everyone left the area? They knew exactly what was going on. Jesus Christ," Murphy mumbled.

Parker updated Hamilton and Girard when they arrived while Murphy called Shevchenko. She had warned him that Haidt could be a problem. It was not a question of 'I told you so,' it was a question of to whom Parker should report what he had seen. No one knew it was getting worse by the second.

Sun fled her store out the back door, taking her delivery van home. The racist assault had shaken her, but the wrath of the growing crowd was terrify. She felt small and vulnerable, a Brown woman in a sea of white faces twisted in anger. She felt a cool wave of relief as Kettering shrank in the rear-view mirror.

The crowd was just getting started. Amid the provocateurs were average Kettering residents. They began by listening to Haidt, and they ended by knocking over planters and throwing public trash cans into the streets. An old woman grabbed a sidewalk sign for a bookstore—a bookstore she often went in herself—and threw it into the street. A young man brushed past her with a metal patio chair raised above his head. He hurled it at the bookstore window, cracking the glass. A man in white coveralls rushed beside him and kicked the window in. "Fire in the hole!" He threw a petrol bomb into the bookstore and disappeared. The old woman raised her hands up to protect her head as she shambled away from the fire that now seethed through the books.

Further down the street, young men stood in front of the bank and kicked at the glass. A smoldering car was splayed across the road, bleeding smoke and gasoline. When the gas caught fire, flames rushed to the car, and it exploded. The men scampered from the bank like cockroaches in the light. Across the street, two women with sticks were trying to smash their way into a clothing store.

The Fire Department was overwhelmed. It was not just the fires in stores and trash cans. It was the crowds that gathered at each truck, throwing stones and garbage and shouting religious passages and insults. Frustrated, they turned their hoses from the fires to the protesters, knocking them down with the force of water. But like punching bags, they sprung back every time the hoses returned to the fire.

Murphy, Girard, Hamilton and Parker sat in the atelier watching the CBC news coverage. They already had a news helicopter over Centre Street, filming the riot while an anxious street reporter shouted to be heard.

"We're losing," Parker said. "There aren't enough cops."

Murphy said that they have more and they are coming. Much of the last year's Northshore Police budget was spent on riot helmets and nightsticks.

This would come to an end soon. It had to.

The live news broadcast tracked a cube van arriving at Franklin and Centre. It showed more than a dozen people clambering out with banners and signs for the right-wing Christians By Birth group. They were joined by people who had been in front of headquarters.

"Here we come!" Parker shouted excitedly. Police Van 15 arrived as close to the scene as they could, and ten officers scrambled out. Officers formed a single line and slowly headed down Centre Street, herding people back down the street. If someone avoided the police by entering a store, an officer would head in, demanded they leave, and order the store to close. It well exceeded their authority, but they did not care. Public safety above all.

The team watched the events unfold during the live broadcast. Murphy kept her face stoic, but her heart was hammering in her chest. She tried not to imagine a truck mowing down innocent people as they fled. She tried not to imagine an orange car blowing people into pieces. Murphy blinked rapidly and shook her head, and rushed to her office, whispering, "This is not the same. This is not the truck attack. This is not the bomb. This is not the same. We are protected, we are safe, we are together! Breathe, breathe. In...out...in...out. Keep going. In...out. Keep breathing."

She looked into the atelier, and everyone immediately looked back to the screen. They had watched Murphy as she struggled to stand, watched as she shook, watched as she clenched her fists and mumbled to herself. "Ah fuck," she said.

Murphy walked into the atelier. "I saw you all watching me. I am okay. When I was growing up in Ireland, there were riots, car bombs and a lot of murders. This is just freaking me out a little."

Murphy cleared her throat, trying to decide how much of her own emotional anguish to share. She decided it would not be much. "When I see people pulling the same shit here—arson and riots and assaults on a large scale—it's like people have forgotten history. People like Haidt aren't new. Hatemongers aren't new. Gullible angry followers aren't new. None of this is new. It makes me angry and so sometimes I need to take a breath. I need to shake it off. So be patient with me."

Girard stepped forward and gave her a hug. "What? No, no. Adam," she protested. Girard did not let go for a few more seconds.

"I'm with you. There is nothing we can do about Haidt as detectives, but as human beings we can remember," he said. Murphy and Girard were close, but showing even this level of vulnerability made Murphy uncomfortable. "And I promise I will never hug you again."

Murphy burst out laughing and slapped his back congenially. "Deal."

CHAPTER ELEVEN

Murphy covered her cast with a plastic bag and stepped into a cool shower. Adjusting the showerhead to the softest stream, she let the water alternatively soothe and refresh her. She finally stepped out and patted herself dry.

Walking downstairs, she found Del, Thomas and Jens sitting together having a drink. They discussed what the news had to say about the riots both in and out of town.

"We're getting international coverage," Jens said. "Check this out." He switched to the BBC News, which, within minutes, returned to the story of riots in Kettering.

"Violence erupted early today in the quiet Canadian town, leaving businesses destroyed and residents in shock. Chaos ensued after a young man drove his truck…"

The rioters in Kettering had burned the Sparkling Unicorn, the Dickery Dockery Bookery bookstore, and a synagogue on the outside of town. Seven stores had suffered damage, and a small mosque had graffiti written on it. Dozens of people were showing up at the hospital and local walk-in clinics with cuts and bruises.

Jonathan Haidt continued to fan the flames on his radio show. His rhetoric about abominable lies from 'the other side' stoked the righteous indignation of his followers. Murphy was still uncomfortable with Miller's apparent connection to Haidt. She had to decide how best to proceed without becoming obsessed with the man. So far, he was not breaking any law she could arrest him for.

"Local authorities are considering a curfew…"

"Is there going to be a curfew?" Del asked.

"I don't know. Hey, did you get to Toronto today?"

"Protesters in white painter coveralls vandalized downtown stores, banks, and set fire to a bookstore and trash cans during a religious protest that police struggled to control…"

"No. Bob is in an induced coma. When I called last night, I lied and said I was his sister. They have amputated both legs, and he has sacral nerve injuries," she said. Del knew a lot about spinal and nerve injuries, and explained what it meant for Bob.

"He is going to need months in rehab, probably in Toronto, because we don't have those kinds of facilities here. He might be able to walk with prosthetic legs, maybe. But, I don't know, he seems like he would be up for the fight, but it's going to be a fight like he's never had before."

"Well, he has you to look up to," Thomas said.

"And help. You are going to give him so much advice and tips," Jens said.

"Protest leader Jonathan Haidt said he was fighting the criminalization of religious freedom…"

"You know, if Bob was thirty-two, it would be different. But he's sixty-two. He already struggled with living alone," Del said.

"Oh god yes. At least a dozen times during the COVID lockdown, I would go over to see him, you know, talk through the window, and he would just be splayed out on the couch, barely moving. All this trash around him."

"Yeah, no. Bob doesn't do alone very well at all."

"Authorities worry additional protesters are on their way from other Canadian provinces, and the United States…"

Murphy sat in the chair, only half listening. The words jumbled together and became nonsensical poetry. She was exhausted.

"What do you think?" Thomas asked. Everyone was intensely staring at her.

Murphy roused herself after dozing off and not hearing what they were now asking about. She could either agree, disagree, or ask for more information. She chose the latter. "I need to think about it, to talk about it a bit, you know?"

"Yes, fair enough. It's a big deal. We'll talk about it later," Del said. Murphy wondered what she had missed, but let it go. It was for another time.

"Okay, yeah, let's do that. I have to grab a bite to eat. Excuse me," Murphy said. She rooted around the fridge and settled for an apple, some cheese, and made a tuna sandwich. She retreated to her bedroom and called Sun.

"How are you doing?" Sun asked with concern in her voice. "I heard about what happened on TV. Cops were injured. Are you okay? Please tell me that wasn't you."

"It was not me. We are all fine. I'm fine," Murphy said. "What about you? What happened when we were talking?"

Sun told her about the slur and the slap. The personal attack initially shocked her, but that wore off quickly and fear had set in. She had watched the news all day, and it looked like they spared her store further damage. "But the Unicorn is gone," she said. "And that bookstore across the street. They burned it out!"

"I am so sorry, babe. I wish there was something I could do to help."

"I can fix the flower shop, but what am I going to do? What if this rioting continues? Or there is another attack?" Sun asked. They talked for a while, with Murphy offering vague reassurances that things will be fine. Sun was upset, hurt, and frightened. Murphy fell asleep mid-conversation.

When she awoke an hour later, the phone had slipped to the floor. Murphy felt empty and alone. She could help no one. She had the bad guy, but it was just not enough. She even fell asleep trying to emotionally support Sun. Murphy did not know if she had more. Slowly, she got up from the bed and made her way to the bathroom. She undressed, applied more ointment to the wound on her hand, and then looked at herself in the mirror. The woman who stared back at her was scarred and tattered, exhausted physically and emotionally. She had made a herculean effort to stay detached and unemotional. There was no screaming when she heard Bob was hurt in the attack. There was no wailing when she walked past the blood-stained sidewalk. She did not yell when her lover's store was attacked. She kept everything inside.

Murphy wanted to scream and shout and hit and punch and bite and kick and rip and tear. She gritted her teeth, walked back into her bedroom, and screamed into her pillow until she fell asleep again. She said no prayers for the dead.

Murphy woke up Wednesday morning with the familiar disorientation that came with her nightmares. It was not every night, but was becoming more frequent and more disjointed. Her left arm was extended beside her and she stared at it. Her eyes followed the cast up her arm, then skipped to the bedsheets, which were stained here and there from the antibacterial ointment transferred from her hand, and sweat.

She groaned as she sat up, her body aching. Her internal turmoil was taking an external toll. It took ten minutes for her to stand up and find her phone. She read the messages, emails, and news accounts from overnight.

Painfully, she tended to her wounds, got dressed and walked downstairs. It surprised her to see Thomas making breakfast. "Good morning. Where is Maria?" Murphy asked.

"I stayed over last night, slept on the couch. Thought I would make breakfast," he said.

"Cool thanks," Murphy said. Kissing Del on the cheek, she grabbed an apple and yogurt from the fridge and said goodbye. She hurried to the Brawler because of the rain and pulled out of the parking lot and onto Highway 11. It was eerily clear in both directions.

Murphy pulled into the Goose Gas and flipped a switch to unlock the gas tank door, and got out of her Brawler. She looked around for Sergei, but could not see him. Sergei was a homeless Russian man, a retired war veteran who lived in a homeless camp near the gas station. Murphy could count on him to come to pump her gas in exchange for food from the station. She had never not seen him there, no matter the time or weather. With no one around, she felt confident to leave the gas filling her Brawler while she went inside.

Out of habit, and a bit of concern, she gathered a sandwich, a bag of candies, and two litres of pop. "Is Sergei around today?" she asked the clerk.

"I haven't seen him since yesterday," he said. "You can try out back."

Murphy nodded, paid for Sergei's food, and headed out to her vehicle. The overflow switch on the pump had snapped off, meaning her tank was full. She sighed when she looked at the cost: almost two hundred. She was glad the police reimbursed much of the expense. Murphy pulled the Brawler around the back of the station and waited near the garbage bins, revving the engine. The Brawler sounded distinctive, and she hoped it would call Sergei out of the woods. After a few minutes, she gave up and left the bag of food with the clerk. "If he shows up, give him the food and call me, please. Northshore Police," she said, handing him her business card. She hoped it would be enough to keep him honest.

Parker and Hamilton were both in the office when Murphy arrived. Girard had the day off. "Hey, you alright? How was this morning?" she asked. She left the question open to interpretation more out of habit than premeditation.

"Have you spoken to anyone about the lighting of the fires on Centre?" Murphy asked Parker.

"No, I have to call them. Lance Robinson from the Ontario Fire Marshall's office," Parker replied.

"Get that done soon. Are you both doing the Miller work?" Murphy asked.

"Yes, for sure," Parker laughed.

"Okay, give me an hour to get through all the emails and review the reports again. We'll go over what we need in the case. I feel like the riot knocked everything on its head," Murphy said. She retreated to her office to focus on the Miller case. She re-read all the emails and reports from the investigation, and ignored the emails from Human Resources. After forty-five minutes and an instant coffee, Murphy headed back into the atelier.

"Cleo, Michael, let's cover Mr. Perry Miller. We have his basic information like age, home address, he didn't work and didn't go to school. He had no friends and the neighbours won't talk to us. But that's more about hating us than liking him. The only motive he gave was hate, but I suspect he wants fame. I expect his lawyer will try to mitigate with a claim of mental illness. Adam and I drove the scene and believe it's possible he targeted some people, and just randomly hit others."

"And he played a first-person shooter game, La Guerre Infinitus."

"Right. Do we have anything more on that?"

"No boss," Hamilton said. "We are waiting on Mitch Tremblay and the gaming company for any chat and saved video information."

"Our working theory is, he went for a drive with intent to harm, came into Kettering, saw a sign for the drag show, and mowed people down. That is based on the suspect interview really," Murphy said.

"And this theory is what might get us to Hate-Motivated charges, right?" Parker asked.

"Yes, exactly. And that is where Jonathan Haidt comes in. Miller is a listener, and then Haidt shows up spouting hate, and there was a riot. There is still a riot," Murphy said.

"Could they be co-conspirators? Could Miller be acting on Haidt's orders?" Hamilton asked.

"Boss, that old man that stopped me from going to the fire. I really think he knew something was up. Maybe he was a Haidt follower, maybe there was a plan that some people knew about," Parker said.

Murphy nodded and considered the possibility this was all planned. "So we need to know if Miller's cell phone ever called the radio station. CRST, is it? Christ. Ha! See what I did there? Okay, I want his landline and cell line checked for calls to the radio station. And we need to find out who Haidt is, get his phone numbers, check for any communication. Check emails, social media messages, everything. Michael, you do that."

"Yes, boss. Haidt has been linked to three previous public mischief incidents, but those were preaching on the street corner. No charges, just fines," Parker said.

"And we need to have Haidt investigated for hate speech. That's not us. Who would it be?" Murphy said. No one answered. "I'll talk to Supt. Shevchenko, find out whether there will be a special task force set up for the riot, or if related crimes will be handled through normal channels. I'll do that."

"I spoke to the man who sold Miller the truck. He said he parked the truck in his driveway by the road, stuck a for sale sign in it, and sold it to the first person who stopped. I did a quick background check on him, not so much as a parking ticket," Cleo said.

"Okay, thanks. Now, let's get on to interviewing the survivors, if we can. I'll call Adam and see if he got anywhere." Murphy headed back to her office and called Girard.

"Hey boss," Girard said.

"Sorry to call you on your day off, Adam. I wanted to ask if you interviewed any of the Miller victims?"

"No, I never had the chance," Girard said. "I can do that—"

"No, tomorrow, when you come back. You rest. Sorry to bother you," Murphy said. After a few more minutes of conversation, she hung up and called Shevchenko.

"Sir, good morning, I was—"

"Not a good morning, Murphy. Not good. There have been two more buildings looted, a sporting goods place, and a shoe store. Seven assaults, three sexual assaults," Shevchenko said.

Murphy was shocked. "Is a task force being—"

"Yes, a task force has already been established. You are not on it," Shevchenko said.

"Yes, sir. What's the communication plan?"

"I'm on the task force, so you go through me," he said. Murphy then advised him that Parker was witness to the riot and fire, and that Haidt had been there, stirring up the crowd. Shevchenko told her Parker should make an appointment to see him.

"Haidt could have his fingers in this," she said.

"You brought that up at the meeting," Shevchenko said. "Hate crimes, yes?"

"Sir, we are going to check for a pre-existing relationship between Haidt and Miller. We might bring Haidt in for an interview," Murphy said. Shevchenko sighed loudly in her ear. "If there is anything that connects them, that is. Calls, texts, that kind of thing."

"Alright, but tread carefully."

After hanging up the phone, she told Parker to contact Shevchenko, and settled in to a day's work.

Murphy called Mitch and had her send over digital copies of her draft report. It was going to be easier to search the data rather than print it out and look for possible contact with Haidt visually. Within minutes, Murphy's email dinged, and she opened the cell phone report from Mitch. She searched the police database for anything on Jonathan Haidt, but he had no record, just as Parker said. A search of the internet and local newspaper archives was a different story.

Haidt wrote a newspaper column for the Northshore Redeemer, a weekly Christian newspaper. Seven years ago, his rhetoric was much different. He advocated making the church more accessible to youth and covered interfaith gatherings. Four years ago, his tone changed. She printed and marked the article in which Haidt said Jesus Christ had spoken to him and that he was now possessed by the Holy Ghost. It was his turning point. Thereafter, he wrote less about redemption and more about revenge. Revenge against those who would speak against religion, and against those who were not of his religion. Murphy printed a few of the more strident articles.

Haidt disappeared from local newspapers until last year. He wrote a letter to the editor of the Northshore Gazette decrying sinning in the area.

Murphy wondered where Haidt had gone to for those few years and she broadened her search. Haidt had travelled to Nova Scotia, where he had extensive news coverage of his actions. He disrupted the worship services of churches in Halifax, Lunenburg, and Peggy's Cove. An ex-follower unsuccessfully sued him for threatening to 'bring the fires of God upon your head.' The newspapers loved every minute of the scandal.

Haidt was divorced and remarried. His marriage to another evangelical preacher had been unsuccessful. He and his first wife wrote a blog together—In God We Haidt. It covered disappointment, spiritual exploration, disciplining naughty kids, and being accused of impotence. They had no children themselves, but certainly had a lot of opinions about disciplining them. Local ministers portrayed Haidt and his ex-wife as cult leaders.

Haidt had come alone to Northshore, according to the last post he wrote on In God We Haidt. 'I leave behind a woman possessed by the Devil himself, fornicator with Asmodeus, king of demons and denier of God's Plan!!!' he wrote. It sounded to Murphy like he had suffered a mental breakdown and was delusional. She knew better than most that the line between mental illness and faith could sometimes be desperately thin. She would keep her opinion on his mental health to herself, reasoning she was not an expert on the subject.

His current website included blog postings, daily prayers, and scripture interpretation. He and his new wife, Jessica, were on the 'About' page, although that was her only presence. It was all about him. The site also hosted videos shot by followers and professional news outlets. Fight videos, extreme weather videos, strange lights videos: anything that he could fit into his own narrative. Murphy watched a few videos, wrote some notes, and moved on.

Murphy checked the phone numbers for CRST radio. Miller's landline had called seventy-three times during the previous month. She noted it was always during the three-hour Haidt show. Noting some dates and times, she searched the radio station's website for show archives, and found two of Haidt's shows from the previous week. Murphy downloaded both files, made another cup of coffee, and settled in. She was most concerned about any call Miller made. It might have been broadcast, so she set the playback speed to two hundred percent and listened to hours of vitriol.

They identified Miller only in one program as a caller, and his call seemed innocuous. "I have no fellowship in Northshore," Miller said. That was it. That was the only comment directly to Haidt that Murphy could find. Haidt's response was also unremarkable, saying Christian fellowship was necessary to avoid sin. He recommended Miller continue listening to his radio show and support his sponsors.

By three o'clock, Murphy was done. She had had enough and was going home. Murphy signed off the computer, gathered her files, and walked into the atelier, locking her office door. "I am heading out. See everyone tomorrow," she said.

"Yes boss," Hamilton said.

"Bye," Parker said.

The rain had stopped, but it left a crisp earthiness in the air. The rainwater on the streets was shimmering in the bright sun. Murphy headed across the road to Jacqueline's Pâtisserie to pick up some croissants and a box of Fusion Chocolates for Del. She stopped into a pharmacy down the street and bought more ointment, bandages and sought an opinion on the status of her hand. Everything was healing well, the pharmacist said. "Keep doing what you're doing," he said. "It's working."

Murphy walked back to headquarters and got into the Brawler to drive home. She was anxious: everything was upended. Murphy pulled onto the road and headed home.

CHAPTER TWELVE

D el was alone, to Murphy's surprise. Ever since the truck attack, Del had Thomas and Jens with her, but now there were no cars but her own wheelchair accessible van in the parking lot. All that talk the other night came floating back to Murphy in bits and pieces. Murphy had been too tired to think, but not too tired to hear. Only on replay was she beginning to understand what was said. They were trying to figure out what to do about Bob.

Del and her friends were nowhere near in accord with one another on the issue, and Murphy had no firm opinion. Long-term care home, assisted living housing, or living on his own with support, like Del. That is always the best, Murphy thought, but Del was a force to be reckoned with. Not everyone could thrive after such devastating injuries. Murphy parked the Brawler and walked to her home.

Within seconds she was in the house, saying hello to Del. "No Maria again tonight? Where are Thomas and Jens?" Murphy shouted out. Without Maria to help her get ready for bed, to hook up her catheter or massage her legs, Murphy wondered if Del would be alright. But she had learned long ago not to question Del's ability to care for herself. The woman could fly a goddamn plane: she knew what she was doing.

When she popped her head into Del's room, she was surprised to see a blend of frustration and anger on Del's face. Murphy wondered if her own face was anything but weary. "Hey," she said.

"Hey," Del said.

The defeat in her voice shocked Murphy. Instead of stressing out, Murphy nodded and walked back into the kitchen. She wanted to turn off her emotional involvement and listen with a detective's ear. A tone of voice or particular choice of words meant a lot to Murphy. Paying attention to something small like that could mean the difference between a murderer confessing or walking free. She wanted to believe there was nothing to it, that the sound of Del's voice was just fine. But she knew it wasn't.

"Where are the Boys?" she asked.

"They both had to go home to check on things," Del said.

"Do you need to get away from all this stress?" Murphy asked.

"Oh, fuck do I! But whatcha gonna do?" Del said with a laugh.

"Have you had dinner?" Murphy yelled. "I have to put my stuff away. I'll be down in a minute to get dinner." Murphy headed upstairs to put her gun away and change into jeans and a t-shirt. She was not planning ongoing anywhere tonight.

She took her phones downstairs with her and headed to the fridge. "Grabbing dinner!" Murphy dug through the bottom freezer. "Hey! Do you—" When Murphy popped her head up, Del was sitting right next to her.

"No need to yell. It's my legs that don't work, not my ears." Del stuck out her tongue.

"Ha ha, sorry. You can be so quiet sometimes. Dinner?"

"Yeah, I'd love that. Maria must have left a million frozen dinners in there."

Murphy needed her life to be simple, and Maria was a big part of that. She crouched down and Del came closer to look into the freezer with Murphy. "How about... menudo blanco?" Murphy said, holding up a package of green and white.

"You know, it's delicious, but I just can't do tripe right now. What else?"

Murphy picked up a pie and searched for a name written on it. "Curried Chicken Pot Pie. Not exactly the blueberry I was thinking it was," Murphy said with a grin.

"That sounds great. Yes, curry tonight."

"Okay, it will take... an hour and a half once the oven is hot. Okay?" Del agreed, and while Murphy prepared to cook the pot pie, she pulled a bottle of wine out of the small wine fridge. She put the bottle and a couple of wine glasses on the kitchen table.

"Allow me, madam," Murphy said as she opened the bottle.

"My damn what? Ha ha!" It was a silly joke, childish almost, but both women laughed.

"Caitlin, what are we going to do about Bob?" Del asked as Murphy sat at the table. She took a glass of wine and held it up. "Cheers."

"Cheers," Murphy said, clinking her glass against Del's. Del had chosen a semi-dry gewürztraminer, and the aroma was both sweet and peppery. Beyond that, Murphy was at a loss. She sniffed the wine a few times and finally said, "You know, when I am with Sun, I can smell and taste the most amazing things."

"So a good sex life, then?"

"Ha! Funny. Yes, but aside from that, she..." Murphy stuck her nose into the glass and inhaled deeply. "I don't know. Around her I smell flowers, and food and just stuff I have never really noticed before. Like I can't tell if this smells like flowers or peppers, but she can describe which flowers, and which peppers, you know? And when she says them, I can taste them."

"That is kind of weird. It's like she's hypnotizing you," Del laughed.

"Well, there are worse things in the world than to smell flowers," Murphy said.

"Just to almost completely change the subject back, I sent Bob some flowers. I went with whatever the florist said. I haven't even seen them. When I video chat with him, I'll ask him to show me."

"How is he?" Murphy asked as she got up to put dinner in the now hot oven.

Del shrugged. "On the surface, he's alright. Weak. Well taken care of. But you know what he just went through, the pain and the fear. You can feel that in your heart. I know that. You know the right thing to do," Del said. Like she always had the power to do: she was manipulating Murphy's sense of Christian duty. Murphy knew it, but that would not stop Del from trying.

"I know," Murphy said. "And?"

Del's face was fixed, but her eyes gave her away. "And you know what he has coming. You know what the next few years are going to hold for him," she said. The next few years we're going to be years of hell, and Del did not need to say it out loud.

Her wife's compassion for her good, longtime friend made Murphy feel the warmth she rarely felt from Del. She was even tougher than Murphy, and her compassion often came with a hard edge. But not this time. "He needs me," Del said gently.

"He needs you," Murphy repeated. She knew the explanation would come soon enough.

"I think we should get divorced."

Murphy frowned for a split second. That was unexpected. "What's that now?" she asked.

"If we get divorced, then you could marry Bob and he could have access to your benefits," Del said.

Murphy smiled and shook her head. "No way. For sure, someone in HR would go 'oh look, this lesbian just divorced her wife in a wheelchair and now married a guy in a wheelchair. Not suspicious at all.' Sorry Del, but that would raise way too many red flags. I could lose my job over benefits fraud."

Murphy knew she had a lot to make up for in the world for being Catholic. But her good deeds were arresting killers, giving some sense of closure to victims' families, remembering the dead and treating people with respect. Her good deeds did not extend to getting a divorce and marrying a man.

"I have checked out supportive housing in the area. Everything is full with a long wait list, or had so many code violations it's scary. I think he'd have to live in Ottawa or Toronto," Del said as resentment rose from the pit of her stomach. She pursed her lips to keep the words in her mouth. "God," was all she could muster.

"Hey hey hey, what's really going on?" Murphy asked as she reached out to hold Del's hand.

"You might not believe this, but the worst part of my accident was not the accident, and it was not the idea of living the rest of my life in a wheelchair. It was right after the accident. The worst was not knowing where I was going to live and who was going to step up to help me. It was being afraid that I would end up in some shit hole of a care home waiting around for someone to wipe my ass. It wasn't about losing my legs, it was about losing my independence."

"But you didn't lose your independence," Murphy reminded her.

"Exactly. Once I had a plan on where and how to live, it was so much easier. Then when The Boys came into my life, it was like everything was...was sprinkled with fairy dust," Del laughed.

"So you want to be there for Bob," Murphy said. She swirled the wine a little in her glass and took a sip. "I think we'll be finished this wine before dinner is done."

"We don't have another bottle of gwertz. We'll have to switch to something else," Del said.

"What has Bob said?" Murphy asked.

"We have not really spoken directly about it. I promised him I would take care of it. Whatever it is," Del said.

"So the 'it' is where and how is he going to live. At least to begin with. Right?" Del nodded, and Murphy continued. "Let me think on it. Between us we will come up with something great. I just need some time. We don't have to figure this out right now. Right?"

"Right."

The oven timer dinged and Murphy got up to get the curried pot pie. It smelled delicious and homey. As the women ate, they video called Maria to thank her for the meal and check how she was. She and her kids were safe in their fourth-floor apartment. The next call was a video call to Girard, who was home with his family. Murphy and Del chatted with the entire family. Everyone was fine. Steven and Allan behaved badly and noisily danced and sang. Ruthie squealed and smacked the phone out of Girard's hand.

"I'll be in the office tomorrow," Girard said.

"You are amazing, catching that terrible driver," Ruby yelled over Girard's shoulder.

"Ruby, you do not know what Adam means to me," Murphy said. "You know I love you guys." Ruthie shrieked and laughed, while her brothers ramped up their singing. "Okay, gotta go. Adam, I'll be in touch."

She hung up and leaned back to relax. "Are you going to call Sun?" Del asked.

"Yeah, but I think I'd like to go upstairs for that."

"Oooooh, shekshy time," Del laughed.

"Ha, I sure would like that. But I don't know. Is it really the same on video?"

"Of course it isn't the same, but that doesn't mean it can't be good. I have accounts on a couple of chat sites. I come every single time because it's me touching me," Del said. "I'm sure the two of you can figure it out."

Murphy banged her cast against the couch and laughed. "Maybe. But maybe I'll just call her regularly first. I'll be back down in a while to help you get ready for bed."

"Okay, thanks. Take your time, there's a western that's just about to start," Del said as she grabbed the TV remote.

Upstairs, Murphy thought about what Del had said. She climbed into bed, arranging the pillows behind her back. She took a deep breath and tapped on Sun's number.

"Hey," Murphy said when Sun answered the video call. Murphy had changed her mind and used video chat.

"Oh Caitlin! How are you? Oh my gosh, thank you for... What? I'm on the phone! Hang on a minute, Caitlin. What are you looking for? On your bedside table by the clock. Sorry. I swear, that boy will never really grow up," Sun said.

"How is Chris?" Murphy asked. In her eagerness, she had momentarily forgotten Sun lived with her son, his girlfriend, and their daughter. There would be no video phone sex tonight.

Everyone was alright, Sun said, and she was thankful she lived on a quiet road, away from rioters. She had stopped watching the news because the broadcasts were upsetting. Instead, she checked the local news site's headlines once every two hours. She had set a timer, she said.

That had Murphy laughing so hard she dropped the phone.

"Stop that, stop laughing at me," Sun said with a smile. "Seriously what can I do? I am scared to go back to my store."

"Oh no babe, that's easy to fix. Buy some rolling shutters for the store. You know, those metal covers over a storefront."

"They are ugly as hell. No one will want to go to a flower shop with a big metal grate. I always thought it made a street look dangerous," Sun said.

"The metal rollers aren't that different from a garage door on a house. Push a button, up they go or down they come. Just on a bigger scale. Hire a local artist to paint flowers and the store name on it." Murphy had seen the shutters in Ottawa like that. She thought it would be good advertising.

"How expensive are they?"

"You got me there. I have no idea. Probably depends on the size you need. Block your doorway too. The whole width of the store. I am thinking of would be less than twenty thousand for everything."

"I don't have that kind of money Caitlin. And I am more concerned about when I am there, not when I am not there," Sun said.

"We will figure something out for you. Sooner rather than later. Let's keep you safe," Murphy said reassuringly.

After almost half an hour of chatting, the news timer dinged in the background. Sun and Murphy ended their call with air kisses and a promise to call tomorrow. Murphy looked at the clock. It was ten thirty, too late to call her parents too reassure them she was fine. She looked at 'Chicken Eyes, Symmetrical', one of her father's quirkiest paintings. It sat on the mantle of her fireplace, staring at her with its decidedly unsymmetrical eyes. There were so many pieces of art on the wall from friends and family. It sometimes felt like she lived in an eclectic art gallery instead of above one.

Murphy headed downstairs to help Del get ready. "No, that tube runs over here," Del said as Murphy switched the leg bag to the night bag. "I've heard of the automated bags. They tell you when your bag is full, and it uses a pump instead of gravity to drain the urine. Which is probably not what you want to hear after a sex call with Sun."

The women both laughed. "No sex, just a call. She lives with her son's family, that's why we don't meet at her place. It's hotel rooms every time."

"That must be getting expensive," Del said. She rolled over to the bed, and with a bit of help, transferred herself. Murphy pushed the wheelchair slightly back and made sure the alarm button was within reach. "Hand me my phone, would you? I'm not sleepy yet," Del said with a wink.

Murphy kissed her wife's cheek and headed up to her own room. Her work phone had unread message after unread message, relaying updates on the chaos. She knew that if there was a homicide, someone would call. Until then, Murphy could relax

She laughed to herself. There was no way she could relax. The best she could do was accept there was little she could do. Murphy pulled back the curtains and let the dark flood into the room.

Turning off the light and looking out the bedroom window, she breathed a sigh of relief when she saw no flames. She opened the window and heard echoes of shouts and screams. Murphy did not know if they were real, or throwbacks to her childhood trauma. It was easier to shut the window than figure it out. As she turned away, a flash of light caught her eye. Instinctively, she ducked.

Murphy replayed the image in her mind and quickly realized it was vehicle headlights. She looked out. A truck had come around a bend and was slowly making its way down the road. The headlights swept the ragged treeline. Murphy was relieved when it drove past. She pulled the drapes and crawled to her bed.

Kneeling, she prayed. "In your hands, O Lord, are humbly entrusted our brothers and sisters..."

CHAPTER THIRTEEN

Murphy was in the office at 6:00 a.m. The computer buzzed into life while she grabbed an instant coffee and sat down at her desk. She opened her email first, but froze. NSPD EMERGENCY. Murphy stared. Her mind was racing, but her hands weren't moving. The latest NSPD announcement had shocked her.

NSPD EMERGENCY: Code X-Black…

She could not read past the first few words. Her phone dinged, but she could not look at it. The emergency code meant a law enforcement officer was dead: the X meant it had been a homicide. Her eyes flicked from side to side as she went through the next words. *Was it one of theirs? Have they arrested the killer? Did she know the victim? Did they have a chance, or was it an ambush? Was this the beginning of a nightmare attack on cops?*

Murphy's hand twitched, and she took a deep breath. She tapped the message.

NSPD EMERGENCY: Code X-Black. OPP officer down Highway 11. OPP on scene. Paramedics on scene.

The words were simple and devastating. Murphy looked again at the message. An Ontario Provincial Police officer, not yet identified, was the victim of a homicide. He or she died on a provincial highway, their death would be investigated by the OPP. Murphy read the text again. And again. No matter how hard she tried to rewind time, to change the text, to stop the message, it was still there. It was a stone in her stomach, tumbling wetly as she read the words.

The air was suddenly too close, too hot. Murphy got up on shaky legs and dragged herself to the window, throwing it open and sucking in the air. She wanted to scream, to tear the curtains from the window and smash the panes. She wanted to stomp her feet and kick and scream like a child, like the child she had been when she got the news that her uncle Seamus had died in the line of duty. Stripped raw, she felt unsteady on her feet and turned around to stumble to the desk.

She lay her face down on the desk for a few minutes before remembering she was no longer a child, no longer that child with glass spikes in her back. She could sit up, she could sit back, there was no glass. But she did not turn. Instead, she clenched her fists and cried. She cried like when she heard the news of Seamus's murder, when she vowed to herself to keep her vulnerability hidden.

Tears at first blurred her sight, but then flowed so freely they ultimately washed away the decades-old visions. Murphy stared at the ceiling, letting the ghosts of Seamus and Roisin flow back into the past. A hot chill bubbled over her and she sweated and shivered and gasped for air. Finally, her breath steadied, and she cleared her throat of the mucus that had pooled. Murphy sat up and took a few deep breaths before grabbing some tissues and blowing her nose.

She went to the washroom and washed her face, then grabbed her phone. She was ready again to look through the rest of the email messages, ready to be brave again. She looked at the clock. It was 6:30. Stop wallowing, she told herself. People will be here soon.

"Good morning," Girard said as he walked into the atelier an hour later.

"What the hell are you doing here so early?" Murphy asked, shocked.

"A day at home is a week off my life," he joked. He laughed and turned to see a fierceness on Murphy's face he did not recognize.

"An OPP Officer was killed on a highway. Code Black X. In your email," she replied. Her PC dinged. Another email.

NSPD EMERGENCY: OPP Sergeant Doris McKay pronounced dead on the scene. Our thoughts and prayers go to her family. OPP have suspect in custody.

"Wow," Girard said as he closed the email. "Did you know her?"

"No. Just what's there."

"I'm going to check the news sites and the OPP Twitter feed. I will let you know when they release more information," Girard said.

Murphy buried herself in work. She spent hours reading over witness statements gathered by her team. No one knew Perry Miller or the Miller family well enough to provide insight. None seemed to be ultra right or ultra left on the political spectrum.

To handle Haidt's repulsive radio shows, Murphy went to the CRST website and downloaded more of his archived shows. She fired up VerbatimVox and loaded the first audio file. The voice to text software immediately began transcribing the preacher's radio show. Thanks to a sophisticated algorithm, VerbatimVox could run at double speed. It would take an hour and a half to transcribe Haidt's three hour show.

Murphy watched as the first words appeared on the screen, then minimized the program and let it run in the background. She would then do a simple word search in the transcript. It would give her enough tertiary evidence to tell her if recommendations for hate speech charges against Haidt could be forwarded on.

"You want some lunch? I am heading to Thai Tiger," Hamilton asked as she stuck her head into Murphy's office. It startled Murphy. *When had she arrived? Was it lunch time?*

"I sure do. Coconut Panko Shrimp please," Murphy said. She dug fifteen dollars out of her wallet and handed it over. "Thanks."

She checked the VerbatimVox program: it was finished the second show, and she loaded the third. The phone rang. "DI Murphy speaking."

"DI Murphy, this is Dispatch Operator 78. Pathologist Dr. Chen is requesting your attendance. A body has been found at Lac Sainte-Marine, under suspicious circumstances. He is close to the southwest parking lot three," she said.

"Right, thank you. I will call Dr. Chen to advise," she said. By the time she got the basic information from him, Hamilton had returned with lunch for the team. Murphy walked into the atelier and picked up her styrofoam takeout container. "We have a case out at Lac Sainte-Marine."

"Where? That is almost seven thousand hectares of water," Girard said.

"Southwest parking lot three. I want you all at the scene."

"You don't want me and Hamilton in the office?" Parker asked.

"Let's face it, we are all getting cabin fever. It's been a minute since we had a real investigative case," Murphy said.

"I know I want to get back at it," Hamilton said.

"Alright. Eat," she said as she plopped down on the couch and tucked into her shrimp. "So, have we found a connection between Miller and Haidt?"

"We were thinking, maybe Miller was connected to Haidt. But maybe he was connected to the CBB," Hamilton said with a mouth full of cashew stir fry.

"Or any other religious fruitcakes," Parker added. "No offense, boss." Murphy frowned and stuck her tongue out at Parker. She might be religious, and she might be a fruitcake, but she was not a religious fruitcake.

"Anyway, has anyone found anything showing Miller and Haidt had a reciprocal relationship?" Murphy said.

"No. He seems to have listened to Haidt's show, but I have seen nothing that shows he ever even met the guy," Hamilton said.

"Me neither. I have found no connections back to Miller. It all seemed one way, just a radio listener," Girard said.

"I have been running some of Haidt's radio shows through the VerbatimVox, but I haven't run the keyword search yet. Michael, maybe you can do that? The text files are on the server, in the case file under 'Transcripts'."

"Yes, boss. Can I still come to Lac Sainte-Marine?"

"Yes. Are we almost done? Does anyone need a ride? No? Okay, let's meet there," Murphy said as she threw the rest of her food into the garbage.

The lake was only twenty minutes away. Murphy took the highway to Lowland Road, rounded a bend and drove down Holler Lane. Ahead, the Forensics Unit van was parked in southwest parking lot three. She waited for everyone to arrive and they headed over to the team working the scene.

"DI Murphy! What a delight to see you and your team. Delight. Did you know, a Missouri man survived being picked up by a tornado and dropped three hundred and ninety-eight metres away? Survived," Chen said.

Murphy quickly glanced at her team but knew from their faces that they also did not understand the relevance of Chen's statement. Murphy looked around. There was no sign of a tornado. "Is that how he got here?" she asked.

"No, of course not. I do not know how he got here, but I believe we can rule out the weather. That would be quite remarkable," Chen said.

Samuel de Champlain chose to name Lac Sainte-Marine after a Catholic saint who had been beheaded for her faith. They said that a spring of water appeared at the site of her martyrdom. There was a surreal air of calm to the scene. Dr. Chen's staff were bent, unmoving, in their white coveralls, looking more like icebergs than humans. The only movement came from the rippling lake and the curious detectives. The beach was narrow, not more than five metres wide. Large granite rocks glistened brown, red and green in the slight spray of water rising from the lake.

It seemed a melancholy place to die, despite the searing sunlight. For some time, Murphy stood quietly on the rocks that overlooked the scene. The winds were blowing enough to push the water around, commanding it, bending it to its own will. Across the uneven beach of Lac Sainte-Marine stood a large, bare, perpendicular rock. Someone had set a pair of Northshore chairs on the top of it, to watch the beauty of the early morning stretch across the water.

The beach was sharp, and getting to the body had been a short but treacherous walk. The rocks let you walk but only under threat of breaking an ankle. They lay smashed and strewn by the water's edge, some flat but others tilted and leaned. A distance from the body, a single pine tree stood out against the Canadian Shield.

Murphy and the team looked at the body. It appeared to be a fully clothed man lying on a large boulder. From the blood around his head, it looked like he had slipped and fell, hit his head and died.

"Dr. Chen, why do you suspect a homicide?" Murphy asked.

"Tillson, show the good detective the photographs of how we found the body," Dr. Chen said with a wave of his hand. Obediently, one of his technicians walked over to the detectives with a camera.

Tillson angled the camera so the detectives could see the review screen. The body had a t-shirt over its face.

"Not accidental? Just the way he fell?" Murphy asked.

Dr. Chen laughed, stood up and waved Murphy to an area past the crime scene tape. He lit up a cigarette, inhaled deeply, and exhaled with great satisfaction. "Cigarettes have been a source of joy to me for years. The comfort they provide far exceeds the years they take from my life. We both know, detective, there are no guarantees about how or when we die. Years," Dr. Chen said as he took another drag.

"He was not wearing the t-shirt. It was laid over his face after he fell. Someone put it there."

"Is there a cause of death?"

"As I said, there is a wound to the back of the head. There is presumed blood and brain tissue on the stone by his head. Initially he looks like he fell backward, hit his head, died. Then someone covered his face, including part of the wound. Head."

"So the shirt covered part of the wound?"

"Correct. We still need to do a full analysis of course, but it would appear to be a possible homicide," Chen said. "There was no identification. It is all rock and water around here, so there are no footprints we could see. Would you help by looking for any garbage or any objects that might be related to the scene?"

"Yes, of course. Thank you, Dr. Chen." They returned to the body, and the detectives fanned out to check the area. A search of one hundred metres in both directions and back to the parking lot revealed nothing.

Murphy turned back to surveying the scene, standing at the periphery of Dr. Chen's area, respectful of the space the team needed to work. She looked at the dark goo on the rock.

"He died instantly." Dr. Chen had correctly guessed her unasked question. "He has not been here long. I will take the body back with me. This scene is giving me nothing. There are no useful tire tracks as the parking lot is asphalt, no footprints, or other signs how he got here." Chen stood up and walked to the edge of the water. "As you can see, the water is shallow, and we have found nothing here. No phone, no identification, nothing at all about who he is. Not yet."

Murphy looked at her watch: they had been at the scene for an hour. "Okay, we need to get to the office. Dr. Chen, thank you." Before she could ask, Chen said he would have the postmortem by the next morning. With a last glancing survey of the area, the team headed into Kettering and the office.

When Murphy unlocked the door to the office, the air seemed to rush out, welcoming the detectives back. The detectives went to their respective desks and began drafting the computer files on the new case.

Murphy reviewed her emails and saw one from the IT specialist working on the Miller case.

"Mitch Tremblay," she said when she answered the phone. Mitch was a civilian who worked with all the police units.

"Mitch, it's DI Murphy, Homicide."

"Hi! Thank you for calling me back. Mind if I come up and show you a few things?"

"Sure, yeah come on up," Murphy said. Within minutes, Mitch walked into the atelier with some paper printouts.

"Hi everybody," she said as she walked into Murphy's office. Once again, Murphy was blown away by her body. Maybe she was a weightlifter. Mitch sat down in the leather chair across the desk from Murphy. "I found a brief chat and some saved gaming video in the La Guerre Infinitus game Miller played. Before he signed off, he got into an argument with other players. It seems he used his weapon to shoot a swastika into a wall, and a few other players attacked him. Someone called him a 'nazi faggot' before he signed off. Frankly, it's not unusual language for players. But it might speak to duress."

"Excellent, Mitch, thanks for letting me know."

"Also, I sent his keyboard to the Forensics Unit because there was blood on it," Mitch said.

"Okay, I will follow up with them."

"Great. I don't get to see the sun too often during the day, you know? It's a nice change."

"Well, you are welcome anytime." Murphy immediately regretted saying it. The last thing she needed was a bored IT technician hanging around.

"Great. Do you have any more IT work? I'm happy to help," Mitch offered.

"Sure. I have some Jonathan Haidt VerbatimVox files that have to be searched. We are looking for any mention of Perry Miller. Anything about attack, taking up arms, trucks, vans, vehicles. Maybe just search for synonyms for attack and include all of those words. The transcripts are on the server, under the Miller file, under 'Transcripts'. Can you work with Michael to get access?"

"Yes, sure thing! Thanks. So, you think Haidt might have used his radio program to direct Miller in his attack?" Mitch asked.

"Honestly, I doubt it. This is more about incidental findings that can be passed on to the RCMP Hate Crimes unit, or whoever the hell might take that on. How long will the keyword search take?" Murphy asked.

Mitch sighed. "Maybe ten minutes?"

"What? Why so fast?"

"I'll go to the Merriam Webster website, find synonyms for attack, truck, vehicle, arms, war, maybe assault. That's a five-minute search. I'll copy every word into a delimited text file and use the Grep commands to search. Maybe another five minutes of my time," she said. "The rest is just the computer working."

"Grep? What the hell is a Grep? Is that a company name?"

"No. It's a command that comes pre-installed on Linux machines. I have a Linux machine at my desk. Grep is a series of computer commands.

Global, regular expression, print. Grep. It will print all the lines matching a specified pattern. So you can see context," Mitch said.

"And we have this magical software? I am amazed," Murphy said. "Okay, that will take ten minutes and not days. Alright. Can we run that on the interview with Miller? You'll have to run the audio through VerbatimVox, but... maybe there's a keyword or something that they share," Murphy said.

"So some kind of trigger word? What words would I be looking for?" Mitch asked.

Murphy shrugged. "I have no clue, just rare words. Can you do it?"

"Sure thing, I will work with Michael on it." The pair walked into the atelier. "Michael, can you work with Mitch on transcripts and keywords and Grep commands on the Miller case?"

"Grep commands?" Parker asked.

"Someone named Linus wrote it. Or some shit. I have no idea. Pardon my language. You two work on that, please. By tomorrow. It only takes ten minutes once you start? Okay, go do your ten minutes of work, make sure the Miller file is up to date and then check a little more into Haidt's online presence. His website hosts other people's videos. See if Miller ever posted anything. Thanks."

"Okay, my desk," Mitch said. She and Parker walked out. Murphy stared at Mitch's ass as she walked out of the office and then turned around quickly to see Girard also staring.

CHAPTER FOURTEEN

"Okay, folks. We have Miller and now this John Doe. Let's call him Lac Sainte-Marine Doe. Adam, I—No, I don't like that name, it's too long. Marine Doe. That will do, Marine Doe. We won't get the postmortem until tomorrow, but if the forensics are available, start on that. Cleo, check all missing persons' reports from the last couple of days."

"Yes boss," Girard said.

"Let's aim for a few hours of work and then call it a night," she said. Girard and Hamilton sat together at Girard's desk while Murphy headed into her office.

Twenty minutes later, Mitch burst into the atelier, with Parker trailing behind. "Chinese!" she shouted as she held up large paper bags.

"Did you just go out and buy us dinner?" Girard asked.

"You bet. Michael said he was hungry, so here we are. Here, take this," Mitch said as she handed him two bags. "Do you have plates?" she asked.

"I'll get them," Parker said, excited by the sight of the foil takeout containers.

Murphy walked into the atelier, puzzled. "I thought you were working."

"We worked, but now we are done. Michael and me. So, who wants deep fried shrimp balls? Here, there are some vegetarian spring rolls here. And this," Mitch said as she peeled off the white cardboard lid, "is barbeque spare ribs. Moo Shu veggies here, god I love these little pancake things. Eggplant in garlic sauce, and General Tso chicken, of course." Mitch also laid out vegetable fried rice, beef chop suey and Shanghai-style fried noodles.

Everyone sat on the now-crowded couch and passed around plates, cutlery, and food. The fragrant smell of scallions, garlic, soy sauce, and ginger floated through the air. Tremblay and Hamilton opted to eat with the disposable wooden chopsticks provided by the restaurant. Everyone else settled on plastic forks. They chatted and compared opinions on the food. While the General Tso chicken won the majority—only Hamilton voted against it—the Moo Shu was the next most popular.

After forty minutes, the containers were empty, and the stomachs were full. "It's time I head out. I don't get overtime. DI Murphy, it's been an honour to work with you and your team," Mitch said. "The Grep program will run overnight. You will get a report in the morning."

"Send it to Michael, please," Murphy said.

"You bet. See you all later!" Mitch said as she left the atelier.

Within an hour, the team was ready to give a preliminary report on Marine Doe, and Girard called Murphy into the atelier.

"Male, white or Hispanic, likely between twenty-five to thirty-five. Dr. Chen will give us a better idea tomorrow," Girard said as he stuck the photographs of the dead man on the link board. "We have searched missing persons database and there are no matches. His fingerprints were subm—"

"Oh shit!" Parker shouted. "Shit shit shit!" he barked as he jumped back to his computer. "I just saw that guy. I just saw him!" Parker began clicking on Haidt's website.

"Here! This is him." Parker played a video of a man and woman in a home, talking to the camera.

"That's definitely him," Murphy said.

"This is sick, watch."

Murphy frowned. *Sick?* She and the rest of the team watched as the video cut to the same couple yelling at a man. "Fuck him up, Eugene!" the woman yelled. In response, Eugene punched the man in the face and kicked his legs out from underneath him. The camera jostled as the woman filmed her feet, kicking the downed man in the head. As they ran from the scene, the video flailed.

The credits rolled over the couple as they sat in their back yard drinking beer. "This video is fictional. We compensated all people for their time."

No one spoke for a moment. Whoever 'Eugene' was, he was their homicide victim. Murphy added an arrow to Marine Doe and wrote 'Eugene'.

"You were looking for Miller videos, but we found our Marine Doe? Haidt is in the middle of everything," Murphy said.

"He posted under the name Eugene Baptiste," Parker said.

"There are no missing persons name Eugene or Baptiste in the NSPD database," Girard said after checking with his computer.

"I will go through the videos more, check comments," Parker said.

Murphy wondered what the chances were that Haidt knew and would share the identity of their victim. She stared at Eugene's photographs. In one, pulled from the website, he was smiling, and in the other, he was dead.

"Michael, work with Mitch. I want each of his videos transcribed and searched for names. See how he knew Haidt or if he knew Perry Miller. Find out if that woman's name is ever mentioned. Or if any of the victims, or actors, or whatever the hell they are. Tell me where the videos were shot. Everything," Murphy said. Parker immediately got on the phone to Mitch and left a message asking her to help with the search.

"So we have a fight video. This guy posted a fight video. Why? Does he have other videos? Play the videos on the screen," she told Parker. Parker turned on the projector, then shared the video output from his computer. The team watched a video titled 'Street Beat Down'. Eugene was filmed happily swinging a baseball bat in the air and heading into a laneway. The videographer followed and filmed the chaotic attack. Eugene snuck up on the sleeping man before screaming at him. As the man jolted awake, Eugene swung the bat and hit him in the legs. The short video, less than sixty seconds long, showed two more blows to the man's body before Eugene and his conspirator fled, laughing.

"Hi, I got your voicemail," Mitch said as she walked into the room and headed toward Parker's desk. No one responded. They were riveted by the videos. She booted up the PC at the desk next to Parker and sat down.

The next video was similarly short and brutal. It was an attack on a young Black woman wearing a BLM t-shirt. Eugene was barehanded in this attack: he punched her in the stomach and, when she doubled over, kneed her in the face. The videographer filmed her own feet kicking the woman twice before the couple ran away.

In the third video, Eugene waved an empty wine bottle at the camera. The couple snuck behind a tree and waited for their victim. A young man called out, "Are you there?" just before Eugene jumped from behind the tree and struck him in the head with the bottle. The head wound bled, and bright red blood flowed through the young man's hair as the videographer zoomed in for a close-up.

"Sweet Jesus," Murphy said. "Mitch, thank you for coming back. So Eugene makes street fight vid—"

"Unprovoked assault videos," Hamilton said.

Murphy nodded. "Eugene makes unprovoked assault videos. He might be pre-selecting his targets."

"The blond guy said something before the attack, what was it?" Girard asked.

Parker scrubbed the video backward and played it again. The man said, "Are you there?"

"He was meeting someone there?"

"The man or the woman? Or both?"

"Michael, Mitch, can you get a date on the last video?"

Mitch took control of Parker's computer. "It was posted June tenth this year," Mitch said. "I can see the metadata. It has the same date. They put some text at the end, so that is only the day the video was finished, not the day it was filmed."

"Adam, check for reports of assault this year, spring to summer, where the victim is a blond man, a Black woman or a man in an alley."

"Yes, boss."

Girard's search turned up Crystal Bradford, a twenty-one-year-old Black woman who reported an assault in June. "Boss, I have one possible victim. I can talk to her."

"Not yet. She is a potential suspect. Build a file on her. Check social media and news outlets. He must have found her somehow, had a reason to target her," Murphy said.

Mitch's reverse image search on the internet for Eugene returned thousands of faces. Hamilton's search of various missing persons databases came up empty. The postmortem report would not arrive until the next day. Forensics was busy with all the cases arising from the truck attack and would be some time before their items would be processed.

"Thank you, everyone, for all your work, but it's time to go home. Mitch, thank you for coming back. Stay safe. Hey everyone, stay safe, get home safe. We'll get back into it tomorrow."

Murphy walked out to the Brawler cautiously. The riot was over and most, but not all the protesters were gone. There would be a dozen reports from all levels of policing and government on the riot. Public groups would want their say on the quality of policing, the economic fallout and the religious implications. She wondered if the Association of Canadian Taxpayers would complain about the policing costs. They had raised a stink during a press conference announcing finding the remains of Cardinal Horn. She would put nothing past them.

On her drive home, Murphy called Sun. She was excited about reopening her store. "The flowers in the coolers should be fine, as long as there was no power loss. All the hard products should be fine, after they are thoroughly cleaned," Sun said.

"Will insurance cover anything?"

"It will cover the window, since that was before the riots or protests or whatever the hell that's been."

"Hell is a good word," Murphy said.

"Yeah. I need a police report, but you guys are a little busy."

"Ha! No kidding."

"I heard an officer lost his life," Sun said.

"Yes, a woman. The OPP are handling it."

"Oh! I thought it was you. You aren't involved?"

"No. We'll go to her funeral, but it's not our investigation. I'm glad. I never want to investigate the death of a cop, never," Murphy said. She was tearing up. "Hey listen, I'm almost home. I have to go."

"Caitlin?"

"Yeah?"

"I'm really glad you're okay."

"I'm glad you're okay, too. Bye."

"Yeah bye. I—"

Murphy hung up the phone, then realized she cut Sun off. *Oopsy,* she said to herself. Murphy pulled into the parking lot and saw Maria's car. "Oh, bless you Maria."

When she walked into the kitchen, Maria rushed over to hug her tightly. Murphy winced. "Oh Caitlin! Del told me everything! I never knew how that truck man rammed your truck. Your arm. Are you okay? How are you?" She would not let go. Murphy hugged Maria back, the scent of her hairspray drifting lightly up. Her fingers trembled, although Murphy did not know if it was good or bad.

"Maria, thank you so much for coming over," Murphy said, separating herself from the grasp.

"Oh of course, of course, as soon as I could. Please sit, I'm making pasta. Just some butter and garlic and spices. I could not buy any fresh groceries. Stores closed."

The women sat and talked and ate for a couple of hours until it was almost time for Maria to leave. She insisted on helping Del get ready for bed—it was her chance to make sure Del was physically well and that the catheter was properly in place. She said goodbye and, with tears welling in her eyes, she said she would be back tomorrow.

"Okay, what the what? Is that our Maria?" Del said as she and Murphy lay on her bed.

"Yes, that seemed very, uh, motherly. I think the riot really freaked her out."

"No shit, Sherlock, it's freaked a lot of people out. It freaked me out. I talked to Thomas and Jens earlier and they are, well, they are both really stoned. Thomas asked why I was speaking Klingon."

"Ha ha! Were you speaking Klingon?" Murphy asked.

"It was French. I told them they were 'con comme la lune'. Ha ha! Those two," Del laughed. She looked at Murphy's questioning face and laughed again. "They are as stupid as the moon."

"Oh well, that makes sense," Murphy laughed. She knew a few French phrases, usually related to food or friends. Being called a stupid moon was a new one.

"What am I going to do with The Boys?" Del asked. "I mean, I have to help them. When I came to Northshore, they adopted me. Thomas found this wheelchair accessible home and helped me turn the front rooms into a gallery and studio. Bob did research on all the government funding programs for the renovations and filled out a ton of forms. Jens helped with medical forms, and they all took turns taking me to appointments until I could buy my van. I owe them so much, and..."

Murphy held Del as she cried, rocking back and forth gently. "The COVID lockdown messed them all up, but now, it seems like the entire world wants to kill us. The Unicorn has been destroyed, and that meant the world to them. They are older. They never really embraced online socializing or anything."

The pair continued to talk and watch television for a couple of hours before Del said she was tired. With a kiss on the cheek, Murphy left Del's bed and went to her own.

After saying the names of murder victims, she fell into a tortured sleep. In her dream, she was standing in front of Sun's flower shop, watching the Sparkling Unicorn go up in flames. She felt the flower shop window explode behind her and she curled up in a ball, waiting for the shards of glass to come. When they did not, she looked up and saw Mitch in a police uniform. She was looking down at Murphy laughing, her arms out in a Jesus Christ pose, protecting her. Mitch's back was peppered with glass. Blood trickled onto the sidewalk.

"Run with me," Mitch said. Murphy sprung up, and the women ran down the empty street. The road bucked and folded as they scrambled. In front of them, a gaping chasm opened up. Mitch lay across the gap and Murphy ran over her back and across the fissure. Turning back, Murphy saw the fissure was now the raging Niagara River, and Mitch was standing on the opposite side.

Murphy turned and ran until she saw St. Mary's Infirmary. When she ran past the iron gates, she was in her office. No one was about, but all the phones were ringing. Murphy tried to answer each one, but the more phones she picked up, the more appeared. Desperately, she scrambled to answer the phone on her desk. "Hello?" she shouted to be heard over the ringing.

"Hi Caitlin! It's me," Roisin said in a joyously happy sing-song voice.

Murphy jerked awake, sweating and breathing hard. Roisin had died—been vaporized—decades ago in a car bomb explosion, but she sounded like the happy six-year-old Murphy knew. She sat for a few minutes, perplexed by the mashup of old memories and new horrors. She huffed and got out of bed to shower and wash away any remnants of the dream.

Murphy got dressed and went downstairs. Del called out as she passed by. "Hey! You okay?"

Murphy stuck her head into Del's bedroom. "Yeah, you?"

"Nice try. Come here for a minute. I heard you shout. Are your dreams getting worse?"

Murphy shook her head and shrugged. "I do not know. I used to have the same dream over and over, but now it's changing. Last night, the IT technician, Mitch, was in it."

"I don't suppose that was a scream of passion I heard?" Del asked.

"Ha, no. But damn, that woman has a body. That's a strong woman there. Anyway, no. Nothing like that. It was Roisin. She called, but all these phones were ringing, so I had to shout 'hello' so she could hear me. That's probably what you heard."

"She called? Did she say anything?"

"She just said 'hi, it's me.'"

"I think you need a therapist," Del said.

"I need a dream therapist. Gotta go. Breakfast at the Goose Gas awaits."

"I do not know how you can eat at that place. It's disgusting."

"Yes, it is, but that's part of the charm. I want to check on Sergei too. Last time I was there, he wasn't around," Murphy said. She kissed Del on the cheek and headed out the door. As she pulled out onto the highway, she saw Maria arriving in her car, and waved.

Murphy pulled into the Goose Gas parking lot and stopped in front of a gas pump. Sergei hobbled over to the pump and grabbed a gas pump hose, waiting for Murphy.

"Sergei, I'm glad to see you. I missed you before," she said as she swiped her credit card in the machine to activate the pump. She pressed a few buttons, and Sergei began filling her tank.

"It was a hard time for me. They came to the park, they came here. I had to run into the forest. I hurt my leg," he said. Murphy looked down to see that his pants were ripped and bloodstained.

"Have you been to the doctor?" Murphy asked. She had no idea who 'they' were.

"No, how do I get there? It's too far to walk on a hurt leg," he said.

"Ambulance? No? If I take you, will you go to the hospital?" Sergei said nothing, concentrating now on pumping the gas. "Did you get the sandwich I left for you?"

"Yes, sandwich and pop and candy. You are always good to me," Sergei said.

"Okay, Sergei, I will make a deal with you. Let me drop you off at the hospital so they can look at your leg. I will give you two sandwiches, two pops and two bags of candy. Deal?"

"How am I to come back?" he asked.

"I can get you a taxi ride. They will bring you back here. Will you do that? Come to the hospital and then take a taxi home?" The gas pump handle snapped: the tank was full.

"Three sandwiches, two pops, one bag of the chewy candy and a box of crackers. The cheese kind. Plus the taxi ride back here. Leave in twenty minutes. I have things to do," Sergei said.

"Deal." Murphy walked into the diner and paused before going to wash her hands. She was reluctant to use the bathroom, given the state of the diner. She'd never dated.

"It's cleaner in there than out here," Emeline said from behind the counter. Murphy walked into the washroom and saw that it was true. The washroom was a single-user room with sparkling white wall tiles and a glistening white floor. Even the toilet glimmered in the soft florescent light. Murphy held her hand under the automatic hand soap dispenser to receive a dollop of lightly scented soap, then pivoted to the automatic water tap. A steady stream of warm water shot out, and Murphy washed her hands. She then had a choice between an automated air dryer or a paper towel dispenser. She opted for the paper towel, swiped her hand underneath the sensor, and tore off the paper that came out. Drying her hands, she then swiped her hand at another sensor and the door opened.

"Well, I would never have guessed you would have anything so fancy here," Murphy said as she sat at her booth. Emeline arrived with her coffeepot and poured Murphy a cup.

"The owner's wife got COVID early on and was really sick. He took all the COVID money he got from the government, you know, for renovations and safety precautions, and put it into the bathroom. He still has someone on contract to clean it once a day. Full steam clean, with a machine."

"Wow, that's kind of amazing. Thanks for the coffee."

"Amazing or stupid, your choice," Emeline said as she went back behind the counter.

Murphy nodded, sipped at the greasy coffee, and pulled out her pencil crayons and colouring book. She flipped to the last page she had been working on: a mouse with oversized ears. Grabbing the lavender colour, she shaded in the inside of one ear. She used a darker shade of purple to colour the fur on the outside of the ears and then something in between for the rest of the mouse's fur.

She was almost finished by the time Emeline arrived with her breakfast. Two eggs, sunny side up, two sausages and some hash browns. Murphy thanked her, put away the colouring book and ate her breakfast. She was shocked at how good it tasted. "Hey Emeline, is Tony still the cook?" she asked.

"No, we hired a new guy. Hey you, what's your name again?" she shouted through the kitchen window.

"Jamal. Is there a problem with the food?"

"No, great food. Great food," Murphy said, waving her fork back and forth to emphasize that there was no problem. She wanted to say it was worlds better than anything Tony had ever cooked. "I think I'll try to come here more often. Delicious," she said. She wolfed down the food, paid Emeline for the meal, and headed outside. Sergei was waiting for her by the Brawler. She waved and walked inside the convenience store to buy him his food.

Hustling Sergei into the Brawler, he insisted on sitting in the back seat "like a king," he said. "Drive on." Murphy laughed as she pulled out of the Goose Gas and headed toward the hospital. It was a ten-minute drive that took Murphy only seven minutes. She pulled up to the emergency drop-off and hopped out.

"Your highness," she said as she opened the door for him.

"Thank you for the ride," he said as he shuffled toward the door. Through the glass, she saw Jasmine watching. Murphy pointed toward her leg, then at Sergei. Jasmine nodded and greeted Sergei at the entrance. Murphy gave Sergei a taxi chit, said goodbye, and drove off.

CHAPTER FIFTEEN

Murphy sat in her office, instant coffee on her desk, going through reports on the Miller van attack. They had contacted each of the victims, including two who had chosen not to speak with the police. There were fifteen reports, with fifteen medical notes outlining the injuries suffered. Issues ranged from a sprained ankle to the catastrophic injuries Bob had suffered. He had suffered the worst of all the survivors. Murphy read the statement he gave to Parker. A notation showed he had given it to Mitch, who used VerbatimVox to transcribe the recording.

"I don't know what to feel. I can't really make sense of it. I don't know if I am angry or sad or scared. I can't believe it. It was really scary, everything happened so fast. I was just sitting there, having a drink. It was a beautiful day, and I was with my two best friends and we were laughing and joking and then there were all these horns. Car horns. And suddenly you could hear screaming, like shouting. And I felt this heat. My ears kind of popped, you know, like they would if I was on a plane.

"It felt like I got punched by a giant, like just...boom! It was like the universe collapsed on me. It was dark and there was so much screaming. I... it was weird. I was trying to stay so calm, I kept thinking it's okay Bob, just take it easy, you can figure this out.

"I could smell gasoline, a car engine. Well, truck. And I kind of looked up, and I saw all this metal, like bars and sheets of metal. And the tires. There were tires by... fuck. There were tires by my head and tires on my legs and all this metal and it was hot and stinking and this black smoke was all around. It was horrible. It was getting hard to see, and I was choking and screaming and it sounded like a freight train. I remember thinking, how the fuck could I get hit by a train? I knew something bad was happening, but I didn't know what.

"I thought, I have to stop screaming. I am screaming and screaming and screaming and I have to stop, but I can't. I can't make myself stop screaming. And then the truck was gone. I could see the sky, the blue sky and it was so clear and so beautiful that I thought, okay, you can die now. It's okay to die because the sky is so beautiful.

"But I didn't die. Not yet, anyway. The doctors have not said much. I have no legs. They did not ask if they could take my legs. I have a broken back. Lots of things are wrong. So much is broken, I'm broken. He shredded me to pieces."

"Sweet Jesus," Murphy mumbled as she wiped away tears. She tried not to think about what Bob was going through, what all the living victims were going through. She grabbed her bag and pulled out her colouring book and coloured in the first thing she turned to.

Finally, her coffee was gone, and the entire butterfly was one colour of lime green. She put the book away and looked into the atelier. Everyone was busy at their desks, studiously not looking into her office. Murphy cleared her throat and closed the file on the computer.

Murphy believed Miller should face one first degree murder charge and seventeen attempted murder charges. He would get life in prison for the murder charge. The attempted murders might get him twenty years each. But everything would be served concurrently. The Supreme Court of Canada had ruled just a few years ago that the maximum period of ineligibility for parole was twenty-five years. No matter the guilty verdicts,

Miller would get life with the chance of parole in twenty-five years, and nothing more.

The charges, Murphy reasoned, were not for the punitive value. Miller would feel no more remorseful or regretful if he spent fifty years instead of twenty-five years in prison. The charges and guilty verdicts were for the victims. It was important that each victim felt like their injuries, their suffering, mattered. If Miller was found guilty of attempted murder for Bob, then Bob would feel like he had been seen and heard by the justice system. That was the theory, anyway.

Murphy would have to run all the charges past Shevchenko and then present it to the Crown prosecutor. She looked at the other detectives and decided Girard could make the presentations. "Adam, in here please," she called out.

"Yes, boss?" he said, walking into her office. She motioned for him to sit down.

"How well do you know the Miller file?" she asked.

"Fairly well. We have forensics from his car and home, and the crime scene. We have autopsy results on Kitty. We have medical reports on the survivors. We have his timeline, including CCTV and video reconstruction of the crime itself. We have his statement with confession. There is no evidence anyone planned it with him, but we are looking at Haidt for incitement. And based on the religious rhetoric and Bible clippings, we believe the crimes were hate-motivated," Girard said.

"Excellent summary. What charges would you recommend?"

"First degree murder, and attempted murder for all survivors. We could add a million other charges, like damage to property, assault police, resist arrest, threatening..."

"We will add those charges later. And we will add them because of insurance claims and whatnot. That might help with claims, make the business owners feel better. I agree. Would you like to present this to the Superintendent, the Chief and the Attorney General's office? All separately, of course," Murphy said.

Girard was taken aback. "Really? I haven't done that before, not to the AG. Yeah, that sounds great."

"Good, I think you're up to it. Read over every single detail twice. Make an appointment with Supt. Shevchenko. Only after you've outlined the case, do you make an appointment with Chief Valencia. And after that, an appointment with the Crown counsel," Murphy said.

"Yes, absolutely."

"And if any of them have even a single question, you go back and rewrite the report to address the concern, and move forward again. Keep me updated. Yes?"

"Yes!" Girard said proudly. Presenting the case to the Attorney General was something Murphy had always taken on. "Any special reason?"

"Well, first off, I think you will do a great job. You need the experience. But I have a friend who was injured during the attack. I think it would be better with an unbiased eye on it," Murphy said.

"Are they okay?"

"No, nope. I won't tell you who. I just want an extra pair of eyes on this. So you have to be extra thorough in going through everything. Unbiased."

"Yes, absolutely. I understand. You can count on me," Girard said with a confident nod of his head.

Murphy smiled. "I know that, Adam. Thank you. I want every T crossed, and every I dotted. Every fact cross-checked. Let's go," she said. They walked into the atelier.

"Heads up. Adam will present the Miller case to the AG. Cleo, please help if need be."

"Yes, boss," Hamilton said with a respectful nod toward Girard.

Girard felt electric. Since the killer was caught immediately after the attack and had confessed, it was not the hardest to prove. The amount of evidence made this one of the largest homicide cases in Northshore history. Had it not been for the other teams assisting, it would have taken months to get as far as they had. Girard knew there would still be more evidence required, there always was, but it was certainly enough to go forward to the Crown to discuss charges. Excitedly, Girard explained everything to Hamilton, and the pair got down to work.

With that off her desk, Murphy knew it would be easier to clear her mind. She remembered the car that had interfered with her pursuit of Miller and called Traffic Safety. During the pursuit, she had given the emergency operator the license plate of a car that had tried to block her path and brake-check her. She wanted to make sure the NSPD were pressing charges. Back in her office, she called Sgt. Kendall to ask for an update. Kendall advised she had sent an officer out to get the other driver's side of the story. Subsequently, the driver was charged with aggressive driving and stunt driving. His driver's license was immediately suspended for thirty days and his vehicle impounded for fourteen. That made Murphy a little happier.

It was not five minutes before her phone rang. "DI Murphy."

"Detective Inspector Murphy. This is Francis Hagano from Special Investigations. I would like to speak with you about the Miller case. Can you come to my office?"

"Yes, of course. When?"

"Now," he said with a laugh.

"I will be there in ten minutes," Murphy said. SIU was in a small office building three doors down. There were four offices in the two-storey structure, and SIU took up two on the first floor. On the second floor were an accountant and an architect.

"Heading out to speak with SIU. Back never," Murphy said as she walked out. Minutes later, she walked into SIU, introduced herself, and was taken to Hagano's office.

"Sir, nice to meet you," Murphy said as she stuck out her hand.

"I do not think I have ever heard that from law enforcement," Hagano said. "Please, sit down. This interview is being recorded. This is Hagano speaking with Detective Inspector Caitlin Murphy. Murphy, Can you please recount the events of July 15 to the best of your recollection."

Murphy liked Hagano's no-nonsense style. She gave him a high-level recounting of the events. It included Miller's attempt to ram her truck, him driving into a field, and him slipping in the ditch. She tapped on her cast a few times to emphasize that her injury had been greater than his.

"Did you at any time hit Mr. Miller?"

"On Sunday July 16 at the Uniondale Federal Penitentiary, Supt. Shevchencko and I interviewed the suspect. At that time, he physically attacked us. I retreated from the table and put my arm in front of my face to defend myself, and he lunged forward, across the table and into my arm. Prison security immediately subdued Mr. Miller. I did not hit him, but he did hit my cast when he tried to attack me. There is probably video, of course."

"Yes, I have seen the video, actually. DI Murphy, you have quite the reputation in NSPD. You are a solid and honest person, a good cop. Everyone says that. I do not see too many good cops in my line of work. I have already spoken to Mr. Miller and viewed the tape. He is not making a complaint," Hagano said.

"I appreciate the words," Murphy said.

Hagano reached over and clicked a button. "Recording is off. This interview is a formality. I actually do not think you appreciate my words, DI Murphy. I have never had anyone say it was nice to meet me. And you are only the second person who has shown up without a union or legal representative. You are not defensive. You gave an account that is matched by testimony from Mr. Miller and Supt. Shevchenko. It matches the Forensic Unit report on your vehicle. I do not think I have ever spoken with someone whose suspect was injured twice on two different days, who I do not hold responsible for those injuries. Not including Mr. Miller's black eye from an incident at the prison. You are a good cop. You have an excellent reputation. I cannot tell you how refreshing that is."

Murphy was surprised. When did they test her vehicle and were they going to tell her she could get it fixed? Hagano reached over and pressed the button to continue recording. "DI Murphy, thank you for your time. A report will be sent to Chief Valencia." Hagano again reached over and turned off the recording.

"Thank you, detective. Have a good day," Hagano said with a handshake. Murphy walked out thinking that was the easiest five-minute career save she had ever made.

Back in the office, Murphy picked up a voicemail from Chief Valencia, asking that she come to see him. There was another voicemail from Sun, this one on her personal cell phone, asking if she would like to meet for lunch or dinner. Del had also left a voicemail, saying she and Maria were heading to Toronto to visit Bob.

Murphy texted Sun to say yes. Lunch sounded great, when and where. She hit the send button and headed upstairs to see the Chief. His assistant, Sandra, told her to go right in.

"Sir," Murphy said as she entered and stood in front of his desk. Valencia did not invite her to sit down.

"I will nominate you for the Medal for Police Bravery. I've seen some of the paperwork. I have a preliminary report from SIU."

"Already? I just spoke to Francis Hagano," Murphy said.

"It was just a formality. You had a suspect try to ram your vehicle, although why he thought his piece of shit truck would do any damage to your Brawler is beyond me. He tried to kill you. You could have shot him when he pointed a gun at you, but you did not. You could have left him in the vehicle with gasoline leaking, but you did not. You could have let him drown in that damn ditch. You did not. When he leapt at you in the interview, so much could have gone wrong. And it did not. You kept your cool. You stayed professional. You made me proud."

Murphy's heart swelled. "Thank you, Sir. I am not sure if it rises--"

"Update me on the Miller case."

"Girard is preparing to present to Supt. Shevchenko, then you, Sir. I am sure he will make an appointment for first thing next week."

"That was an extraordinary turnaround," Valencia said.

"Thank you Sir. Supt. Shevchenko's teams were a great help."

"Good. And this latest homicide? Why am I getting calls from reporters asking if it was a gay attack? A queer bashing?"

"No idea, Sir. I will check that angle. He is a social media guy who films fights. Well, attacks on others. Pathology and forensics are still outstanding. If you are getting calls, someone notified the media, and it wasn't us."

"Right, yes. Okay. Suspects?"

"Nothing yet Sir. Early days," Murphy said.

"Right. Get on it. Dismissed."

Murphy headed back downstairs and read an email from Dr. Chen. He was ready to report his autopsy findings and requested her presence. "Michael, with me. Eugene's autopsy. Are we any further along on videos?" she asked.

"Mitch is still working on it."

The pair walked to the Coroner's Office, just down the street from headquarters. Dr. Chen was happy to see them. "Detectives, welcome,

welcome. In 1912, John Morton bought the formula for Chapstick lip balm for $5. But it was his wife who told him to make it easy to use like lipstick. Five."

"No. I had no idea. Was he wearing Chapstick?"

"No. Do you have a name for him yet? What are you calling him?" Chen asked.

"We think he is Eugene Baptiste."

"Okay. Eugene Baptiste it is for now. Male, between twenty-five and forty years old, based on pubic symphysis and dental analysis. He died where he was found, on July twentieth. An anonymous call came in. Paramedics arrived at 9:45, I arrived on scene at 11:10 a.m. The beginning of rigour was noted at the scene, so he had been dead only two to six hours previous," Chen said. He moved the dead man's arm as he spoke.

"Postmortem lividity in the posterior and back of legs indicate he was not moved after death." Chen rolled the body over to show the purple skin on the buttocks and legs.

"He is one hundred and seventy-two centimetres, almost five feet eight. Fifty-seven point six kilograms, one hundred and twenty-seven pounds. Seven. Caucasian, black hair, brown eyes." Chen pried the man's eyelid open to reveal a dead brown eye.

"He suffered one significant blow to the back of the head. He either fell or was pushed and hit his head and suffered a life-ending impact. Blood, hair and brain matter found. Found."

"Suspicious, but not necessarily homicide."

"Overall good health. Minor lacerations and bruises on the hands but healing. They did not happen at the same time. He was recently in a fight. No new defensive wounds, no bruising, no contusions."

Chen walked over to an x-ray and held it up for Murphy to see. "X-rays indicate healed minor fractures in the left leg and right arm. Probably from three or more months ago, and not treated by a doctor. There may be something on the clothing, but the Forensic Unit took that yesterday."

Chen walked over to the body again and pointed at the chest, then made a fist. "There is slight bruising on his chest. He may have been punched. I am running touch DNA tests, but that will take some time. Touch. There were palm prints and fingerprints in blood on Baptiste's chest, but I will need amido black to bring them out. His fingerprints have been taken and submitted to the system."

"Dr. Chen, thank you. That was remarkably clear," Murphy said. "So, suspicious death?"

"I am closing the death as undetermined suspicious for now. Death."

Murphy and Parker headed toward headquarters. Murphy's phone buzzed, and she read the text from Sun. *Pete's Coffee, across from her store, in thirty minutes.* She texted Sun back, agreeing to meet her there.

"Michael, I'm going for lunch. I will meet you back at the station, and we will look at the clothing."

"Yes, boss," he said as he set off in a jog toward the station.

CHAPTER SIXTEEN

M urphy headed to Pete's Coffee, and Sun. As she passed people in the street, most seemed almost to have forgotten what happened just a week ago. A woman glanced over her shoulder when a truck passed, and another pulled her child a little closer. But most simply walked on.

The air was sultry and getting hotter as the sun beat down. The sky was bright and empty and the heat roared like a forge fire. Murphy squinted: her sunglasses were no match for the sun. No matter how we might kid ourselves, Murphy thought, no one is tougher than the sun. She turned on to Centre Street. There were fewer people walking and more people standing. Many of them had orange t-shirts.

People stood on the street corner talking while others stood at curbsides watching. Murphy popped into a convenience store and bought a bouquet. She would have preferred to buy her flowers at Sun's flower shop, but it was still closed. Finding another dedicated flower shop seemed almost like cheating. She chose a convenience store to buy a bouquet for Kitty Meyers.

As with every one of her homicide victims, Murphy laid flowers at the scene of where Kitty's body was found. There were already a dozen bouquets, a stuffed teddy bear and some candles that had long blown out. Her flowers joined the rest. Murphy knew the entire scene would be cleared in the next day or two. She looked briefly at the hording that had gone up around the Sparkling Unicorn, a barrier between then and now.

As she stood, two people in orange t-shirts passed by. On the back, in bold black text, were the words Northshore Ganawendan: Protect Northshore. "Excuse me," Murphy said as she caught up to the walkers. "What do the t-shirts mean? I've seen a few people wearing them."

The pair stopped to talk. One gave Murphy a flyer. The other person said that they are Indigenous volunteers protecting Northshore against the far right. "We want to be an extra set of eyes and ears for the NSPD. You know, like helping them out and being aware of what's going on."

"People are nervous after the attack and the riot. We all saw how it started and had no way of preventing it. The police cannot reach community members by themselves. Being visible in places that might be risky, showing up. We are making sure everyone feels safer. We let people know we take our roles of protectors seriously," said the other.

"The bright orange t-shirts remind people they're on indigenous land. We have a strong tradition of taking care of our community. It's all about respecting and being aware of the history and the people who lived here before us."

"We want to make our community feel secure and happy. Just by being around, we hope to give everyone a sense of comfort. We want to create an environment where people feel good and supported."

"Take a flyer. It explains a bit more. Remember, if you ever see any of us in these orange shirts, know that we're here to make a positive difference. We care about Kettering, and we're doing our best to make it a better and safer home for everyone."

Dutifully, Murphy took a flyer and thanked the pair for the information. Somehow, a citizen street patrol had been birthed out of the chaos of the last few days. She wondered if it was reactive or proactive. She put the flyer in her pocket, crossed the street and headed to Pete's Coffee.

"Hi beautiful," Murphy said as she sat down opposite Sun at the bistro table.

"Well, hi beautiful right back to you," Sun said with a slight smile. She looked worn down, the weight of rebirth carried on her shoulders.

"Hey, you okay?" Murphy said as she held out her hand, palm up, waiting to be held.

"It's a lot," Sun said. She reached out to take Murphy's hand, then withdrew it quickly as the waiter approached.

"Are you ready to order?" he asked. He stood beside the table, and although he had an order pad in hand, he was looking indifferently out the window. He was a young man, barely out of his teens. On his forearm was a shaky line tattoo: 'what doesn't killed me makes me stonger'. Murphy smirked.

"I'll have the kale, pumpkin seed and chickpea salad, and a cup of coconut curry spinach lentil soup please," Sun said.

"Soup and salad. For you?" the waiter asked, looking briefly at Murphy before returning his gaze to the nothingness outside.

"Burger and fries."

"Is there any chance you can help me at the store? There is more to repair than I realized," Sun said after the waiter was gone.

"Maybe in a day or two? We caught another case," Murphy said. She suddenly wished she'd ordered a drink.

"I'd appreciate any—"

"Hey Caitlin!" Mitch's voice boomed in the otherwise hushed murmurs in the cafe. "How are you? Hi, I'm Michelle Tremblay," she said, holding her hand out to Sun.

"Sun Kumar," she said, shaking Tremblay's hand. Her grasp was firm and confident.

"Sun. Call me Mitch. Hey Caitlin how—"

Murphy held up her hand. Her phone was ringing, and she had to answer it. "Murphy."

"Are you and Caitlin friends?" Sun asked. Mitch was wearing jeans and a tight t-shirt and Sun was taking all of her in. The muscles on her arms and legs were thick and well-defined. Her smile was bright and white and charmingly crooked.

"He is where now?" Murphy asked. She got up from the table, phone pressed to her ear, and walked to an empty area of the cafe.

"Oh, not just friends. I work with the Homicide Unit. I am in IT," Mitch said with pride.

"Hey, Sun, I've got to go. Sorry," Murphy said as she returned to the pair. She reached into her wallet and threw two twenties onto the table. "That should cover it," she said.

"I did not mean to interrupt," Mitch said.

"It's not you. I have to go. Mitch, I've ordered a burger. You can have it. Keep Sun company. Gotta go," Murphy said. She walked out as Mitch sat down.

"Wow, a free burger with a pretty lady. I don't know if my day could get better. So Sun, where are you from?"

"Across the street. Sun Flowers."

"Oh yeah, that's your store? Glorious name. Sun. Sun Flowers. It took a hit in the riots. If you need any help to fix it up, just let me know," Mitch said. The waiter did a double take when he arrived with the food, then internally shrugged and put the food down.

"You know how to install windows, do you?" Sun asked. She liked Mitch was trying to impress her, but she was more than happy to call the woman out.

"Oh yeah. Windows, tables, counters, shelves. Brick work, plumbing, electrical, whatever." She took a bite of the hamburger. "Mmm, good," she mumbled through a mouth full of hot food.

"And where did you learn to do all of that? Online?" Sun said as she took a bite of salad. She would not let Mitch off the hook.

"Ha ha. Army. I've built schools and hospitals in Mali and Uganda. From scratch. But only one hospital had windows. I helped build a sea wall in Sri Lanka too. That was cool."

Sun was taken aback. "You've done all that?"

"I was in the Army for five years. We travelled all over. In Mali, I helped doctors set up a clinic. You know, protect them. They were a target. But we also helped the locals build a one storey hospital, some place for the docs to work. Uganda was a school one time. Same thing, protection. And a hospital another time."

"I have to say, I'm impressed," Sun said. "I never really understood what you do, what the Army does. And Sri Lanka, too." She sipped a spoonful of soup. It was cooling.

"Yeah. There was that tsunami in oh-four, and we went ten years later, in fourteen, to help rebuild a sea wall. It was damaged, it was breaking up into the sea. So we rebuilt it. We checked out a couple of other sea walls to figure out what worked. Well, the engineers did, we just kept them safe. We went to India to see what they had done. Up the coast from Nagapattinam to Puducherry. Beautiful," Mitch said. She took a bite of her burger and wiped her face with a napkin.

"You were in Puducherry? Where?"

"Uh, Pondicherry seawall. That's as far north—"

"You were in Pondicherry? I was born in Pondicherry!" Sun exclaimed. She was surprised to hear that Mitch not only knew about Pondicherry, but had also been there.

As Sun and Mitch got to know each other, Murphy walked back to headquarters. Jonathan Haidt and his followers were on the steps of HQ demanding answers about the riot. "Who were the rioters," he shouted. Murphy shook her head: he started all this crap, she thought. She really wanted to speak to him, but with everyone's eyes on him, now was not the time to ask for an interview. Murphy walked into HQ. She tapped her employee card at the card reader to unlock the door.

"We have a bit more information on our victim, Eugene," Hamilton said to Murphy as she walked into the room. "I confirmed his name as Eugene Baptiste. He is on alt-right social platforms under that name, with the same avatar image. He is an active CBB member and part of his thing—their thing, since he was often with a woman—is to attack people, then post the video."

"Any link to Haidt?" Murphy asked.

"Just his website so far."

"Has anyone reported Eugene missing? No? Okay, do we have anything on... What was her name? Crystal Bradford."

"Local social activist with some news coverage this year. I found three news articles in the Northshore Gazette, including an interview after her assault," Girard said.

"We need to interview her, but I need coffee first." Murphy made herself an instant coffee and realized she was hungry. She took a couple of quick sips and walked downstairs to the locker rooms, where a lone vending machine stood against the wall. The aged machine, which still had actual buttons to push instead of sensors to press, was not plugged in. Murphy looked at the offerings anyway, since it was simple enough to plug it back in. There were five chocolate bars and a bag of peanuts, with an expiry date from four months ago stamped on the cellophane.

Jacqueline's Pâtisserie it was. Murphy walked outside and across the street. The Pâtisserie sold a variety of items catering to the lunchtime crowd. It was open from ten until six every weekday, and then nine to nine on weekends. Murphy bought a cheese and mushroom pizza for the team.

Back at HQ, Murphy brought the pizza to the atelier, grabbed a slice, and left the rest for the other detectives.

"Boss, here is the file we were starting on Haidt, as a possible instigator of Miller, and for a connection to Baptiste," Girard said. He leaned in to grab his slice of pizza, followed then by Parker and Hamilton.

"Great, thank you. How is the Miller case going?"

"Oh, great boss. I have met with both Supt. Shevchenko and Chief Valencia. The Chief wants us to include IT's report on the computer porn. We have an appointment Monday morning with the Crown Prosecutor, Ryan Babcock, to take him through everything," Girard said.

"Excellent work."

Right, okay, Eugene Baptiste," Parker said as he downed the last of his pizza. He looked at everyone else who was still eating, then at the pizza. There were two slices left. "Hey, anyone mind if I take another slice?" he said as he reached.

"No, no, go ahead. You're still growing, you need the energy," Murphy joked.

"The Forensics Unit report there are fingerprints and DNA on the t-shirt that was found with Eugene," Parker said. He printed two photographs from the report. One was the t-shirt lying on Eugene's face at the scene, the other was the t-shirt lying on the analysis table at their lab. "They are running a DNA test. It will take a few weeks," he added.

"There are nine E. or Eugene Baptistes in Northshore," Girard said. "I have eliminated six based on either gender, photos from driver's licenses, or age. That leaves us three." Girard pulled up a driver's license photograph on his computer. The man in the picture had long shaggy hair and an unkempt long beard. "This Eugene Baptiste is a possibility. The eyes are right, but everything else is too hairy to compare."

"Okay, and the other two?"

"This is Eugene Baptiste," Girard said, calling up a photo of a bleached blond man with a brilliant smile. "Maybe in the eyes, and around the ears." Everyone looked at Eugene's photo on the board. "And this is Eugene Baptiste," Girard said as yet another image appeared for everyone to review.

"These guys all look the same, don't they? Except for the hair, they could be the same person," Murphy said.

"You said it, not me," Hamilton laughed.

"Ha. Everyone pick a person and call, see if there is anyone we can't reach," Murphy said as she walked back into her office. Within minutes, the team had narrowed it down to hairy Eugene Baptiste. He was the only person who did not answer the phone.

"Adam, with me, we will go to his home address. You two, find out more about this Eugene Baptiste. Let us know if you find anything." Murphy and Girard headed out.

"Are you angry at me for some reason?" Girard asked as they drove to Eugene Baptiste's home.

"What? No, of course not. Why?"

"Are you sure?"

"Adam, if I was pissed off, I would be in your face about it. What makes you think I am?"

"Well, you have been working a lot with Michael, doing things with him when normally you would take me."

"Like?"

"Like asking him to go to the postmortem," Girard said.

Murphy laughed. "Well, for fuck's sake, Adam. That is basic work, stuff a detective constable should do, not a staff sergeant. I gave you the opportunity to present the Miller case all the way up because you need the experience. You need to get out there and get your name known. I'm trying to help you."

"Why do I need my name known?" he asked.

"You will not get a promotion, or move up the ladder, if you do not stand out. It is the start of your move up," Murphy said. She was perplexed.

Girard remained silent. "Adam, what?" Murphy asked. "Adam? Adam, do not make me pull over. You do not want to make me pull over."

He laughed. "Okay mom."

"And…"

"I do not want to move up. When I see some of the crap you have to do, some of the crap you have to take, no thank you. I love my job just like it is. I still get days off. It is not too busy and if I ask for time, you give it. I get along well with Michael and Cleo. We have a great solve rate, it is fantastic. Why would I want that to change?"

"I get it. I really do. I thought you might want more money, maybe a desk job, after the riots and attack. It has unsettled lots of people."

"I know. But you are handling it well."

"Barely! But you know I am there for you, Adam. And you are there for me."

"You see? You think about me, you think about us. I will never find that kind of caring and help behind a desk," Girard said.

"What? Like if you staple your tie to the photocopier?" Murphy said. She was relieved when Girard laughed, breaking the growing emotion.

Girard stuck his tie out and rocked back and forth. "Help me! Help me!" he shouted in mock fear. "Hey, boss —"

"Nope. Do not say it."

"Caitlin, you know you are amazing. You are in my heart."

"If you call me Caitlin again while we are working, I will bust you for insubordination," she teased.

"There's the place," Girard said.

"That place that we just passed? Great, thanks for the heads up." With a quick safety check and seeing no one around, Murphy hit the brakes and began backing up.

"If you write me up for insubordination, I'll write you up for reversing on a highway," Girard said.

"Deal." Murphy turned into the driveway of the home and drove up the long drive to the small building. It was not much more than a shed with a crooked sign on a post announcing 'Baptiste'. As they got out, an elderly woman was eagerly standing at the door, ready to welcome her guests.

"Hello my dears, I extend a heartfelt welcome to the Baptiste home and love sanctuary." She had obviously rehearsed her welcome speech and used hand gestures and even a twirl to emphasize her words.

"My name is Evelyn Baptiste, but you can call me Evie. Come with me. Embrace the wisdom of the ages as we embark on this extraordinary love journey together. May your spirits be uplifted and your hearts be enriched by the sacred traditions that grace these hallowed lands."

"Oh, no ma'am. Sorry. Evie, we aren't here to..." Murphy paused. She did not know what Evie Thompson was offering.

"You aren't here for the couple's retreat?"

"No. Sorry, no. We are with Northshore Police."

"Oh dear. Who are you looking for?" she asked.

"Does Eugene Baptiste live here?" Murphy asked.

"Oh no. Eugene and his wife moved out a couple of months ago. Just down the way. I'm his grandmother. Is there something I can help you with?"

"Do you have his new address?"

"He and his wife are at 17 Hawthorne Drive. Is he in trouble? Is it those damned videos?"

"You know about the videos?" Girard asked.

"Where he beats people up and thinks he is some kind of Internet influencer? That is not my grandson, I can tell you," Evie said. "I kicked him out. It's that rotten wife of his, if you ask me."

"Do you have a recent photograph of him?"

"Why are you asking?" Evie was far more suspicious than Murphy was expecting.

"Can we go inside? Please?" Murphy asked.

Evie's hands started shaking as she brought the detectives into the little house. The cramped quarters were cluttered with old family photographs and heirlooms. She had nothing of financial value, but clearly every item had worth.

"Can I get you a tea?" Evie asked as she led the detectives into her kitchen. There was a small table in the corner, piled high with clean laundry. There was just enough space for one person to sit and eat.

"No tea, thank you," Murphy said.

Evie stood in front of the refrigerator and, with trembling hands, plucked a piece of paper off the fridge door. "This is the most recent one I have."

Murphy took the photo from Evie and showed Girard. His face tightened. He then used his phone to take a photo of the photo. "Evie, would you like to sit down?" Murphy guided her to her chair and then crouched in front of her. "Evie, I am very sorry."

"No."

"Eugene has been found at Lac Sainte-Marine. He has passed. He is dead. I am very sorry for your loss."

"Oh dear. No. Are you sure?"

"Yes Evie, I am very sorry," Murphy said.

Evie paused for a moment and then asked how her grandson died.

"He hit his head. We are trying to find out exactly what happened. We need to find out why he was there, what he was doing. Do you have any idea why he was at Lac Sainte-Marine? Was it a special place for him?"

Evie sank back into the chair, shaking her head, and Murphy stood up. "The lake means nothing. I mean, I've never heard of it, but there are a lot of lakes around here. His mother died young, and I raised him. I'm a widow myself. It wasn't easy. When his father showed up a few years ago, I knew it would end badly."

Evie explained that Eugene's father, Alexander, had used drugs after Paula drowned in Dundar Lake. She took Eugene in and everything was fine until Alexander returned, drunk and addicted. "He put ideas into the boy's head. A criminal, you know? Taking advantage of everyone and everything. You know the type."

Evie told the detectives that Eugene and Alexander had a falling out after Alexander made a pass at Karen. In his sorrow, Eugene turned to a local radio preacher—she could not remember his name—only for him to make a pass at Karen. "I'll tell you why. She is an evil woman. All me, me, me. Full of greed, that one. Willing to take advantage of a man. That woman is the most plain Jane woman you will ever meet, but she has large bosoms. Excuse my language, young man."

"Yes ma'am, not a problem," Girard said.

Murphy got contact information on Alexander Baptiste and Karen Baptiste, and asked if Evie had anyone she could call for support. She replied she would call her friend. While waiting for her friend's arrival, they got a list of names of Eugene's old schools and his workplace. After a few minutes, there was a knock on the door. Evie's friend had arrived.

Murphy and Girard headed out to the Brawler.

CHAPTER SEVENTEEN

"We have ourselves a bit more background on our victim," Hamilton said once everyone was at the atelier. New photographs were on the link board, and she stood in front of them as the team talked. "Eugene Baptiste, thirty-two years old. Recently moved to 17 Hawthorne Drive with his wife of three years, Karen." Hamilton pointed to the photograph of a smiling blonde woman.

"Evie was accurate with her description," Murphy said.

"No children. He worked at Kettering Trenchless Concrete Services for five years, and Timeless Landscaping before that. The landscaping company is out of business. We are not sure about his banking details yet, and not sure if he had a cell," Hamilton said. "Based on his videos, he likely had one." Murphy silently cursed for having forgotten to ask Evie.

"Online, he seems to have had a dozen different accounts that I have been able to locate. This is public facing research, so anyone can be anybody, but he seems to have accounts on the top ten social media sites. His Facebook account linked to most of the other sites. Some have not been used in a while. The Haidt website was the one most recently posted on. That was a comment on Jonathan Haidt's video from Tuesday the eighteenth. Two days before Eugene died," Parker said.

Parker held up five pages of one- and two-line comments, taped together. "This at the top is Eugene's last comment. 'Hebrews 13:4 John 2:4.' It set off a firestorm of reaction."

Murphy laughed. "Go on, I am sure you looked it up."

Hamilton cleared her throat. "Hebrews: Marriage should be honoured by all, and the marriage bed kept pure, for God will judge the adulterer and all the sexually immoral. John: Whoever says 'I know him' but does not keep his commandments is a liar, and the truth is not in him."

Murphy stood up and gestured at Parker's printout. "Those are fighting words. What reactions did he get?"

"Some reactions are Bible verses like 'Romans 1' and 'Hebrews 13:17'. But most are calling him a nonbeliever, saying he is the one who wants to sin. 'Talk to Jonathan face to face', 'repent and return'. That kind of thing," he replied.

Everyone stared at Murphy while she thought about Eugene's comment. "I think Eugene is calling Haidt an adulterer and saying he is a liar and sinner. What is the subject of the video?"

"Marriage and fidelity," Parker said with a laugh.

"Is Haidt now a suspect in the murder of Eugene?" Girard asked.

"Mmm," Murphy said. "Haidt could have taken that comment down but did not. I want to know why."

"If that many people are commenting, maybe he felt it would have stuck out if he removed it," Hamilton said.

"Cleo, make a list of the names of persons of interest. Jonathan Haidt, Karen Baptiste, Alexander Baptiste, Crystal Bradford. The alley man and the drug dealer. Have we identified those two people?" Murphy asked.

"No. We could not find any complainants matching them," Hamilton said.

"And have we heard from Karen Baptiste? Has she reported him missing?"

"No."

"Okay. Let's collect alibis. Adam and I will take Jonathan Haidt and Karen Baptiste. You two take Crystal Bradford and Alexander Baptiste. Just for a death notification and alibi," Murphy said.

"What about the two unknown people?" Parker said.

"Let me check with my guy, Sergei. Maybe he has heard something. I will call and let you know, either way," Murphy said.

Girard and Murphy drove south to Goose Gas. Sergei came up behind the Brawler, ready to pump gas. "Sergei, did you hear about a couple of people getting beat up in the last month or so? A guy in an alley, maybe older. Hit with a baseball bat?" Murphy asked as she swiped her card at the pump.

Sergei pumped the gas. "Maybe. People are always getting beat up." Murphy's question was too vague for him.

"What about a young blond man, maybe a drug dealer, in a park? Hit with a wine bottle."

"What about them? Why do you care?" Sergei asked.

"I want to find out who did it," she said.

"Bullshit," Sergei said as he yanked the nozzle out of the gas tank. "You don't care."

"Hey! Yes I do. I think I know who did it, but I need to hear from them as victims. I only want to speak to them as victims of assault."

Sergei looked hard at Murphy. "The old man died a couple of days ago. In hospital. I don't know his name. I don't know about the blond man. Too many blond men are dealing drugs."

"Okay, thanks anyway. You want the usual?" Sergei nodded, and Murphy asked Girard to buy him a sandwich, pop and bag of candy. While he was gone, Murphy asked Sergei how he was doing. He said he was alright, but Murphy could sense a change in him. He was not okay. After giving Sergei his fee, the detectives drove north to the Baptiste home.

On the way, Murphy called the office letting them know she struck out. She asked Parker and Hamilton to check with the morgues and hospitals in Kettering and Ravensburg. They needed to look for a man whose death might match their laneway video victim.

The pair approached Hawthorne Drive. They had only to travel a few minutes from the gas station. The house at 17 Hawthorne Drive was at the farthest edge of the property from the road, serviced by a long, narrow lane. It was well-hidden by the large Red Maple trees and bushes, although Murphy knew it would become more visible every autumn and winter when the leaves fell. The sides of the Brawler brushed up against the overgrowth as she drove to the building.

The house had no sense of home. Clearly, it had been rented out for years to tenants with no interest in caring for the old structure. Murphy decided the house had been used for activities best not seen by police and nosy neighbours. The only eyes to see anything here belonged to wildlife and birds.

Murphy parked and she and Girard stepped out of the 4x4 and into the yard. It was very brown. Sun would hate this, Murphy thought, though that seemed more from growing wild on its own, and less from a human hand. Sticks and stones lay scattered about the long grass, making for uneven walking. Murphy rapped sharply at the front door and stepped back, waiting. It was only seconds before Karen Baptiste opened the door, smiled and welcomed them in.

Karen was in her mid twenties and wore a short, tight tank dress with matching headband. Its neon yellow colour washed out her light skin tone, making her look sickly and grey. She wore neon yellow slip-on running shoes to match. Her thick blonde hair fell past her shoulders and down her back.

"Hello, are you—"

"Come in," Karen said, and then turned back into the house and walked away. Murphy and Girard stepped into the narrow hallway and were bidden to follow Karen to the living room. "I guess you are the police? Evie called me," Karen said.

"I am very sorry for your loss, Mrs. Baptiste," Murphy said as she stood by the couch. "Would you like to sit down?" The bay window looked to the east and would catch the morning sun filtering through the trees. The sun was resting momentarily on the back of an old wingback chair Karen sat in.

"I am Caitlin Murphy. This is Adam Girard, from the Northshore Municipal Police Department. I am sorry to tell you we believe your husband was found dead on Thursday."

"What do you mean you believe it's Eugene? You don't know for sure?"

"No, we have not yet made a formal identification. But we are quite certain," Murphy said. "If you can, we would like you to come to the Coroner's Office and make an identification."

"See him? Can't you just use DNA or something? I saw on TV that you can use DNA," Karen said. Her face was small and thin and unremarkable. Her mouth was neither large nor small, her teeth a dull off-white. Karen's eyes were green when the sunlight caught them just right, but looked brown most of the time. Her makeup was perfect, yet bland. As a discerning detective, Murphy could easily see she was pretending to be beautiful.

"Yes, of course. DNA will take some time, though. Months, possibly. As long as you have one of those financial emergency funds in your name, you will be fine," Murphy said.

"What do you mean?"

"Sometimes, and I do not want to be indelicate, but sometimes, women who have just lost their husbands end up struggling financially. The banks will lock up his accounts, the credit card company will freeze his cards. It leaves the widow without enough to pay the bills," Murphy said.

"If you identify the body, someone can often issue the death certificate much faster. That just gets everything going faster. The executor can begin winding down the estate. Read the will... Did Eugene have a will?"

"Yes. He was very forward thinking that way," Karen said.

"Excellent, things will be easier for you. Did he have life insurance too? That can be collected much faster than closing the estate. Depending on the company, of course," Murphy said.

"Yes, he did. It is with Blue & Jameson. Do you know if they are fast? I will need some money soon," Karen said.

"They have been very good in the past and pay out as soon as you provide the death certificate."

"And that happens faster if I identify him?"

"Yes, the sooner they officially identify him, the sooner you get the certificate, the sooner you get your money," Murphy said. "Now, I would like to ask you a few questions. There are just a few things that aren't clear to us." Murphy noted Karen had asked nothing about his manner of death. It was possible she got some information from Evie. Or she was the killer.

"Okay. Can I get you coffee or something?" Karen asked.

"No, thank you. Did you report Eugene missing?"

"Oh no. You have to wait twenty-four to forty-eight hours to report someone missing. Unless it's a child, then you can report sooner, you know," Karen said.

"I do not know where that myth came from," Murphy said. "Probably some TV show from the 80s. You do not have to wait. Can you tell me about Eugene?"

"Do you mind if I get myself a glass of water?" Girard asked. It was a classic ploy that almost everyone fell for. It would give him a chance to look surreptitiously at other rooms.

"Oh, sure, the kitchen is through there, glasses in the cupboard above the sink. Sorry, what was the question again?"

Girard got up and made his way to the kitchen. It was clean, bare. Almost unused. There were no dirty dishes in the sink, and no crumbs on the floor. So unlike his own home. He snuck into the hall and glimpsed into the main bedroom and bathroom. Nothing seemed amiss. They set another room up with computers and lights. This was where they filmed some of their videos. He headed back to the kitchen.

"Evie said you found Eugene yesterday at a lake. He slipped and fell," Karen said. "Hit his head on the rocks. Oh my God, he is actually dead!" Karen began to shake and cry. She flung her arms about, occasionally burying her face in her hands. "He's really gone."

Girard heard the crying, and, grabbing a box of tissues, returned to the living room. He put both the tissue and the water onto the side table near the chair. Karen grabbed a tissue and blew noisily. "I'm very sorry for your loss," he said.

"Thank you," Karen said as she coughed and caught her breath.

"Tell me about Eugene," Murphy said.

"Me and Eugene met about four years ago. He was a nice guy, you know. Very attentive, he really love bombed me, you know? I wanted to do whatever I could to keep him happy. Me and him both had a great online presence. And he helped me grow mine so I could make a living."

"Is that how you made a living? Online?"

"Yep. We made great money. Like, about $15,000 a year. I know it may not look like it, but we have a lot of money in the bank. We will be able to... I will buy a house soon, without a mortgage."

"I'm sorry to have to ask, but I have some tough questions for you. Where were you Thursday morning?"

Karen said she was asleep when Eugene left. He had not told her where he was going or what he was up to. She last saw him Wednesday night, when they had gone to sleep just after a movie. On Thursday she called him, but did not get an answer. He was often busy, she said, and did not always answer phone calls or texts quickly. She had woken up, gone for brunch with friends, and live-streamed for much of the evening.

"Do you know why he was at the lake?" Murphy asked.

"No, I do not know."

"What about those videos he did? Was he making a fight video?" Murphy asked.

"Oh those. So horrible. What a terrible thing to do. I don't know. I don't know if he was filming one. I wish he had never started," Karen said.

"We have seen a couple on the web. Do you film them for him?"

Karen drew a sharp breath and clutched her invisible pearls. "I would never do such a thing! That was all him. He thought it would make him famous."

"Do you know who filmed him? Or who the others in the videos were?" Murphy asked. She was careful not to call them victims: the video credits suggested they were actors, or at least willing participants.

"No."

"Do you know who he was going to meet on Thursday?"

"No."

"Did he ever discuss his videos with you?"

"No."

"Do you know why he posted them on the Jonathan Haidt website?"

"No," Karen responded after a noticeable pause. She cleared her throat and dabbed at her eyes with a tissue. "Is this going to take much longer? It's just so much."

"Sorry, just a couple more questions. Can you tell me how he and Mr. Haidt knew each other?"

Karen paused for a moment. She looked down, inspecting her long manicured nails. She explained that she and Eugene were having marital problems, and had sought Haidt out for couples' counselling. Karen confided Eugene had unnatural desires, although she did not specify what they were. The couple had gone to Haidt at the beginning of the year, but Eugene had dropped out. Karen continued to receive spiritual counselling. It was after the break with Haidt that Eugene started posting his fight videos.

"Okay, thank you. One last question. Do you know where Eugene's cell phone is?"

"No."

"Okay, thank you for your time. Do you have someone who can stay with you?" Murphy asked as she rose from the couch.

"I will reach out to the pastor," Karen said. "He can help me through this."

The detective extended sympathies and provided information on officially identifying Eugene. Murphy also asked Karen for both her and Eugene's cell numbers. The detectives left the Baptiste house and headed back to the office. Once there, Murphy provided an update to the team.

"Karen Baptiste has just risen to the top of the suspect list."

Murphy sat down on the couch in the atelier. "No confession, but lots of suspicion. Cleo, can you take notes? The first thing we talked about, which I raised, was his identity and death certificate. She was keen to get it quickly to her life insurance company and to handle the estate."

"You yourself said it was important because she might need money to pay the bills," Girard said.

"I said that. But I expected her to ask about her husband first. We spent ten minutes talking about the death certificate. Michael, call Blue & Jameson Insurance, find out how much the life insurance policy is on Eugene and when it was opened. Ask if Karen also has a policy. They might tell you," Murphy said.

"Yes, boss," Parker said, as he picked up the phone.

"Karen said Evie told her Eugene slipped and fell. I did not tell Evie that. So either she made it up and told Karen, or—"

"Or Karen knew," Hamilton said.

"Next point, though, and maybe part of the same problem. Karen said he hit his head on the rocks. I just said he hit his head. We need to check what Evie said to Karen. Adam? Please call and ask."

"How do I ask her without being obvious?" Girard asked. "Or do you want me to be obvious?"

Murphy shook her head and thought for a moment. "No. That is something we will have to keep in mind. Maybe we can talk to Evie later, if it matters. Adam, what did you think of her crying?"

"That was fake. My four-year-old fake cries better than her. She even faked blowing her nose. No tears, no snot, nothing in those tissues. They were bone dry. And that whining? I know that ewww-eh-wehhhh sound," Girard said, mimicking his son.

Murphy nodded. "Agreed. Significant to me, she denies she is the woman in the fight videos. Michael, pull up the fight video of Eugene and Crystal Bradford." Parker played the video. "Stop! There, where the videographer is kicking her while she is down. The shoes."

"Those are the same neon yellow running shoes she was wearing today," Girard said. He was incredulous.

"Right, but she denied involvement in the video. Who spoke with Crystal?"

"I did, boss. Let me double check her complaint," Hamilton said.

"Michael, insurance?"

"The manager will call back."

"Okay. When was the first fight video posted? Cleo, you keep taking notes. Michael? The date?"

"Mitch helped me out with that. She said February 22, of last year."

"Did the complainant describe the female attacker? Karen said Eugene made the fight videos after a falling out with Jonathan Haidt. Which is our next big issue. Karen told us she and Eugene received marriage counselling from Haidt and that Eugene stopped going and started making fight videos. Karen said they went to Haidt at the start of this year, and only afterwards did Eugene start to make fight videos. But his first fight video was posted an entire year earlier. She is lying about her relationship with Haidt."

"Which may be why Eugene's comment is about infidelity and lying," Girard added.

"Got it, boss. Crystal described a white woman, long blonde hair, in a bright yellow dress and yellow shoes," Hamilton said.

"She is looking good for this. You spoke with Crystal about where she was?"

"At home watching television. She was texting her friends from ten p.m. until quarter past two. I do not have screenshots, but I looked at it while I was there. It was very consistent: every five or ten minutes. We can get her cell phone location because it certainly was in use the whole time," Cleo said.

"Yes, please. What about Alexander Baptiste, Eugene's father?" Murphy asked.

"He has been incarcerated at the Central East Correctional Centre in Lindsay since June tenth on charges of cheque fraud," Parker said. "I let them know about his son. They said they would tell him."

"Okay, Alexander is off the list. Crystal is probably off the list. What happened to our possibly dead laneway guy, John Doe?"

"One man in the Ravensburg morgue, four in Kettering, matching the general description. It is too vague. A possibly unkempt man, likely between the ages of twenty and seventy, who died because of blunt force trauma, possibly in an alley, somewhere," Hamilton said.

"Same problem with the blond drug dealer with a head wound. That is just too vague."

"The Narcotics and Organized Crime squad could not identify him? No? Okay, make a note to keep on them," Murphy said.

Standing up and approaching the link board, Murphy tapped at Haidt's face. "He is the last one left to check." She looked at the clock and sighed. "He will be on air right now. Okay, it's time to go home, everyone. We have made significant progress today. Fantastic. Go home, relax, and enjoy your lives."

CHAPTER EIGHTEEN

Instead of leaving, Murphy sat at her desk, coffee in hand, flipping through the information gathered so far on Eugene Baptiste. Still outstanding were his finances, cell phone, and two unknown victims. He could have been killed during a scuffle with his latest fight video victim. And Karen was hiding something. She just did not know what.

Murphy called Del and told her she would be home late. "That's nothing new," Del said. "But Maria had made an extra serving of quiche for you. It's in the fridge for you."

"Thanks, tell her thanks. How are you doing? Did you see Bob today?"

"Yes, Maria and I flew down. We were there for a couple of hours. They think he has a couple of more weeks in the hospital until they send him to the Toronto Rehabilitation Hospital. He'll be there until at least mid October. We have until then to find a place for him," Del said.

"Is he for sure coming back to Northshore?"

"Yes, he wants to come back. He has no other family. We're all here."

"We have a bit of time to figure it out."

"You are joking, right? Time will fly by."

"Yep, you're right. We will figure it out," Murphy said.

"Promise?"

"Pinky promise. Okay, I have to go. Thank Maria for me." Murphy hung up. She did not know what to do about Bob. Thomas and Jens were about as useful as a screen door on a submarine. She was not sure that Del really appreciated how lucky she was to have a large insurance settlement and her deceased partner's life insurance policy payout. Topped off with Murphy's benefits and the income from the art gallery, Del was financially secure. She did not know about Bob's finances.

Before she headed out, she called Sun. "Hey hi, how are you?"

"Good. Fantastic. What are you doing?" Sun asked.

"Thinking about you. What are you doing?"

"Thinking about you naked."

"Ah, and what can I do to make that thought come to fruition?" Murphy said with a grin.

"You can book a room at the Serene Inn. I'd really like to... What? There's some in the freezer!"

Murphy laughed. "This is why we use a motel. Okay, I'll book it and text you the room number."

"That sounds great. See you soon," Sun said. Murphy booked a room through an app and texted Sun the room number. She said she would be there in about thirty minutes.

Murphy arrived at the Serene Inn first and signed into the room with her app. She had a quick shower and tried not to look at her work phone. There was a knock on the door, and Murphy quickly threw a robe on, looked through the security door viewer, and saw Sun's smiling face.

She unlocked the door and Sun walked in. Sun smiled and nuzzled Murphy back into the room. Keeping her eyes on Murphy, Sun reached behind her and locked the door. Without a word, she walked up to Murphy, put her hands on the robe's belt and slowly pulled the knot apart. She looked up and drew in Murphy's lips by desire alone.

Murphy's fingers tingled, and she reached out to hold her lover, to squeeze and pull and press. She grabbed hold of Sun's shoulders and pulled her even closer, kissing her hard. She opened her eyes to see Sun's passionate face. Her robe slid down her body and fell to the floor.

Unsheathed, Murphy could feel the cool air and Sun's fiery touch all over her body. She felt an unfamiliar flame ignite in her heart. She pulled Sun suddenly onto the bed and both women worked frantically to remove Sun's clothes.

Murphy slipped her tongue into Sun's mouth and her fingers into Sun's warmth. She moved her fingers in and out, gently and slowly at first, then harder and deeper. Murphy could feel the blood rushing to her hands, taking over from her mind, moving with instinct and passion. She felt Sun arch and slipped her left hand under the small of her back, pulling her body harder toward her hand. Sun moaned softly, growing louder and more jagged. Murphy moved her mouth near Sun's, breathing in her orgasm, allowing her pleasure to pass into her. Murphy felt a wet pull on her fingers, pulling her deeper, swallowing her up. Sun arched up again, slowly, deliberately, and held the position for a moment before bucking and groaning.

Sun's back collapsed against the bed, her mouth dry and her lungs burning. She gasped for air. Murphy hovered over her face, watching as her eyes were resurrected from their shrouded ecstasy. Murphy leisurely slipped a finger into her mouth, devouring every bit of Sun that remained, and then the next, and the next. She leaned down and gave her lover a lustful kiss. She pulled at Sun's lips with her teeth, strong at first and then tenderly.

Murphy was lying on her back, and Sun was tucked under her right arm, curled up against her. "Hey," Murphy said. "Can we talk?" Murphy slid her hand down Sun's back.

'Can we talk' should never come right after sex. Sun paused and turned around to stare fully at Murphy. She felt panicky, as if at any moment everything she had would come crashing down around her.

"That sounded scarier than I expected," Murphy said when she saw the fear in Sun's eyes. "I did not mean to scare you. This is just really hard to talk about. I am not sure I can do this." Murphy's voice cracked slightly, and she hoped Sun had not noticed. This was very scary territory for her. But this would not be the first time she was an asshole to someone she cared deeply for.

"What is it?" Sun asked. She turned her gaze to the black television screen. She wished it was on. Sun wished there was something else to see, to hear. Her heart pounded. She wanted to block out what she felt was coming. She wished hearing 'let's talk' was unfamiliar, was not part of pain from the past. Her throat was dry, and she couldn't swallow.

"When we first met, one thing you told me was that you had a terrible time dating men because--"

"Is this about me being bisexual? I haven't--"

"No, let me finish. You had a hard time with men because they expected some kind of sexual... magic, I guess. They expected you to be erotically gifted. I remember that phrase. Erotically gifted." Murphy spoke with a hesitancy that she knew was making it worse.

"Caitlin, I am not sleeping with men right now. I am not sleeping with other women. Just you. You are the only one," Sun said. "It's Mitch, isn't it? You're sleeping with her and you want to drop me."

"What? No! Stop. Let me talk, okay? Let me talk. Look, I'm trying to say, you... I... I find you very sexy, sexual. You bring something out in me that I never even knew was there. And every time I see you, or even think of you, I think about touching you and kissing you and fucking you and getting fucked by you. And I kind of feel like shit because I do not want you to think I am some racist asshole who thinks of you only as a fuck. You mean a lot t--"

Sun pushed Murphy's arm away. "You scared the shit out of me for that? I cannot believe it. What's wrong with thinking I'm the best lay you've had? I mean, is that what you are saying? Am I the best you've had?"

"No. I mean yes, yes you are. But I just mean, I do not want you thinking that I am trying to enforce a racist sexual standard on you."

"Please just stop," Sun said, laughing.

"What? Why are you laughing? What's funny?" Murphy asked with a smile.

"Caitlin Murphy. Caitlin. Okay. I am going to tell you the truth. Are you open to hearing it?" Murphy nodded. "You are a middle class, almost middle-aged white woman living in a white country. You are a Christian living in a Christian country. You are a cop in a country that over-polices and oppresses people of colour through the legal system. You represent so many racist systems. You perpetuate structural racism. You. Personally." Sun paused and squeezed Murphy's hand.

"Can I keep going? Okay," Sun said. "I set boundaries with you at the beginning. I am more than sex. I will not have a conversation with you or any white woman, white person, about race if the only thing you want to hear is what a great ally you are or how you are not racist."

"I am not trying to do that here," Murphy said.

"Stop. I know. You are trying to say this little Brown woman is a hot fuck, but you aren't sure how to do that, because I set boundaries. And that is challenging you and making you feel uncomfortable. So let's make a pact. Say whatever you want to me, and if I think it's racist crap, I will call you on it. And you may not, cannot, tell me I am wrong. If it hurts your feelings, tough," Sun said. Her zeal caught Murphy off guard.

Murphy was a bit confused, but nodded in agreement. Sun was not wrong about any of it. And just like she said, Murphy's feelings were hurt.

She felt defensive, but kept her mouth shut about it. "So, it's okay for me to say you are a hot fuck? Because you are a hot fuck."

"It is absolutely okay for you to say I am a hot fuck because it's true," Sun said as she kissed Murphy hard.

Murphy sat up and rolled Sun over and gave her a one-handed massaged on her shoulders. "I'm sorry about that." She kissed Sun between the shoulder blades.

"Mmm, nice," she said as she closed her eyes.

"Covers?"

"Yes, please," Sun said with a smile. She was falling asleep, and Murphy pulled the covers over Sun, turned off the lights and crawled into bed for a couple of hours' sleep.

In the morning, Murphy nudged Sun, kissed her and smiled. "I have to get going," she said.

"So early? On a Saturday?"

"Yes. I have one thing to do, but then I will be free," Murphy said.

"Alright. I'll be at my shop today. Mitch and I are fixing it up."

"Mitch?"

Sun laughed. "Mitch. Michelle, your IT friend?"

Murphy laughed. "I know who she is. She's helping you with the shop?"

"Yes, she said she has some building experience, so she's going to help with the repairs. You're welcome to come by yourself and lend a hand," Sun said.

"I will see what happens with this thing I have." Murphy had to contact Jonathan Haidt and set up an interview—she knew he would rebuff anything casual. And she wanted to talk to the Baptiste's neighbours at both their current and former locations.

She felt weird—jealous?—about Mitch helping Sun. She kissed Sun and walked out to her Brawler. As she headed to Little Cane Road, Murphy wondered what the hell happened last night. The sex was fantastic, but the conversation was tough. She hoped it would get easier over time. She put it on the list of things to think about and cleared it from her mind.

Murphy potentially had the entire weekend open. She hoped for a weekend of sex and food with Sun, but realized she might have as many arguments as orgasms. The relationship was draining her, and she was touching a nerve. The first few dates had been fantastic, but something had changed. She wondered if it was familiarity: Sun had become comfortable and somehow open to fighting. The energy she was putting out to keep Sun placated was exhausting.

Murphy had to set boundaries and keep them. Sun was trying to creep into her work time, impede her work life, like a weed infesting a garden. Murphy was not having it. She liked her boundaries. They were an important part of keeping her life organized and in control. She had seen far too many cops not keep their boundaries. Each fell into an abyss of drugs, alcohol, corruption, or depression. For Murphy, her boundaries kept her alive.

She remembered the first time she felt truly pressed up against her own boundaries. She was a rookie, with less than two months on the job. Her first partner retired after having a heart attack. She was then partnered with a man who attempted to catch every drug dealer or user he saw. He would pull the cruiser over to the dealer, take the drugs, and let them go. She lasted only a week with him before suddenly developing a back problem. After two weeks off, she returned to a new partner. It was the only way she could think of to get a new partner without confronting a drug-stealing cop. She was not stupid, and would not end her career to bust him. Not as a rookie.

Now, with more experience under her belt and a much higher rank, she could create the honest, hard-working team she wanted to work with and keep them. She wanted nothing around her that did not belong, and she worked hard to keep the undesirable things out. Sun seemed to blur the boundaries, a concerted effort maybe, and Murphy did not like it. Then she wondered, *am I the asshole here?* She did not have an answer.

Murphy spent an hour talking with people on Little Cane Road. One neighbour said a lot of cars would drive in and out of the property, but she could not be specific about when or who. Another neighbour said the internet was saying Karen did it. "It's always the spouse," the woman confided. When pressed, she had nothing but a rumour to offer.

Murphy walked to her Brawler after wrapping up the last interview. She spotted a local television news reporter standing at the 4x4. "Detective Inspector Murphy, my name is Jenny DeFrey, CFFG TV. Are you investigating the death of Eugene Baptiste?"

"Northshore Municipal Police Department received an anonymous phone call regarding a possibly deceased person. Mr. Eugene Baptiste was found deceased at Lac Sainte-Marine on Thursday, July 20th," Murphy said. "It is unclear how Mr. Baptiste came to be there, and we are looking for answers."

"That is almost exactly what the NSPD press release said. Eugene was an online provocateur. He filmed himself assaulting people. Why didn't the NSPD ever charge him?"

"I cannot comment on past actions by the Northshore Police. I can tell you it is unlikely he will be charged with them now," Murphy said as she opened the door of the Brawler and pressed the button to start the engine.

"Do you think one of his victims killed him?" DeFrey asked.

"Mr. Baptiste's death has been classified as suspicious, not as a homicide."

"There is a lot of chatter on the internet suggesting it is retribution for his assaults," DeFrey pressed.

"Chatter on the internet. If you find credible information, Ms. DeFrey, the Northshore Municipal Police Department would be glad to hear about it. Do you have credible evidentiary information for me? No? Then thank you for your interest in the matter, but I have to move on now," Murphy said. She got into her 4x4, closed the door and drove away.

She dialled Chief Valencia and explained that the reporter had spoken to her at the Baptiste home, and there might be a snippet on the evening news. Murphy also advised him she would call Haidt to have him come in to help with the investigation.

"You know he will bring a dozen lawyers," Valencia said.

"Not a problem, sir. He is not a suspect. Just a potentially helpful citizen," Murphy said.

"Do not let your personal feelings get in the way Murphy."

"I never do, sir," she replied. With the Chief apprised, Murphy called Jonathan Haidt's office and spoke with a receptionist. Murphy explained the matter and said she would like to speak with Haidt at headquarters. "If he knows the man," Murphy added. "Just email, letting me know if he can make an interview at headquarters to assist in a police investigation. Or if he cannot help, again, a quick email please."

By getting the information in writing, she would have something concrete to fall back on if everything went wrong. Murphy drove toward Evie's house and began stopping in at neighbouring homes. Eugene had not lived with his grandmother for some time, and no one recalled any useful information. She stopped working for the day and met up with Sun at a town park after convincing her to leave the store in Mitch's hands. The park was meant for families with kids and neighbours who wanted to stroll past flower beds and manicured bushes. Last year, Murphy worked on the homicide of Cindy Gilray, who was found strangled to death in one of those manicured bushes.

As they meandered along the path, Sun pointed out flowers and grasses the town had planted. "See the plant with white striped foliage and that double orange red bloom? Beautiful. It's Hemerocallis 'Variegated Kwanso', a daylily. The scent is subtle, but worth the effort."

"What's that one? The tall one with the leaves there," Murphy asked.

"Acanthus mollis. Bearsfoot. Its leaves are so beautiful. They were the model for the Corinthian leaf motif you see in ancient Greek and Roman architecture," Sun said. "It's a rhizome. They make great cut-flower bouquets." Murphy nodded, not understanding what a rhizome was. It did not matter. She just loved to hear Sun talk about something she loved so much.

Sun then talked about the repair of the flower shop and boldly suggested having a place together in the basement. "It's a little small, and there are only two small windows, but when Mitch and I were down there, she thought we could fix it up. Some deep cleaning and some paint would take care of most of it. Imagine having a place of our own, not a hotel room. It would smell so amazing. What do you think?"

Clearly, Sun had put some thought into it. And clearly, she had talked about it with Murphy's co-worker. Once she began describing what type of furniture she wanted, and the colour of the sheet set she had her eyes on, Murphy stopped her. "Sun, no. We both have our own homes. You have your son and daughter-in-law and a grandchild. I have my wife. My. Wife. Look, I have a commitment, and even though Del and I are not sexual, it is a commitment."

Sun did not like that answer. She had put a lot of thought into the basement love nest, envisioning herself tending her flowers until Murphy arrived for love and sex. She pouted and fussed for the rest of the walk. At dinner time, she picked at her food. Murphy knew not to suggest she had the emotional intelligence of a fifteen-year-old: she had said that once and it had not gone well. But she did not care for this petulance.

"Did you just take the last samosa?" Sun asked. They had ordered a sharing plate of mini samosas at the restaurant, and the restaurant provided five. Not six, not four, not a number divided by two. But five samosas, and Murphy had just taken her third.

"Oh, yeah, do you want it?" Murphy held it out, dripping tamarind sauce on the tablecloth.

"No," Sun said. With that, Murphy popped it into her mouth, eating it in one bite. "Does it not occur to you to share?"

Murphy stopped chewing for a moment and looked down at her plate. There were three peas sitting in a smear of masala, and a few bits of curried potatoes. She began chewing again, then swallowed the samosa. "I asked if you wanted the samosa. You said no. We can order more," she offered. She looked at Sun's face. "This is not about the samosa. What is it about?"

"You didn't ask me," Sun said. Murphy clearly did not understand. "You did not think about me. You did not think 'hey, that looks delicious. I wonder if Sun wants it.' You thought, 'hey, that looks delicious, I'm eating it.' I never even crossed your mind and I am literally right here in front of you."

Internally, Murphy groaned. "Okay, I got it. I should be considerate, to consider you. Right?"

"Well, if you know the answer, why did I even have to bring it up?"

"It's just food."

"No. Just food is eating a sandwich while you are working on the computer. This is a meal shared between two people. When we sat down, we committed to more than wolfing down some food. We committed to conversation and consideration, to thinking about each other and being with each other," Sun said.

Murphy was taken aback. She thought for a moment. Was this a race thing? A cultural thing? An Internet advice blog thing? "I understand, I'm sorry." It was a half-truth.

Murphy was glad they were almost at the end of their meal. The petty argument left an unpleasant taste in her mouth. She had no problem apologizing, even when she did not understand what she was apologizing for. But that Sun turned the food down and then continued to complain, meant she just wanted a fight. Sun seemed to enjoy them, she thought. Murphy knew she needed relationship help.

"Oh, hang on," Murphy said, reaching for her phone. "Murphy. Yes, yes. When? Okay," she said. There had been no call, but she needed a way out of the evening. Since she often had her phone on vibrate instead of a ring, the absence of noise was not suspicious. She hoped. "I'm really sorry."

"Don't tell me, it's work. I understand, babe. You go. I'll be fine."

"Sorry I have to go." Murphy bent down and kissed Sun before heading out.

Murphy was grateful to get into the Brawler and head home. When she walked in, she was greeted by Del, Maria, Thomas and Jens sitting in Del's room, chatting.

"Hey wifey," Del said.

"Hey lifey," Murphy responded.

"I know that face. What is up?" Del said. "Sit down, talk to momma."

"You are not my momma," Murphy said with a smile.

"I'm your momma!" Jens said. "Sit down. What's the gossip?"

Murphy collapsed on the couch and stretched her legs out. "Okay, advice please. Sun starts pointless arguments all the time."

"About what? What are the arguments about?"

"Stupid shit. This last one was because I ate the last samosa. I did not even eat it before she started complaining that I took it," Murphy said. "I do not know what the problem is. She said it was because I took it without thinking about her, but what the hell does that mean?"

"She was mad because you did not eat the samosa?" Del asked.

"We had five samosas, for starters. She had two, I had two, and then I took the last one because it was getting cold. And she's like, 'hey, why didn't you ask me if you could have it?'"

"Ask her if you're allowed to eat? That's controlling," Thomas said.

"I meant, she wanted me to offer it to her instead of just taking it for myself. To think about her before I thought about myself. I said she could have it, but she just kept going on and on about how I am supposed to think about her when we are together."

"She's insecure. She wants to know you are paying attention to her," Del said.

"No, she's a narcissist. She is saying 'pay attention to me all the time'. She is attention seeking," Thomas said.

"I think she just wants to be part of your life, you know, sharing. Sharing food is a very intimate act. If you aren't sharing, you are leaving her out of your life," Maria said.

"You said you did not know why she's arguing? When you don't know something, ask," Jens said.

Murphy burst out laughing. "I asked, but the answer was not exactly clear. But just so I am clear: Sun is controlling, insecure, narcissistic, feeling left out and wants me to think about her all the time. Is that right?"

"You are not exactly the easiest person to deal with. Maybe she is just trying to figure you out," Del said.

"I am so easy. Do everything my way, when I want and how I want. And I should not have to tell you. Just read my mind. Easy," Murphy joked, eliciting laughter from everyone.

"Is the sex good? If the sex is good, I can put up with so much bullshit from someone," Jens said.

"True. Never underestimate the value of a good orgasm. It's harder than you think," Thomas said with a wink.

"Yeah, how much do you like this woman? Is she worth the effort?" Jens asked.

"No, no, relationships are not about being worth the effort. It's about affection and love," Maria said. "Every relationship is work."

"Do you love her?" Del asked.

"No," Murphy said very matter-of-factly.

"Are you sure? Have you ever been in love?" Thomas asked.

"And that is my cue. Good night everyone," Murphy said. She got up from the couch to the protest of her friends.

"Get back here, you coward," Del said.

"Can't hear you, my head is in the fridge," Murphy shouted as she grabbed the quiche that had been left for her.

"Caitlin, get back here," Thomas said.

"Microwaving my meal, can't hear you."

"Caitlin!"

"Going upstairs, can't hear you. Have a good night," she said as she brought her food up to her room. She was not hungry and set the food aside. She quickly scanned her dozen books: nothing on relationships. Murphy locked up her gun and badge and changed into shorts and a t-shirt.

Murphy knelt at the edge of her bed and clasped her hands in prayer. "In your hands, O Lord, are humbly entrusted our brothers and sisters. Welcome them into Your paradise, free of pain and worry. Grant these souls eternal rest: Harry Hamshaw, John Pearce, Mary Rathbone, Tiffany O'Brien, Tyrone Peake. Amen."

CHAPTER NINETEEN

On Sunday morning, Murphy woke up early and slipped out of the house. She walked through the backyard to her art studio and unlocked the door. The smell of paint was thick in the air and slowly oozed out the open door.

Murphy pulled on paint-covered coveralls, pulled the hood tight around her face and slipped on her mask. Her cast felt awkward and the arm of the coverall was tight. She quickly opened her paint buckets, then put her sports equipment cum art tools into the buckets, and prepared her canvases.

Without thinking further, Murphy grabbed a hockey stick and slammed it against the wrestling dummy she had strung up in the middle of the floor. With a satisfying thwack, blue paint flew and splattered on the canvases. She tossed the stick back into the blue paint bucket.

With both hands, she grabbed the baseball bat in the white paint bucket. Her eyes widened, and she stepped forward quickly, raising the bat above her head. She slammed the wrestling dummy in the head twice. Her actions were as fast as a bullet. Bam! Bam! It was a swing so powerful it would have killed a human.

Murphy replaced the bat in the white paint and grabbed the lacrosse stick in yellow. She skipped swiftly to the side and swung, causing the lacrosse stick to launch its paint onto the canvas on the side wall before she hit the dummy. She rocked quickly in the opposite direction and sliced the air with ribbons of yellow paint that shot across the breadth of the canvas hanging on that wall. Murphy sprung forward as if her target could move and body checked the dummy before punching the figure with her cast. A sharp pain shot through her wrist and she grunted. She staggered back and swung at the dummy wildly. She missed, and a spray of yellow hit the canvas on the ceiling.

Tossing the lacrosse stick to the floor, Murphy grabbed the tennis racket that was standing in the green paint. She swung it in a violent arc, sending a stream of green paint spraying onto the canvas above. It then connected with a sharp snap on the dummy's arm. Murphy kicked the figure and flung the racquet at the canvas to her right. It slipped noisily to the floor.

Murphy's senses were sharp as she scanned the studio, the creative fire burning through her. She turned and snatched the baseball bat in one hand and the hockey stick in the other. Although her left hand was unable, she spun her right wrist around and around, spraying blue paint everywhere. She felt powerful as she took deep breaths to prepare herself for her last battle. Sweat poured down her neck and cascaded down her breasts. She lifted her arms and attacked the figure with all the energy she had left. Slam! She turned and swung. Pow! Colour erupted around the room. Bam! The dummy shuddered under the assault.

She continued beating the figure until she had no breath left in her lungs. Gasping, she collapsed to her knees and ripped her mask away. She dropped on all fours, head hanging, as she desperately sucked the dense atmosphere in. Her heart pounded and her stomach tightened. She felt like she was going to puke. Murphy crawled to the door, and its promise of fresh summer air. Drawing in deep breaths, it smelled of pine, green grass, and dry earth. She crept out the door and onto the ground, turning, collapsing, crashing to the earth.

Murphy lay almost motionless, save for her chest rising and falling as she breathed. She did not move until her heart settled and she could feel her arms again. She waited a few more minutes, then sat up, satisfied and exhausted. After a few more minutes, she stood. Making her way back in, Murphy began the cleanup. She threw the paint covered tools into a heap at the side of the room and put the lids back on the buckets of paint. Everything else would simply dry on its own.

Quietly, Murphy pulled off the sweat soaked coveralls. They were filthy, and she rolled them up and shoved them into the waste bin outside the cabin studio, along with the booties she had worn. Murphy walked back inside the house, locked the door, and climbed the stairs.

She had been painting for hours. The sun was high. The birds and bugs cried out their songs. She was now ready to go back to sleep. Murphy spent most of Sunday trying desperately to relax, but failed. She walked through Del's art gallery to see her newest works. Murphy then tried sitting out back in the sun, but her pale Irish skin complained pretty quickly. Finally, she gave in. Every fibre of her being was telling her to work, and she did.

She searched through the files and records, compiling a list of every name they had associated with Eugene. She collated names, phone numbers and addresses, and began dialling.

The speech was almost identical for everyone. "This is Detective Inspector Murphy with the Northshore Municipal Police Department. Am I speaking to Paul Waters? I understand you are a friend of Eugene Baptiste. I'm sorry to tell you this, but he has passed away. We are uncertain what happened. I am trying to get some background information on him. Just so I can understand him better. When was the last time you saw or spoke to Eugene?"

Murphy would write everything they said. Paul thought Eugene was a narcissist who only thought about himself. "Eugene was always looking at himself on the damn phone, recording himself. He would check his teeth after eating using the phone. He was a jerk, but my girlfriend knew his girlfriend, so there you go."

Paul's girlfriend, Amanda Collier, said, "Eugene was charming. He had a way with words and could easily win people over. He seemed like the kind of person who could do no wrong. Until he started those weird videos. That's when I just kind of dropped Karen and him as friends."

David Johnson told Murphy, "Eugene was a creep. He was really manipulative and deceitful. He used his charm to lure and prey on innocent people. He roofied my sister and took advantage. He filmed it and said he was going to post it if he did not get more sex. I beat the shit out of him. He was an asshole. That was a few years ago but I am glad he's dead."

When Murphy spoke with Sarah Anderson, an ex-girlfriend, she said, "Eugene was very private. Reserved. He was always calm, way too calm sometimes. Like at the baseball game when your team just hit a home run? He would just sit there. He never seemed angry or aggressive. Just always composed and in control."

Michael Ramirez said he worked with Eugene at Kettering Trenchless Concrete Services. "I never trusted Eugene. There was something unsettling about him. He just had a way of manipulating people and always seemed to have an ulterior motive. He gave off an eerie vibe that made me uncomfortable whenever I was around him. The bastard borrowed $500 and said he would pay it back, but he never did. I would not be surprised if loan sharks were after him."

Interviews with Karen Baptiste's friends were no more enlightening. Olivia Carter said, "Karen is incredibly warm and genuine. She has a natural ability to connect with people and make them feel valued. She always takes the time to engage with her online fans and has a kind and compassionate nature. I love her Shout Du Jour channel."

Sophia Reynolds said, "Karen is a creative force. She has an eye for aesthetics and a unique sense of style. Her content is always beautifully curated, and she has a knack for creating visually stunning and inspiring content."

Murphy gave up. She was getting nowhere. No one's stories seemed to match. People lie to the police for a variety of reasons. It might be to maintain privacy or avoid social embarrassment. It might be too much pressure for the person and they panic. With a social media personality, they might protect reputations.

The Brawler made its way along the highway. Murphy stopped at a general store to pick up some flowers, but none were to be had. She had to settle for pulling into a rest stop along the route to Lac Sainte-Marine and pulling flowers out of the ground. She did not know what they were: blue bead-type berries on a long stem, small orange flowers and some round yellow flowers. If Sun were here, Murphy thought, she would explain all of this. Murphy gathered up her wildflower bouquet and continued her journey to the lake.

A few people were walking along the rocks. One was fishing at the water's edge, casting a rod. She wandered along the shore, looking down into every crevice and cranny for a cell phone. Eugene did not have one on him and his wife said she had no idea where it was. The rocks near his death site had mercifully been cleaned both by Dr. Chen's team and by nature. Murphy laid the flowers down and said a small prayer. It included catching his killer.

Murphy stood at the water's edge. It looked so peaceful now. Gone was the buzz of police and the Forensics Unit and flies. Now she heard the soft lapping of lake water on the stones and the far-off hum of highway traffic. Water tickled the crevices between the rocks, choosing to take an unhurried journey.

A ringing phone snapped her out of her peaceful revery. It was hers. "Detective Inspector Murphy," she answered.

"Detective. It's Ellen Longboat."

Murphy pulled the phone away from her face and mouthed 'fuck!', then asked politely, "Ellen, how can I help you?"

"It's my nephew." It seemed to Murphy that Ellen always spoke with a cool, belligerent anger. She probably said 'I love you' as an accusation. She was not always the quietest whisperer so Murphy pulled the phone away from her face and mouthed 'fuck!' again.

"I need to talk to you about my nephew, Charlie," Ellen said.

Who did she think she was? Murphy thought. Calling up the head of Homicide to talk about what? Getting him out of a speeding ticket? "You mentioned that. What's up?" she asked. Murphy did not know why she felt compelled to know. She was drawn to Ellen like a magnet. If it was sexual, Murphy could have understood. But it was not. It was something else that Murphy could not decode.

"He was at Lac Sainte-Marine when that man died."

Murphy's heart jumped, and she looked around. "Where are you?" she asked. She wondered if Ellen was at the lake, watching her.

"At home. Can we meet?"

"Yes. Where is... Charlie, did you say?"

"I need to talk to you first," Ellen said.

Murphy rolled her eyes. Ellen always tried to control the narrative. "Fine. Headquarters in an hour."

"No. I can't be seen walking into the police station. Let's do Verdi Gardens in Ravensburg."

"In public—In an hour," Murphy said. She wanted to say 'In public, how bold' but caught herself.

"One hour," Ellen said and hung up.

Murphy walked to the Brawler and asked WeeSee to find Verdi Gardens. "Berry Gardens, Kelowna," the app responded. Kelowna? That was across the country. Murphy cussed and tried again. "Fear Deep Gardens, Eufala," WeeSee offered.

"Oh, for Christ's sake, Weezy, I've never even heard of Eufala. Weezy, locate Verdi Gardens, Ravensburg, Ontario!" she shouted.

The app paused for a moment before purring, "Verdi Gardens, Ravensburg Ontario." A blue line snaked along the map's roads, showing Murphy what the drive would look like. She tapped the button and WeeSee said, "Proceed forty meters on Unnamed Road, then turn right."

Ellen was waiting in Verdi Gardens when Murphy arrived. "Detective, thanks for coming."

Murphy was floored. Did Ellen just thank her? "No problem. Tell me about Charlie."

"He is my nephew," Ellen said. She turned and ambled away. It was Murphy's cue to follow, which she dutifully did. "He is a troubled kid. Not a great home, a few run-ins with the law. He came over for a visit."

Murphy's attention was fading, and she looked at the flowers. Walking with Sun through flowers was infinitely better than with Ellen.

"We were watching the news and when the clip about the body at Lac Sainte-Marine came up, he started crying. He told me the guy was Ben someone, and he had met him there. He said Ben attacked him and he ran away, but he thought he would be blamed for Ben's death," Ellen said.

"Is he prone to fantasy? Or lying for attention?" Murphy asked.

"What? No. Do you think he is lying?"

"Did you listen to the newscast? They gave the guy's name. It's Eugene Baptiste. Not Ben. So is Charlie lying, or confused?"

Ellen thought for a while before responding. "He is not the most reliable person, but he is not an attention seeker. I am concerned that if he is wrapped up in this somehow, you will find out. And then you will come looking for him, and he will run, and you will shoot him," Ellen said.

Murphy halted suddenly. "You think I would shoot him?"

"Not you personally. But if there is a warrant out for him. I am not sure how that would end. I am just trying to take care of my own. Keep him alive. You can't fault me for that," she said.

"You know, Ellen, it might surprise you to know that I am a decent human being. I don't go around shooting witnesses," Murphy said.

"You know it is not personal. It's complex. It's cops and Indigenous men. They are not a good mix. In fact, can you meet him at his home? Five Deer Road, just outside Kettering. Not the police station."

Murphy relented. It was complex, but it was personal, too. "Okay. Tomorrow at ten a.m. I will meet him at 5 Deer Road. Tell him. We can talk. Okay?"

"Yes," Ellen said. She looked at Murphy for a moment, then walked away.

What a bitch, Murphy thought. Not even a thank you. Murphy headed home and brooded all night long.

The next morning in the atelier, Hamilton had updates. "His legal name is Charlie Belanger, not Charles. Twenty-three years old. Last known address is 5 Deer Road, which is his mother's address. Maureen Belanger. He has some Section 334(b) charges, a few other minor things," Hamilton said.

"Anything serious?"

"Nothing serious. Five shoplifting charges from Goose Gas, three from Doolah's Dollar Store. Two dine and dash, six public drunkenness and one urinating in public," Hamilton said. "He has spent a total of four and a half years in jail."

"Geez, he is only twenty-three. Cleo, please check any known associates to see if he is connected to Eugene or Karen Baptiste, or Jonathan Haidt."

"Speaking of Eugene, the Forensic Unit said there is DNA on the t-shirt. They think there are multiple contributions. They will update us when they can and apologize for the delay," Parker said.

"Yes. They have a ton of DNA from the Miller case. Ask them to prioritize the t-shirt please. Adam, it's you and me off to see Charlie. He could be the last person to see this guy alive. Or the killer. Wear your vest under your jacket," Murphy said.

Murphy punched the address 5 Deer Road into her WeeSee GPS system and within seconds, it gave her two options to get there. One was twenty minutes, the other was fifty. "Weezy, option one," she responded. The device purred and dinged. "Proceed north for two kilometres."

"What is the plan with Charlie?" Girard asked. They were both wearing bullet-proof vests under sports jackets, so Murphy cranked up the air conditioning.

"The plan is no plan. Ellen said he is a witness. But as we know, most people minimize their involvement. So we take it slow."

"Work up to the body?" Girard asked.

"Yes. Charlie called him Ben, so who knows? Maybe Charlie was the target of a video he was filming. We will play it as casually as we can. But it will be your job to keep an eye out for guns."

When Murphy turned on to Deer Road, she immediately recognized it. Mary Rathbone had been murdered at 8 Deer Road three years ago. Her daughter, Lily, found her. The girl was seven. Her father had been given a mandatory life sentence, and his parents moved into the Rathbone house to take care of her.

It was early afternoon, and kids playing street hockey moved the nets out of the way when the Brawler went past. They ran after it when Murphy pulled into the driveway. "Hey, hey! What kind of... What is this?" a little girl asked. Was that Lily?

Murphy got out of the Brawler but left the door open. "It's a Trurock Brawler 4x4. Her name is LouLou."

"You gave your 4x4 a name?" a little boy asked as he peered into the vehicle. When he looked at the dashboard lights, Murphy clicked her electronic key and the engine roared to life. "Wow! That's fucking amazing!"

Murphy threw a look of disbelief at Girard, who said, "I am pretty sure Ruthie's first word was mama, but her second was asshole." Murphy pressed the electronic key a couple of more times, and each time the Brawler roared.

"Look, Hannah does not even come up to the top," one child said, watching another standing near the tire, trying to measure her height.

Murphy spotted a middle-aged woman standing on her porch, arms crossed, watching them. She looked a little like Ellen. "Okay everyone, say goodbye to LouLou," she said. The Brawler roared once more and then the engine shut off. She shut the door and clicked another button. LouLou beeped, and the detectives walked up the driveway.

"Hello, are you Maureen Belanger? My name is Caitlin. This is Adam."

"Yes, I'm Maureen. Call me Mo. I don't think I have met you officers," she said, eyeing the police vests.

"I actually think we have met. I was on scene for the Mary Rathbone incident," Murphy said.

Mo shook her head. "That was terrible, that poor woman. There were a lot of police around then. Maybe we met." She paused for a moment, then asked, "Why are you here?"

"We are here to speak with Charlie," Girard said.

"Oh, for fuck's sake. Charlie! Charlie! Get your ass over here!" she shouted.

"Hey mom, what do you want?" Charlie asked.

The moment Charlie saw the police, his body tensed and his eyes became alert, looking for danger. He was like a rabbit who caught sight of hungry foxes. He was ready to flee at the slightest flicker of movement from these hunters.

Charlie stood very still, waiting. He was compact and, Murphy was sure, made himself even smaller under her gaze. His expression changed from fearful to wary to undecided. He was a young man who had no youth left in his face: there was only fight or flight in his eyes. Murphy stepped back, and that one simple movement, the giving of space when space was needed, instantly relaxed Charlie. He was no longer the rabbit, and she was no longer the fox. He was human again, and he smiled.

Girard took a step forward, and the young man bolted. Charlie could hear the voices behind him, coarse and short commands barked at him. He ran faster, though he did not have a destination. Run! That was the only thing on his mind as he reached the woods. Branches whipped his face and tore at his arms. The voices of his pursuers roared around the trees and finally fell behind him. He was breathless, panting and sweating. His lungs burned and his legs shook, and he finally collapsed into the leaf litter, gasping.

"Damn it!" Murphy gasped as she watched Charlie disappear from sight. The woods were thick and the trees quickly engulfed their prey. She slowed to a walk and then stopped, bent over, gulping air.

"That guy is fast," Girard sputtered as he walked over to Murphy. "I mean, he's young and is not wearing a vest."

"The vest weighs three pounds, Adam," Murphy said, laughing between breaths. "That guy is a freaking rabbit. Zoom, zoom," she said, gesturing left and right.

"What did my son do?" Mo asked as Murphy and Girard returned.

"Nothing that I know of," Murphy said. "Why do you think he ran?"

Mo crossed her arms and glared.

"Nevermind. When he comes home, please, just have him call. Or come in. We are looking for information. That's all." Murphy hand over her business card.

"Homicide? What the hell does Homicide want with my son? Look, he's been in trouble with the law, but it's been minor stuff," Mo said. "He is not involved with a murder."

"We are trying to find out if he knew Eugene Baptiste. He hit his head and died. Adam, show her the picture. This is a photograph of a man we found at Lac Sainte-Marine," Murphy said. "He hit his head on the rocks. We are just trying to get information."

"This guy is dead?" Mo asked as she looked at the photograph on Girard's phone.

"Yes. Do you recognize him?"

"No," Mo said. "When did he die? Why do you think Charlie would know him?"

"Can you just have Charlie come in? He can bring a lawyer if he wants, if he is concerned. Okay?"

Mo nodded silently. Satisfied, Murphy and Girard walked back to the Brawler. "You think he will call?" Girard asked.

"I hope so," she replied as they got into the Brawler and headed down the driveway to the road.

CHAPTER TWENTY

"Whose car is that?" Murphy asked as they drove out. A car arriving in the opposite direction was honking and slowing.

"Detective!" said a familiar voice. Ellen had rolled down her window and was yelling at Murphy.

"I haven't seen you at any road blockades recently," Murphy said. Ellen's incredulous look told Murphy her attempt at small humour failed.

"Yeah no. Standing in front of trucks just isn't a good idea anymore. On a good day, we had a dozen people try to drive through a blockade. Now, with this truck attack, we decided that standing in front of angry drivers in speeding vehicles is not safe. People have changed," Ellen said. "But don't worry, we have come up with another way to stir up shit."

"You are too late, Ellen. Charlie ran from us."

"Sorry about that. I tried calling him, but the phone was off and it went to voicemail. Mo called me and said you were here," she said.

"It's still too late," Murphy said.

"Come back. I will get him to come back."

Murphy turned to Girard and rolled her eyes. "Five minutes." She turned the 4x4 around and pulled into the driveway again. Ellen walked into the forest, yelling her nephew's name. Murphy stayed in the vehicle and looked at her watch. It was ten-thirty-six.

"Detectives!" Ellen's voice boomed in the silence.

"What the hell is up Ellen?" Mo asked. "Why are you involved in this?"

"He's in his hunting stand. He wants to talk only to you," Ellen said to Murphy.

"Just me. And he is in a hunting stand," Murphy said as she got out and pulled the Velcro straps of her bullet-proof vest tighter.

"Adam, call for an ambulance. I want one on site, not thirty minutes away if we need one. No sirens. Parked at the end of the driveway."

"You cannot go alone in a forest to meet with a person who might have guns. This is not okay," Girard said. "There are protocols for a reason. Those are your words. There are protocols for a reason."

"Be sure to complain to Professional Standards. I could use the vacation. Stay here, make sure they stay here. Make sure the ambulance arrives. No sirens. Got it? Adam?"

"I don't like this," Girard said.

Murphy threw her sunglasses onto the dashboard and handed Girard the keys to the Brawler. "Me neither, but you've seen this guy. He will run and he will keep running until he's shot dead by a nervous, overzealous do-gooder who thinks he's helping. I will record everything on the body cam." She affixed and turned the camera on. "DSS Girard, did you have a concern?"

"Yes DI Murphy, I do not believe you should talk alone to the person of interest with known access to firearms."

"Noted for the recording." Murphy grabbed some bottles of water from the back of the Brawler, turned and walked away. As Murphy walked into the woods, she called out, "Charlie? It's Caitlin Murphy. You asked for me? I can't see you."

"Up here." Charlie was in a gigantic oak, sitting on a hunter's stand high on the tree. The branches arched and bridged over the ground. A light wind rustled the leaves, the sun was glowing. To see Charlie, Murphy had to shield her eyes.

"Hi Charlie."

"There's a ladder on this side. Are you alone?" Charlie asked.

"Yes. Do you have a gun?"

"No."

"Okay, can I come up Charlie?"

"Yes. C'mon up," he said, gesturing toward the sky.

Murphy climbed the narrow metal ladder and clambered onto the metal floor of the stand. She scanned quickly and saw nothing but Charlie. "Would you like some water?"

"Yes, please."

Everything looked different from up here. Murphy could see dozens of birds that she would ordinarily only hear. On the ground, everything was brown until it became green higher up. Here, everything was green with only the brown of tree trunks flashing through.

"You know I am a police officer, right? I have my body camera on. You do not need to say anything to me. If you want to just sit here, that's okay with me. I can't give you any favours, and I can't make you any promises. Except that I will be honest, and I will treat you with respect. Charlie? Anything you say to me could be used as evidence. Okay?"

"Yeah."

"Are those the neighbours?" she asked, pointing to a farmhouse in the distance.

"Yeah. They have cattle. Over that way is the lake," Charlie said, pointing in a different direction. "That's Quail Trail over there." Murphy had never seen this area from above, and it was fascinating. The foliage thinned out, and a sloped field took up space. It was a low hill, dark with green and dotted with cows.

"Can you see your house?" she asked as she turned around. She spotted a flower bed with hydrangeas, plants that Sun had once told her about.

There was a small iron table sitting near it, with two chairs, but it had a look of disuse. In the background, a waterjet buzzed through a lake.

"Do you like coming up here?" Murphy asked.

"Yes. My dad put this up before he died. Drank himself to death."

"Hmm, sorry to hear. It's really hard when someone you love dies. But the stand is nice. Do you hunt?"

"No. That's why it's here. It's too close to the house to use as a hunting stand. Dad put it here so no one else would use it, just me," Charlie said. He looked off into the distance and watched a flock of birds pass by. Charlie was the sentinel, watching everything in his domain.

"That was nice of him. Did you get along with your dad?" Murphy asked.

"He was alright when he was sober. Beat mom a lot. She would give as good back, though."

"What about you?"

"Nah, nobody ever hit me. He hit my brothers for being smart asses, but I just did what I was told. It seemed easier that way," Charlie said. His attention was caught by a horse strolling through a pasture to the east. Murphy looked just in time to see its tail flick and disappear behind some trees.

"Did your brothers hit you?"

"No, they protected me. They were nice when I was growing up. Bobby is in prison for robbing a liquor store, and DanDan is, well, I don't know where he is. Toronto, I think. When dad died, they both just kind of..." Charlie's voice trailed off. He kicked at a leaf that sat on the stand and watched as it slowly made its way to the ground.

"So now it's you and your mom?"

"And my two sisters. And all my aunties and uncles and cousins. There are a lot of us. But I can come up here and no one else. I have a key and keep a lock on the ladder. It's just about the only place I have." Charlie pointed at a little spider making its way along the steel railing.

Murphy waved away a wasp that was hovering near her face. "You like being alone?"

"I… no, not really. But I keep getting into trouble when I am with my friends, so mom wants me to stay away," Charlie said. He sounded like a kid, not a twenty-three-year-old man with multiple arrests.

"It sounds like your mom cares a lot about you," Murphy said.

"Yeah, she does. I love her. I love her the most in the world. I would do anything for her."

"Yeah, I think moms have it hard in this world. They watch their kids grow up and sometimes can't help when they get into trouble," Murphy said. Charlie watched as a blackbird announced its presence and then zipped past. Then he stared into the sun, shading his eyes.

"What are you supposed to do when your mom can't help you get out of trouble?" Charlie asked. "I mean, when you do something terrible. She can't help then."

"She can. I don't know your mom, but I bet that no matter what, she would love you and help you. No matter what bad thing happened."

"Do you see up there? Where the treetops almost meet but not quite? My mom told me that's called crown shyness. They are close, but they never quite touch," Charlie said. The statement was not lost on Murphy.

"I am glad I am not a tree. I don't know what it would be like to go through life without touching someone else."

Charlie turned and looked at her with a critical eye. "I read about you in the paper. A couple of times." He reached up and scratched randomly at the bark of the tree. "They always talk about whatever crime you solved, and then they always talk about your wife."

"Yes," Murphy nodded. "The media loves that part of my life. Lesbian detective married to disabled artist."

"Heroic lesbian detective married to disabled artist. They are calling you a hero," Charlie said. "Do you enjoy being married? Even though she is in a wheelchair?"

"Yes. She is the hero. That woman has more guts than I will ever have. She flies a plane."

"No way."

"All by herself. A Cherokee Piper."

"And you, uh, you and her...?" Charlie asked.

"We're married, and that's all you need to know," Murphy said, and then winked at him. "Do you have someone special?"

Charlie's body deflated: his shoulders sunk, his head bowed, his back bent. "I thought I did."

"What happened?" Murphy asked. She waited for a moment and then held out her hand. She let it hang in the air, near but not touching Charlie. He sniffled, and then reached out and took her hand.

"His name was Ben Altimont. I met him online. He lied to me. When we met in person, he said his name was Eugene Baptiste and said he was married. He used me. I mean, we were just friends, you know? I, he..."

Murphy squeezed his hand. "Tell me about Ben. Eugene. Where was he from?"

"Sudbury. I thought so, anyway. We were going to meet up, we did meet up. But he kind of lied about things."

"Aw, I'm sorry that he lied. What did he lie about?" she asked. Charlie again turned to the bark of the tree and tried to scratch a piece off. He worked at it for a while until finally a small piece came free. It flew off the tree and out of his hand, falling to the ground below.

"He said he was twenty-five, but when I met him, he was way older. Like old. Maybe forty. He said he really wanted to meet me. I mean, I lied too. I said my dad was a well-known Mohawk chief. It was…" he trailed off again.

He looked up to the sky again, and let his eye follow the line of a tree down to the ground. "We met there, at the lake. He had a friend drop him off I guess. It wasn't what I thought, but I felt like, that's okay, he's still sort of interesting. He came because he wanted to see me. He said he wanted a blow job."

"When did you make plans to meet?"

"Well, we started making plans a couple of weeks ago. This was going to be so cool. I thought he liked me."

Charlie stood up and pulled Murphy with him. He leaned on the steel railing and looked down. He still had hold of Murphy's hand. She held a little tighter. With his free hand, Charlie pointed to the west. "After I went to Lac Sainte-Marine, we walked out on to the rocks, onto the shore. He had a bag, and he took out this small video camera. He was a nice guy, but, you know, it wasn't what I was expecting."

Murphy nodded. "You were hoping for a connection? Someone to, I guess, touch you? Hold you?"

Charlie nodded. He was tearing up. "He held up the camera and told me he thought I was so hot he wanted to film me taking it in the face. Just casually, he said he wanted to watch it later. I thought that was okay." He stopped to blow his nose clear, letting the snot fall to the ground.

"I was staring at him, you know, just looking. He told me to unzip his pants."

Murphy stepped away from the railing, pulling Charlie with her. She did not like that he was standing so close to the edge. "And then?"

"I thought he wanted to film me blowing him. I knelt down and started to unzip his pants," Charlie said. "He grabbed my head, like put his hand on the top like this. I thought..."

"You thought that was an invitation?"

Charlie looked out at the trees and shifted his weight. The wind stirred the leaves slightly, enveloping them in a soft scent. "Yeah. I never touched his dick, I never touched him, I swear. I did not even undo his pants yet. Then he just freaked out and kneed me in the face. He started calling me names. 'Faggot' and 'cocksucker' and said I was dirty and disgusting. He smacked me across the face and this guy came out of the woods screaming. I just ran. I ran and ran and ran. I ran past his car." Charlie paused as he sobbed.

"I'm sorry," Murphy said. "I am sorry he got hurt. So you ran? Past his car?" No car had been found on the scene.

"Yes. I ran home."

"How did you get there? Did you drive?"

"No, I figured I would walk. It took a while, but it was only about ten clicks," Charlie said. For a young man capable of running as fast as he did, it did not surprise Murphy to hear he thought nothing of walking ten kilometres.

"But he had his car there," Murphy said. "What did it look like?"

"Uh, gold. Beige four door. I don't know what kind. I think it was his car. I only saw it when I left."

"And the guy you saw. Tell me about him."

"Maybe it was a guy. Kind of small, so, I don't know. Just the person yelling. Not too loud but they came out of nowhere. Like I don't think Eugene was expecting anyone. He kind of came out of the woods in a crouch. Like he did not want to be seen," Charlie said. He crouched and crept to emphasize his story.

"He?"

"Yeah. But a small guy. Or a girl. I don't know."

"Did they say anything?"

"Nope. But as soon as I saw him, I took off."

"You saw a person coming towards you. He came from the woods. What did you do?" Murphy asked. She was repeating her questions to catch him in a lie.

"I ran away."

"What did Eugene do?"

"He kept calling me names. How do you get used to people calling you names like 'faggot'? I mean, do people call you names?"

"Sometimes they do. It makes me angry, but I do not react. Unless they are screaming in my face, I walk away. Was Eugene screaming in your face?"

"Yeah. He thought it was funny. He was laughing."

"Did you come back? Did you push him?"

"No. It took me more than an hour to run home. There was no way I was going back to get my phone. I dropped it when he kneed me. I thought I might get it later from him. Maybe Ellen would help, you know? But then I saw on the news that he was dead. Ben was dead, and I got really scared," Charlie said.

Murphy looked up and tried to follow the twisting line of a nearby branch. There were offshoots and buds and things she had no name for. She took a deep breath in and looked at the cows in the field across the way.

"Where is your phone?" Murphy asked. Ellen said she had tried to reach him but could not.

"I dropped it there. I didn't hurt him. He was okay when I left."

"Did you hug him or touch him?"

"No. I never did."

"Did you touch his pants?"

"Maybe near the button? I don't think so."

"What about his shirt? Did you touch his shirt?"

"No. He did not have a shirt. Maybe it was in his bag. I did not touch anything. Not his camera, not his bag, nothing."

She nodded and pulled her hand from Charlie's. He looked in horror at her, fearing he had somehow pushed her away too. Instead, Murphy stood there, arms open toward him. He rushed in and hugged her as tightly as he could. His tears and snot and spit ran down the bullet-proof vest as he cried. He could not stop.

Murphy looked at the bark of the tree while she stroked Charlie's head. The tree was scaly and rough. A line of ducks flew overhead toward the lake. A smattering of bugs crawled along the oak tree, each heading in their own direction.

Now was the hardest part of all: getting Charlie out of the stand without him jumping to his death. She rubbed his back and pushed him gently away from her. She looked into his eyes and gave him a soft smile. "I know your mom wants you home safe and sound. And Ellen wants me to keep you safe, too. Do you want to go see them now?"

"I love my mom, but she doesn't know I am gay. Is she going to find out?"

"Probably. I will not tell her, but eventually, this might come out in court once we find who did this. Be brave for me Charlie. Can you talk to Ellen? Or one of your other aunties?" Charlie shrugged. Murphy hugged him tightly and nodded. It was time to leave the stand.

"Ellen seems like she wants to help. Talk to her." Murphy climbed down first and watched nervously as Charlie carefully climbed down after her. He locked the frame onto the ladder and pocketed the key.

"You're okay," she said as she put her arm around him. They walked back to the house together, to those eagerly waiting for their return. As she walked with him to the Brawler, Mo and Ellen rushed to him, hugging him, crying. "I need your cell phone number and the code to unlock the phone. If that is alright? And can I test your DNA?"

"DNA? Sure. What do you need?"

"I just need permission." As they approached the house, Charlie gave Murphy the phone number and passcode. Ellen gave Charlie a hug. "He is okay. I got some important information. Charlie was really helpful," Murphy said.

CHAPTER TWENTY-ONE

Murphy looked at the time. She had talked to Charlie Belanger for two hours: in the woods, time ran differently, slowing and stretching out. Driving in the Brawler, time snapped back into its usual hyper speed.

She dialled the office on the drive back. "Put me on speaker," she said to Parker, who had answered the call. "I think it's possible Charlie Belanger killed Eugene Baptiste by pushing him. The motive could be self-defence or romantic rejection. But he mentioned a person and a gold four-door car. Check the Baptiste car. Tell me if it's gold or beige."

Murphy could hear someone typing madly on the computer, cursing softly and typing more. "No. The Baptistes have a white 2019 Vento," Hamilton said.

"Karen has been updating her blog with a lot of opinion posts about the Northshore riot. Nothing in particular about her husband, and nothing that indicates she was there on Thursday. There was one video posted yesterday. She talked about how great the CBB was. The riot here was a punishment from God. Nothing about her husband," Parker said.

"Do we have cell phone records yet?"

"An hour ago, they promised I would have it in an hour. I will follow up," Hamilton said.

"Okay, Cleo, work on getting his financials, too. Michael, see if you can track Charlie's phone: he said he dropped it there when he ran away. I will text the number and passcode. Adam, when we get back to the office, you take some uniformed officers and head back to Lac Sainte-Marine. Look for bags or knapsacks, cameras, phones, anything we might have missed. Check the woods. Charlie said a man came from the woods. He said he thought it was a small man, but maybe a woman. Also check the parking lot again. Thank you," Murphy said as she hung up.

"What do you think happened?"

"I think this might have been an attempted assault gone wrong. Eugene Baptiste was filming the encounter, someone came to rob them. Charlie or the robber, maybe Karen, pushed Eugene down and fled. Someone covered him up with a t-shirt, but Charlie said there was no t-shirt. Someone may have the items from the scene," Murphy said.

"So you think it was Charlie?"

"I'm not feeling it, but it makes sense. He makes a great suspect if we can place him there forensically. I do not understand Karen, though. Why did she really not report him missing? Why the fake histrionics? Was she having an affair with Haidt, and is it relevant?" she asked as she parked the Brawler.

Murphy headed to the Forensics Unit with her vest, explaining they needed to compare the DNA from snot on the vest to DNA on Eugene's clothing. Politely, the technician swabbed a large gob and then handed her the vest back. "Oh, you don't clean it?" she asked.

"No ma'am. I recommend you spot clean with a mild detergent," she said. Instead, Murphy took it to the showers and rinsed it off. She then hung it in her locker to dry and returned to the office.

Parker was working on the Haidt website videos, trying to identify any other videos posted by Eugene or Miller. He also noted any videos that Haidt posted that might contain hate speech and asked Mitch to run

VerbatimVox on them. Girard was looking through Karen's Shout Du Jour account, running VerbatimVox on those videos too.

"I have something for you, boss," Hamilton said. "Financial records for Eugene Baptiste. He made $1673 every two weeks from the Trenchless concrete company. He made small amounts each month, $50 to $100, from 'Cliquez sur espèces'. They are an online advertising company. But…"

"But?"

Hamilton put a printout from the back on the link board. "He has purchased a $120,000 GIC every year for the last five years. Each December, he deposits a cashier's cheque for $120,000 and then the next day he buys a GIC. I am trying to get the image for last year's cheque."

"Someone is giving him a nice chunk of change. And he is buying GICs of all things," Murphy said.

"I would have expected crypto, NFTs or at least meme stocks."

"That's exactly what I was thinking. Crypto stocks," Murphy joked.

"GICs are a very conservative investment strategy," Girard added. "I buy them."

"So, Eugene gets a cash infusion every year and immediately places it into safe bank certificates. Alright, thank you."

Murphy returned to her office. She poured over the forensic report for Eugene. There were three DNA contributions on the t-shirt. One male, two female. They found female contributions on the outside of the t-shirt only. The pants had two male DNA contributions, only one on the inside. Murphy assumed only Eugene wore them, but someone else's DNA was on the outside. They should be able to match it to Charlie soon enough.

Murphy looked quickly at her watch. It was almost 7:00 p.m. and the others had already gone. Murphy slowly walked into the atelier, took a mint from the candy dish, and sat down. She rolled the candy in her fingers, listening to the cellophane wrapper crinkle. She was processing all the information, and when she was finally done for the day, she walked into her office.

Murphy called Sun. It was still early in the evening, and she hoped to catch her before Sun ate. She left a message. "Hey, Sun, it's me. It's about 7:10. Are you up for dinner? Let me know."

Murphy left the office for a walk. South would take her to the scene of the truck ramming, and she did not want that. She walked north instead. There were concrete flower pots painted terra cotta, where small bursts of red and purple sprang out. She walked past the Cartier Boutique hotel and peered into the window of the Flagg butcher shop. Slabs of red meat sat in the display case. A woman had her finger pressed against the glass, pointing out which slab she wanted to cook for her family tonight.

Three old men, long finished their coffees, sat on a bench outside of Vinnie's Cafe watching the people go by. The voice of Big Mama Thornton wailed from Jazzin' Vintage Vinyl. The clerk, a young person with bright blue hair and two cheek piercings, stood in the doorway vaping. Through the window, Murphy could see a woman: was that Jasmine? Across the street, a woman stood outside Sweet Honey's Natural Hair, chastising her small dog for snapping at a child. Someone was sleeping in the doorway of a vacant store further up the street. The late July sun was still bright in the sky. It all seemed so normal. Murphy turned around and headed back to the Brawler.

There was no phone call from Sun, so on the way home, she called again.

"Caitlin! Hey Caitlin, come and join us for dinner. We're at Fiddler's Pub. Come and join us," Sun said.

Us? "Oh no, I don't want to interrupt your night out."

"Yes, yes, it's me and Mitch. Fiddler's Pub. I have something to tell you. Hey Mitch! Do I have something to tell Caitlin?" Sun shouted.

"She sure does," Mitch said with a loud laugh. The sting in her heart surprised Murphy.

"Fiddler's Pub," Sun repeated. She then hung up. Murphy turned the Brawler around. Sun was with Mitch, hunky, handsome and friendly Mitch, and they wanted to talk to her. She hoped it would be an offer of a threesome. She decided it was more likely that Sun was going to dump her for her new CrossFit hottie.

The pub was a faux Irish pub that added O' or Mc to everything on the menu. Three Irish beers were on tap beside the standard Canadian brews. Sickly green walls were covered in sports team logos from across the U.K. and Europe.

Mitch and Sun were at a table, laughing. They seemed happy, giddy. Murphy's heart sank. She really liked Sun and saw she was losing her to the IT stud of all people.

"Hi," Murphy said.

"Caitlin!" Sun shouted as she jumped up and gave her a big hug. Sun kissed her passionately. This was a far cry from pulling away from her in a restaurant. "Sit, sit."

They guided Murphy to sit between them. Mitch had a huge smile on her face. Sun had been drinking, but Murphy was not sure Mitch had. The threesome was looking like more of a possibility.

"What's the surprise?" Both women stared at her, grinning. "What? What's the surprise?"

"I love you!" Sun shouted. She let out a laugh Murphy had never heard before.

"What?" Murphy said. Her mind was racing.

"I love you. I am telling you I love you. There is no time like now, right?" Sun asked Mitch.

"That's what I say. Say it when you feel it," Mitch said.

"Mitch has been helping me fix up the flower shop. She is amazing. Did you know she had built schools and hospitals?"

"It's true," Mitch said when Murphy looked at her. Mitch punctuated her short statement by flexing her muscles. Now Murphy was not sure exactly who it was that Sun was saying she loved.

"And did you know Mitch had been to my hometown, Pondicherry?"

"That's true too. Nice place," she said, nodding.

"She is so great," Sun said and flung her arms out .

Murphy was confused. The bar was loud and people were wandering all over the place, causing her to look here and there: a natural precaution. Nothing was making sense.

"I told your girl, if she loves you, she needs to tell you," Mitch said. "So she told you. Wait until you see what's in store. Get it Sun? In store?"

Sun screamed out a laugh and playfully pushed her shoulder. "You are so hilarious, but without you..."

"What are you talking about?"

"Our love nest. Mitch helped me fix up the basement of the flower shop. We can use it for just us," Sun said. She threw her arms around Murphy and gave her a sloppy kiss. Murphy's heart melted. Sun was not leaving her, she was trying to bring her closer.

"Yes! It isn't much, but if you want some privacy and comfort for loving, it will be great," Mitch said.

Mitch looked into Murphy's face. She was as excited as a child. "What do you think?"

"I, uh, I think it sounds great. Why have you done this now?"

"Mitch! She was helping with the flower shop and we got talking," Sun said.

"I went downstairs to see if she had any tools and boom! She told me you two use a hotel room, and she asked if I could fix it up. I thought: Hey!

A cleaning, some paint and lights and a bed. You'll have yourselves a love nest," Mitch explained. "I always wanted one."

"We talked about it before, but I needed Mitch with her muscles." Sun reached over and tapped her arm, prompting another flex.

They talked excitedly about the space and how they had planned the layout. They had to work around pipes and a lack of space. Choosing a light colour paint made all the difference, they assured her. There was enough space for a double bed, a small fridge, and some storage. Mitch had built the bed platform and side table. A TV could be mounted on the wall.

"I have gone online to order a lamp and one of those mattresses in a box. Some linen. God, this is going to be amazing," Sun said, reaching across Murphy to squeeze Mitch's arm.

Murphy was excited and terrified. It was almost like living together. She had only ever lived with her parents, roommates, and Del. This is not moving in together, she reminded herself. This is just a place to fuck.

The trio spent another hour chatting before Sun excused herself to use the washroom. Murphy spoke with Mitch.

"I have to ask you…"

"Oh, don't worry, we did not fuck in your love nest. She's not my type. She's all yours," Mitch said with a wink.

Murphy's heart lightened at the news. "That's great news, but this is about work."

"Ha ha!" Mitch laughed as she slapped Murphy on the back. "You really do always think about work, eh?"

"I guess." Murphy took a quick look for Sun, then leaned in. "I need to know if Jonathan Haidt has subscribed to Karen Baptiste's Shout Du Jour account. Or if he even has an account. Is that something you can check for me?"

"Oh, yes. So he might be associated with Karen? Or Eugene?"

"Both. They were seeing him for counselling. This is confidential, yeah?"

"Yep. Police business. Do you want me to check the local hookup sites for an account?"

Murphy frowned. "What made you think of that?"

"Well, Eugene was found at Lac Sainte-Marine. Lac Sainte-Marine? It's a cruising spot for gay sex."

"And there are apps for that?"

Mitch laughed. "Hell yeah. For men, I mean. Nothing for women. But yes. I thought you knew. Lac Sainte-Marine is a hookup spot."

"Yes. Find out if either Haidt or Eugene had those hookup accounts." She continued as she thought more about it. "A witness said he found Eugene through a dating app. If I get you his username and password, can you search? Eugene should be there." Murphy suddenly had to consider that Haidt was having an affair, or at least sex, with Eugene. Maybe instead of, or maybe as well as, with Karen.

"Yes absolutely. That would make it even easier, too. Send it along."

Sun returned to the table, put her arms around both women and shoved her face between theirs. "My two faves!" she shouted and kissed each woman on the cheek.

Murphy had been through more than a dozen relationships, and while the one with Sun had lasted the longest, the news of a love nest put butterflies in her stomach. Mitch was a knight in shining armour for both of them. She helped Sun rebuild her store and was going to help strengthen their relationship. Sun was laughing loudly, broadly, and her mood was as bright as her smile.

And then there it was. A quick stroke down Mitch's cheek, an extended hand, and a smoldering look in Sun's eyes. *They are going to fuck.*

Mitch might not understand, Murphy thought. She was falling for Sun without realizing it. Murphy watched them talk and drink and laugh and knew how irresistible Sun was. There were so many myths and theories about love at first sight. A tingling, a breathlessness, a sense of knowing. Different people experienced different reactions to seeing The One. Murphy thought Sun was attractive. But there had been no tingling hands or breathless heart palpitations. It was alright, Murphy told herself, Mitch was very fuckable. She could see the attraction.

"Hey, I have a busy day tomorrow," Murphy said. "I have to get going. Make sure she gets home safe, yeah?"

"Hell no. You take her," Mitch said with a grin. Murphy got a sloppy kiss from Sun and they headed out. Before leaving the parking lot, Murphy booked a room at the Serenity Inn. She wished the love nest was furnished and ready to go: it would be so much more convenient.

In the hotel room, Sun wobbled and laid down and fell asleep so quickly Murphy had to undress her. She rolled Sun over and unzipped the dress. With Sun face down, she slipped the shoulders off, then pulled her onto her back.

She worked the dress off, pulling and tugging first the left side, then the right. Murphy dragged it down her legs. Once the dress was off, she laid it over the back of the chair. Sun's eyes fluttered open but softly closed again. Murphy looked at her matching pink bra and underwear and wondered if she should take them off her lover or leave them on. Her hand touched her chest and paused at the front clasp. She leaned over and gave Sun a kiss, then pulled up the sheet. Sun had always slept naked with her, but undressing her while she was passed out felt wrong. Her Catholic modesty came up at the weirdest times.

Murphy stripped and snuggled in beside Sun. Her flesh was warm and enticing. Murphy arranged her pillow to let her head lay right next to Sun's. She silently said her nightly prayer for the dead and had an easy, dreamless sleep.

***

Murphy hung up the phone and rapped her fingers on the desk. She had tried calling Charlie Belanger to ask for his dating app information, but the phone was still turned off. She would have Parker track him down. Murphy was amused by the image of Charlie running through the woods with Parker in pursuit. She was sure the outcome would have been different.

"Boss!"

Hamilton called Murphy out of her office. She walked into the atelier and sat on the couch. "What have you got?"

"TechWave has sent the Baptiste's phone records. Michael took Karen's, and I took Eugene's, plus a second phone in his name," Hamilton said. Murphy was grateful to get the cell phone records finally.

Hamilton began. "Cell phone one for Eugene had phone calls to his wife, his work, grandmother, friends. Nothing spectacular. It is currently pinging off a cell tower here. It's at or near his home." Hamilton circled a spot on the map.

"The second cell phone is a different story. This phone has hundreds of calls to adult phone services. It has two calls to Crystal Bradford, one of his victims. One is prior to the attack on her, one is after. It is pinging off the same cell tower, so it is also still active."

Murphy sat up. "After her attack?"

"Yes. Crystal's complaint report showed her attacker had called her twice. Her attacker called her after the attack to taunt her. It was in her report, but apparently not followed up. One phone number that coincides with the estimated date of the blond man's attack comes back to Randy

Pardoe. Pardoe has numerous drug arrests." Hamilton put his latest mug shot on the board.

"That sure looks like he is the same person in the attack video," Girard said.

"And Eugene had four phone calls to the number you gave us, boss. The one for Charlie Belanger. They begin July third and end July twentieth at 8:30 a.m."

"And Eugene's phones are where right now?"

"They are pinging off a tower near the Baptiste home."

"So he either left it there to meet Charlie or they took it back with them," Murphy said. "Could he have made the call to Charlie at 8:30 and left the phone at home? Maybe," she said, answering her own question.

"Karen's pings are currently at the same cell tower near the house. She has phone calls to her husband, his grandmother, et cetera, et cetera. She has one phone call from Jonathan Haidt, and a half dozen back to him," Parker said.

"We know he was their marriage counsellor. There ought to be some calls to him on Eugene's list," Girard said.

"Seven from Haidt, two to him," Hamilton said.

"I have a thought." Everyone's attention was now on Murphy. She took a sip of coffee and let out a long sigh. "Lac Sainte-Marine is a cruising spot for gay men to meet and hook up. Eugene was there. Charlie was there, he said for sex with Eugene. He said they met on an app. I called Charlie's cell, but it's been turned off or the battery died. I have asked Mitch to check the dating sites once we get the information. Michael, since we cannot reach him by phone, you locate Charlie. Get the dating app information."

"Yes, boss."

"The phones change the track, though. Karen Baptiste is our focus right now. She said she did not know where Eugene's phone was, and it seems to be at home. Prepare the ITOs and get warrants. Phone, cameras, video cameras, computers. We want the Vento processed, including any GPS information. We will bring Karen in for ques—" Murphy was interrupted by the phone on her desk ringing.

"Get the warrants, then we coordinate," she said as she headed into her office. "Detective Inspector Murphy," she said into the receiver.

"This is Tanya Watson with the RCMP Hate Crimes Unit. Please hold for Superintendent Gibson."

Murphy sat in her office chair. Her leather bag lay on the old leather guest chair on the other side of her desk. She absentmindedly compared the two leathers. The chair had a soft patina, worn from all the asses it had held. She was fairly certain it was from the 1990s. It was sturdy and bulky and would probably outlive her. Her bag, which held files, her colouring book and, occasionally, a homemade lunch, was also worn. But its leather bore scratches and marks from being thrown down, kicked aside and, on more than one occasion, run over by the Brawler. Its roughness was a sign of life, Murphy mused.

"Thank you for holding, Detective Inspector. I apologize for that."

Murphy was startled. She was on hold for ten minutes, the music pulling her into boredom.

"Superintendent Gibson, thanks for calling me. Is this about Jonathan Haidt?"

"No, I believe that is with Supt. Shevchenko. I understand you arrested the truck ramming suspect, Perry Miller."

"Yes, sir."

"And you were injured during the arrest?"

"Yes sir, my wrist. Not that bad, just a cast," Murphy said.

"And you drove your truck into him?"

"Well no. He drove his truck into me," she said. "He lost that little game."

"Well, you are either one of the unluckiest sons of a bitch in the world, or one of the bravest," Gibson said.

"Maybe both, sir," Murphy said with a laugh.

"I support Chief Valencia nominating you for that bravery and madness. Good for you. Now, on to Perry Miller. Tell me about his actions, your interview with him."

Murphy recounted the event and her interview with Miller, and high-lighted his hate-filled ideology. Throughout the twenty-minute conversation, Gibson said little more than 'hmm' and 'ah'. When Murphy was done, Gibson remained reticent.

"Send the file to me please, before the end of the year," he said. "I cannot promise anything will happen, but we might well look at it. We may decide to follow the trial. Great work DI Murphy."

And with that, the conversation was over. Murphy hung up and looked at her calendar. The days were blurring together. It was Wednesday, July the twenty-sixth. It had been a week and a half since an asshole changed her world.

Murphy brought her coffee into the atelier. "The RCMP Hate Crimes Unit wants a copy of the Perry Miller file. Adam, it is to the attention of Supt. Gibson."

Girard shook his head. "Boss, there is no way—"

"By the end of the year. You have five months," Murphy said. "They did not tell me what their angle is. You never know with them, but it gives me hope."

CHAPTER TWENTY-TWO

Parker placed a large map on the board. "Boss, we have gone through more of the TechWave information and correlated some of it. Karen's cell phone calls Jonathan Haidt's at 8:00 a.m. for two minutes. Eugene's cell phone number two calls Charlie Belanger's phone at 8:10 for ten minutes. The phone number two for Eugene pinged off the same cell towers at 8:15 a.m., along R.R. 51 to R.R. 80, then 46, here," he said, marking red dots on the map. "They finally stopped here. It's the closest tower to Lac Sainte-Marine. Nothing further south. This is at 8:53 Thursday morning."

"But not phone number one?" Murphy asked.

"No, boss. Number one never leaves the house. Phone two remained at Lac Sainte-Marine until 10:05. Then ping ping ping, the phone makes the trip back home."

"Fantastic! Eugene's phone two goes to the lake, and home again."

"But wait! There's more," Hamilton said. She walked to the board. "This is Charlie's phone. He pings off this tower near his home at 7:09 a.m. We see him ping here and here. He was walking, right? Then he pings off the same tower as Eugene at 9:00. That is the closest to the lake. At 10:05, his phone goes home with Eugene's phone. Same times and towers at the end of the trip."

"Damn, maybe I am getting lucky," Murphy said. "I hope that Karen still has the phones. But that's very compelling. What have we got for motive?"

"Gay hookups?" Hamilton asked.

"If he is keeping the GIC money a secret, it could be financial," Parker offered.

"Either could be a motive. Did we get insurance policy information?"

"Yes, boss," Girard said. "Eugene had a fifty thousand dollar policy. But it went up to half a million dollars in case of accidental death."

"This is like a dream. Wife kills husband over money, maybe infidelity. Do we have Haidt's cell phone data? No? Damn. But are we working on it?" Murphy asked.

"I was checking on him. He had an eight a.m. sermon followed by two hours of Bible study. That's according to his website, it's an everyday thing. We have nothing to put him at the scene."

"Not without his cell phone data, we don't," Murphy grumbled.

"Being objective, boss, there has been no evidence that ties him to the murder. If we tried to get a production order, we would fail."

Murphy shot daggers toward Girard, then huffed. "You're right. You're right. If Eugene's certified cheque is his, maybe that could get us his financials and cell records. But you are right, there is not enough on Haidt. Damn! Did I just say that out loud?"

"The warrants will take an hour or two," Girard said.

"Okay, Adam, ask the warrants squad to put eyes on her. We will have her picked up once we have the warrants in hand, but I don't want her slipping away. What time is it? Yes, the timing is good. This feels good." Murphy's body felt brilliant, and she wondered if the others could see her shining. She was relishing the idea of bringing Karen in, although she would have preferred Haidt. "Michael and Cleo, search warrants for the house and car, and arrest warrant for her."

"Boss, I checked out the image of her house online. There are two outbuildings, at least," Parker said as he projected the computer image onto the blank link board. "Here, and here," he said, circling small dots with his finger.

"Okay, search warrants to include all buildings on the property. Geez, it is amazing what is available to the public. Print it, circle the outbuildings and throw it in the file," Murphy said.

"Hey boss, don't forget about the tribute to Sergeant Doris McKay. It's tomorrow," Hamilton said.

"Right, yes. Will the funeral procession go through Kettering?" Murphy asked.

"Yes. It starts at Kettering and goes to her detachment in Fort Gilgam, about thirty kilometres south," Hamilton said.

"Everyone is to wear their dress uniforms. What time are they expected to arrive in Fort Gilgam?"

"About 2:30 p.m., boss," Hamilton said.

"Okay, dress uniforms. We interrupt whatever we are doing so we can get to Fort Gilgam before her arrival." Murphy retreated to her office and dialled Mitch, hoping to get an update on the VerbatimVox GREP search. Before she finished dialling the last of the numbers, Murphy spotted an email in her inbox from Mitch. She hung up, a little grateful not to have to actually talk to her romantic competition. The image of Sun and Mitch together suddenly popped into Murphy's head, but it cleared after a quick blink. Murphy worked another hour before asking where the warrants were.

"Adam is on the phone with the clerk right now," Hamilton said. They waited impatiently, listening to Girard's conversation.

"That sounds painful, ma'am. Yes. No, we do not believe there is a risk to the public. Yes. No. Okay. Yes ma'am. Urgent. Tomorrow. Thank you." Girard turned to the team, flabbergasted. "Justice Lavigne tripped in his office this morning. He has gone home. He will sign the warrants tomorrow. They can wait because there is no risk to the public." He sighed and put his face in his hands.

Murphy shook her head. She knew Justice Lavigne would hold a grudge if they went to another Justice, especially after saying there was no threat. Murphy realized Girard had still not looked up. "Adam, are you okay?"

"Yeah."

"Liar."

"I... Yes. No. The riots. It was very disturbing even though it turned out okay. I've tried to push what I was seeing out of my head. But when I sleep it comes back," Girard said. "I haven't been sleeping well."

"I have a hard time sleeping after the riots, too. It was not the same for me, but sleeping has not been easy," Hamilton said.

"Not going to lie, I have only had a couple of nights' sleeps since the fire-bombing. I mean, why would anyone do that? And that old man stopping me? Creepy," Parker said.

"I can have some pretty brutal sleeps, but it's been that way since I was a kid," Murphy said. "I still keep trying to sleep, though."

"Does anyone take anything to help you sleep?" Hamilton asked, hopeful for a solution, but there was silence.

"I sleep here on the couch sometimes," Murphy said. "But it's for work. When we had the tip line for Cardinal Horn, I took a call from a psychic at 2:00 in the morning."

"You think she'd have known you were sleeping," Girard said.

"How do you know it was a 'she'?" Hamilton asked.

"I'm psychic."

"Tell me whether I will sleep tonight," Murphy said.

Girard shook his hand and looked at his palm. "The Magic 8 Ball says sorry, maybe next time."

"What is everyone doing for self-care?" Murphy asked.

"I run," Parker said.

"I read," Hamilton said.

"My family," Girard said.

"I'm really glad to hear that." Murphy said.

"One of your friends was hurt in the truck attack, wasn't he?"

"Yes, badly," Murphy said.

"Have you visited?" asked Hamilton.

"Once, before he was transferred to Toronto."

"What was that like? Seeing him?" Parker asked.

"Weird. He wasn't conscious. He had legs then. Parts of legs. But his face. He looked old. He is old, but he looked older. And now they've taken the legs. I haven't seen him again," Murphy said.

"That's terrible," Girard said.

"Your whole life can change in a couple of minutes. That's it. In a moment, it changes from being with friends and laughing, to hospitals and surgeries and scars and missing limbs. Or you're dead. Just dead." Emotions cut through Murphy's voice. "I can see it over and over in my dreams, but I'm not really seeing it. It gets distorted, so it becomes something all its own."

"You can't turn it off," Parker said.

"And it gets scary to go to bed some nights, knowing what might wait for you," Hamilton said.

"But you don't know when it will be there," Girard said.

"There is always more," Parker said.

"The next homicide scene," Girard said.

"The next case to solve," Hamilton said.

"There will always be another, eventually. And we show up. Seeing these things is not simple. It is difficult to walk the streets of your town and remember who died nearby. But we do it because we choose to," Murphy said. "We could walk away, any of us, walk away right now. Just hand in your badge and your gun and walk out and see your family or run or read. And none of us, not one, would think worse of you. The exit door is always open."

"So is the entrance," Girard said.

"We always come back," Parker said.

"Because we choose to," Hamilton said.

"It's a choice to look at the evil things people do, and then to hold them accountable. A choice to fight it," Murphy said.

"I can fight evil," Parker said.

"Me too " Hamilton said.

"Fight the evil," Girard said.

"Forever," Murphy said. "But not tonight. Okay, call off uniform. There will be no arrest tonight. Everyone go home. Rest as best you can. We have a big day tomorrow."

She thought about calling Sun, but instead, she headed home. She had dinner with Del and headed to her room to watch television before falling asleep. She dreamt of a church with millions of lady beetles crawling inside, falling from the ceiling and crunching underfoot.

The next morning, Murphy headed to the Goose Gas to fill the Brawler. She was heartened to see Sergei come out to gas her vehicle up. "Nice to see you," she said as she unlocked the gas tank lid and paid at the pump. "Is there something special you want today?"

"Yes, I would like tuna today. Fish would be nice," Sergei said. With that, Murphy headed into the convenience store attached to the station and picked up a tuna sandwich, some pop, and a bag of candies. She eyed the tuna. It looked a little less than fresh despite having a due date of today. She also bought a ham sandwich, in case the tuna was no good.

"Sergei, how was your trip to the hospital? Did they take good care of you?"

"Yes, yes, they stitched me up, gave me some pills, which I sold for $30, and I got fresh clothes. The pants are a little big, but they found a belt for me, too," Sergei said. *Sold his pills,* Murphy thought. *Well, at least he is honest.*

"Okay, two sandwiches, some pop, and some candies. Thank you sir," she said as Sergei finished filling her gas tank and put the nozzle back in the holder. She handed his food to him and pulled around the side of the station to the restaurant. She brought her leather bag with her into the restaurant and settled into her usual spot.

"The usual, hon?" Emeline asked.

"Yes please," Murphy responded as she pulled out her colouring book. It took just two minutes for her coffee to arrive, and fifteen minutes for her breakfast. She ate quickly, excited at the prospect of arresting another murderer. Murphy wolfed down her food, paid, and headed to the police station.

Girard, Parker, and Hamilton arrived within the hour. Everyone had brought dress uniforms for the funeral. "Folks, good to see you. Are we set to go?"

"Yes, boss. Warrants were signed overnight. I have called uniform and asked they monitor Karen Baptiste. Two Forensic techs will be available. We will have the car towed to our garage. We will meet up there," Girard said.

"I love it when a good plan comes together. Let me gather my things, and we will go. Excellent. Woo! So excited, let's go."

Hamilton and Parker clambered into a van with the Forensic team while Murphy and Girard took the Brawler. The drive flew by for Murphy. Girard talked about his family: his daughter Ruthie had another tooth coming in, and his grandfather Jean lost another tooth. Murphy kept her conversation to a minimum, and when she talked, it was about some roadside attraction they passed.

Girard and Murphy arrived to find the Forensic Unit, Hamilton, Parker, and two uniformed officers waiting. "The subject is still in the house," Officer Dubois said. "We saw her in the kitchen ten minutes ago."

Karen had been peaking out the window when the police pulled up and had her phone at the ready. She also activated the live feed camera on her laptop and said to her followers, "They are heeeeer." She pointed the computer camera down the hallway. With a few taps, her phone began a side-by-side live stream. The camera was aimed at her face.

There was a pounding at the door. She made a surprise face, then a pouty face at the camera. After the second knock, a voice boomed out, "Karen Baptiste, police. Come out. Karen Baptiste!"

"Here it goes, guys." Karen said to the camera. "The door is open! Come on in!"

"Police! Arrest warrant! Police! Show yourself!" Officer Giancarlo shouted. He turned the doorknob and pushed the door open.

"In the living room!" She could hear them scuttling down the hallway. A face appeared and disappeared in a split second. "These guys are so dramatic," she said.

"Karen Baptiste?" An officer finally appeared in full view, hand on his gun holster.

"Hi there. That's me," she replied with a smile.

"Ma'am, we have an arrest warrant for you. Please put your phone down," Dubois said as he held out his hand.

"I am streaming this."

"She has a laptop in the hallway," Giancarlo told Dubois.

"Sorry ma'am. I need your hands. Put down the phone."

Karen held her hands out in front of her just like she had seen on TV. She tilted her head and made another pouty face, waiting for the handcuffs. "Wah, they're going to arrest me," she said. Karen knew this arrest was pivotal. This was the day her online career finally took off. Separate from her husband, she could finally step into the spotlight.

"Come with me please, ma'am," Dubois said. He held out his hand and gestured. Karen stepped forward and let Dubois take the phone from her. She did not mind: the laptop was still streaming. He put the phone face down, but did not turn it off. It streamed the sound.

Dubois led Karen out of the house, followed by Giancarlo. Just before crossing the threshold, Karen turned around. She angled her face past Giancarlo, and said, "See you all soon!" Giancarlo looked behind him and realized she was talking to the laptop.

"Oh detective! Caitlin is it?"

"Yes, DI Murphy," she said as she followed them to the cruiser.

"What happens next?"

"Karen Baptiste, I am arresting you for the murder of Eugene Baptiste. You have the right to retain and instruct counsel without delay. You also have the right to free and immediate legal advice from duty counsel by making free telephone calls. Those phone numbers will be available at the station. Do you understand?"

"Yep."

"You also have the right to apply for legal assistance through the provincial legal aid program. Do you understand?"

"Yes, I sure do," she said.

"Karen Baptiste, you need not say anything. You have nothing to hope from any promise or favour and nothing to fear from any threat whether or not you say anything. Anything you do or say may be used as evidence. Do you understand?"

"Yes, ma'am."

Murphy wondered why she was taking this so lightheartedly. "You understand you have been arrested for murder?"

"Yeah. It won't stick," she said. "But I am going to have some amazing content."

"Okay, pat her down and take her in please," Murphy said as she stepped back.

"Ma'am? I think there is a laptop inside live streaming. She said she was streaming live, and she said goodbye to the laptop," Giancarlo said while Dubois frisked her. "Plus, her cell phone. We just put it down on the table, but she seemed to be on it when we arrived."

"Excellent. Thank you for letting me know," Murphy said. Karen had such a large ego she thought she could beat a murder rap. She probably thought she would be out before the sun set.

"Pasquale, Tillson, glad to see you," Murphy said to the Forensics team. "Giancarlo thinks there is a laptop in the hallway currently live streaming. And a cell phone. Turn them off without looking too goofy or you will go viral. Do a check for any other active cameras. She is a social media person. They could be anywhere. Have you read the warrant?"

"Yes, ma'am," Pasquale said.

"Great. Keep my team updated. Dubois! Giancarlo! Are either of you going to McKay's funeral today?"

"I am," Dubois said. Giancarlo shook his head.

"Dubois, please take Karen in and process her. Giancarlo, can you stay on scene?"

"Yes, ma'am, no problem," Giancarlo said.

"We are planning on attending the funeral for Sergeant McKay," Murphy said. "Dubois, if you leave now, you will have plenty of time to get there."

"We will leave at about 2:00, coming back maybe 3:00, 3:30. Do we have a tow truck coming to bring the car back to the police garage?"

"Yes, boss. It should be here any moment," Parker said.

"Okay, folks, let's get back to the office and into uniform. Then off to Fort Gilgam for the funeral," Murphy said.

The Forensic team headed to the Baptiste house after it was cleared for safety and used a scanner to locate cameras. Only the laptop and cell phones were active. Tillson shut them down, bagged them, and tagged them. "We are looking specifically for cell phones, which were on last time we checked. They may be hidden. Easiest way to find them is to call the numbers. We are also looking for knapsacks or bags, as well as any video cameras and digital recording devices. I want the computer taken, and any hard drives, disks, USB keys and anything that might have video on it," Murphy said as she watched the Forensics Unit begin. "Alright everyone, let's go."

The team took the Brawler back to the office. Dressed in their formal blues, the detectives headed to the funeral procession together. They parked a few streets away from Fort Gilgam and walked. A line of law enforcement stood on either side of the highway, stretching south down the road toward Kettering. The procession would come from that direction.

Down the highway, beyond the people who stood on the shoulders waiting, on a grassy slope, stood horses gazing with wonder. A red horse threw back its head and bolted away, back toward the open field and away from the procession. A raven cawed and landed on a tree branch nearby. It stared, dark-eyed and curious, about the long row of humans standing in the scorching sun.

"There," Girard whispered as the procession came into view. It was making its way along the highway. One person stood taller and straighter, and it sent a wave of movement along the line. The next and then the next stood taller and straighter, facing forward and standing still. Every eye was on the lead motorcycles and the long line of cars behind them. As the hearse carrying McKay's body drove past, each person raised their hand in a smart salute. Each hand stayed there until the cars carrying her husband and children, Chief, boss, and work partner, passed. One by one, the hands went up and one by one, the hands came down.

Murphy's hand snapped down to her side as she completed her salute and she, too, stood at attention. Then Girard's hand, Hamilton's, and Parker's hands, and the others, snapped down, sharply and firmly. Hand after hand saluted as the cars passed and turned into the driveway of Fort Gilgam. Everyone continued to stand at attention until the last of the cars passed and the motorcycle escorts brought up the rear. The bagpipes started as McKay arrived at the Fort. The mournful, supernatural sounds of Amazing Grace carried through the air as the entire band joined in.

Tears slowly wended their way down Murphy's face as she thought of all the times she had heard this haunting sound. Every death of someone she loved, and every End of Watch funeral she attended, was carried in the skirl, and in the skirl Murphy found sorrow and heartache.

The song ended and for a moment, Murphy could hear nothing, as if life itself had ended. But then, a breath later, the sounds of the world came roaring back. Girard handed her a tissue, and she gratefully took it to wipe her tears away. "I think it gets harder every time," Girard said as he put his hand on Murphy's back. "Let's go."

CHAPTER TWENTY-THREE

Karen Baptiste was processed and brought to Interview Room One. Lucas Canet was already waiting for her. She had texted Jonathan Haidt, said police were on their way, and she needed help. Canet was sent.

"How much do you know?" Karen asked.

Canet waved his hand. "I am not a criminal lawyer, and I won't be representing you if the case goes to trial. I want you to be very careful about what you say, okay? Once the police question you, your best defence is to say, 'no comment.' Nothing more, nothing less. We need to see what they have."

"Okay, but I did not hurt Eugene. Just so you know," Karen said. Canet nodded. "Have you seen my Shout Du Jour account?"

Karen and Canet talked for more than an hour in the room. Someone had come by to ask how they were, but that was it. Karen remarked on the plain white walls and said she was impressed. It was much nicer than what you saw on American true crime shows. She would mention that in her next video update.

At one point, Karen saw a camera in the corner of the ceiling and waved. She then waved at the observation mirror that took up almost half of one wall. In movies, the femme fatale would go to the mirror and fix her make-up while the detectives on the other side gawked.

Smiling, Karen got up from her seat and walked over to the mirror. She wished she had her purse and lipstick. She slowly and seductively turned around and fluffed her hair. Canet watched her impassively.

Murphy and Girard walked into the room, startling Karen. "Oh, do not let me stop you," Murphy said as she sat down at the table. Karen was disappointed. Not only was there no detective behind the mirror, one detective was that Murphy woman.

Karen smiled at Girard and sat down. "Nice to see a gentleman who waits for a lady to sit first."

"This is Adam Girard. I am Caitlin Murphy. Northshore Municipal Police Department. This is being recorded. And you are Mr. Canet, is that correct? Did Jonathan Haidt send you?"

"I am Lucas Canet, and who sent me is privileged information."

"Are you doing okay?" Murphy asked Karen.

"Yes, everyone had been very nice. A three star rating so far," Karen said, purposefully oblivious.

"You have some water, but do you need anything else? Would you like some food? I can probably get someone to get you some takeout or something," Murphy said.

"No, thank you Cate. I have plans for lunch," Karen said.

"It's Caitlin. May I call you Karen? Or would you prefer Ms. Baptiste?"

"Karen is fine," she said. She tapped her fingers on the table, and Murphy noticed the sign of her impatience.

"I just want to start off with some basic information, if you don't mind," Murphy said. She explained what her rights were and why she was there. She established the day's date and time. She stated Lucas Canet was present and acting as legal counsel, then moved on to Karen's name, age and address. "And who lives at 17 Hawthorne Drive with you?"

"It's just me and my husband. Eugene," Karen said.

"Do you understand you are under arrest?"

"Yes. For Eugene's murder, you said. Which I did not do," she said.

"Let's talk about Eugene. How long have you known each other?" Murphy asked a series of basic questions that Karen answered happily.

She and Eugene had met four years ago online. He began following her Shout Du Jour account and slid into her direct messages. After five months, they met in real life. Two months later, they got married. They lived with his grandmother until moving out on their own in May. They earned money with their Shout Du Jour videos, although Karen admitted it was not much. And Eugene worked at a concrete plant.

"What about videos that are on Jonathan Haidt's webs—?"

"Detective, is this relevant?" Canet interrupted.

"Yes, and do not interrupt me again or you are out. Got it?" Murphy asked.

"Can she do that?" Karen asked. Canet nodded yes. "Fine. Whatever. Eugene thought we could get a bigger following on Shout Du Jour if we did dramatic videos. I mean, Haidt's followers like fights and mixed martial arts and stuff," Karen said. Murphy write a note indicating Karen contradicted earlier information that she did not know about the videos.

"Did he film those videos before or after you turned to Jonathan for marriage counselling?"

Karen drew in a deep breath. "Before."

"When did you last see Eugene?"

Karen huffed slightly. "He left on Thursday last week. I guess maybe seven or eight in the morning," Karen said.

"Seven or eight on Thursday morning. How did he seem?" Murphy asked. "Did he seem okay?"

Murphy saw a glimmer of a smile cross Karen's face. "He was himself."

"Did you leave your home after he left on Thursday?" Murphy asked.

"No."

"Did he call you or text you?"

"No."

"Do you know where his phone is?"

"No."

"No idea where it is?"

"No. I said no. He always has his phone with him. In case he needs to film. If you don't have it, then I do not know where it is," Karen said.

"We have your phone, Karen."

"I know. I was live streaming when I got arrested. I bet I have a lot of activity now. People will follow me just to see what happens."

Girard looked at his own phone: he was holding it so he could feel the silent buzz of the messages as they came through. He turned and showed Murphy the text: 'Eugene and Charlie cell phones not located.'

"Karen, look at this," Murphy said as she spun the laptop around and played the video of the assault on Crystal Bradford. "Does this look familiar?"

The ghost of a smile on Karen's lips. "No. Never seen it before."

"Okay," Murphy said. This simple word seemed to reassure Karen that she could simply deny everything.

Murphy scrubbed the video back, stopped it, and pushed the laptop toward Karen again. "These shoes. The neon yellow ones." Instinctively, Karen tucked her feet under her chair. Murphy nodded to Girard, who left the room. "DSS Girard has left the room. You are wearing the same shoes as on the video." Canet looked under the table and rolled his eyes.

"No, they just look the same," she said in her defence.

Girard walked in with Maria Pasquale from Forensics. "Ma'am, may I have your shoes?" she asked.

"No way. The floor is dirty."

"Karen, you do not have a choice. Give her your shoes," Canet said. Karen petulantly kicked her neon yellow shoes off and put on the black foam slippers offered by Pasquale. Pasquale gathered up the shoes and bagged them for DNA testing and did a buccal swab.

"Do you know Crystal Bradford? Are you a friend of hers?"

"Never heard of her," Karen said.

"Okay. Let's leave that. So after Eugene left, you did not see him again?" Girard's phone buzzed. Forensics was back at the lab. They catalogued two tablets, one phone—phone number one—and a laptop. There were three video cameras, a hard drive and various storage media. He passed that information to Murphy in a whisper.

"Karen, did you see Eugene after he left home?" Murphy asked.

"He isn't such a gentleman after all," Karen said as she smiled sweetly and tilted her head at Girard. "Whispering is rude. And no. I. Did. Not. See. Him." She emphasized each word as if the detectives were stupid.

"You told me a moment ago, he always had his phone. But we found his phone in your home," Murphy said.

"So he forgot it."

Murphy flipped through her file and pulled out the documentation on the TechWave account. "Two phones for him, one for you. See? But the question is, why was his phone at your home? You said he had it with him."

"I guess he had one phone on him and left another phone at home," she said.

Canet leaned over to Karen and reminded her to say 'no comment'.

"Check this out. We have a map of all the cell towers showing those phones on Thursday. It shows his phone at Lac Sainte-Marine on Thursday morning." Murphy waited for it to sink in. Karen was so shallow she did not have to wait for long. "He had his phone with him when he died, but you have the phone at home after he died. We will find it, Karen. And phone number two was at Lac Sainte-Marine and now it's at your home, and we will find it."

Canet sat back and shook his head. "Say no comment," he advised.

Karen cried and accepted the tissues offered by Girard. Murphy silently gestured at Karen and mouthed 'real?' to Girard. He nodded; those were actual tears.

"Karen?" Girard said softly, "What happened?"

Karen looked down at her hands and tears ran down her cheeks. Between sobs, Karen explained. "Eugene was blackmailing people. Men. He was blackmailing men for years. Since before I met him. It was a great sex scam. He would hook up with straight guys, married men, for sex. But he filmed them and then threatened to post the video if they did not pay up."

"Karen, just say 'no comment.' Stop talking," Canet urged.

"Oh, you shut up. You don't even know!" she yelled at her lawyer. She turned to the detectives. "Jonathan Haidt is posting for him. You know why?" She turned to her lawyer. "Do you know why? Because Jonathan liked butt sex! Eugene filmed him doing it to Jonathan! That bastard preacher liked to take it up the butt!"

"Stop! Stop!" shouted Canet. Canet's mouth continued to open and shut without a sound. He was now in a position where he could not speak to Haidt about the murder without risking disbarment and possible jail time. Once she said that, the truth came flowing out. Canet tried unsuccessfully to quiet her, but he had no choice but to allow her to talk. He was beside himself. Haidt was paying for his legal services, but his legal obligations were to Karen, not Jonathan.

It took every ounce of control Murphy had not to burst out laughing. Imagine that, a homophobic preacher who liked to get fucked up the ass. It was almost a joke by itself.

Karen said that she and Eugene went to Haidt under the guise of marriage counselling. Eugene had talked about having thoughts about sex with men. Soon enough, Haidt wanted to consult only with Eugene. Ostensibly it was to cure him. In reality, they had sex. And Eugene secretly filmed every time.

In March, Eugene began blackmailing him. He threatened to tell Haidt's wife, Jessica, if he did not hand over $1,000. When Haidt easily made the payment, he upped the amount again and again. It was up to $10,000 by the time Eugene died.

"Did he do this with other men?" Murphy asked.

"Hell, yes. He was making a shit ton of money by the end. I never really saw it. He was saving up for a house. They are like two million dollars these days. And we only targ—" Karen stopped talking when she realized she implicated herself in the blackmail scheme.

"Who did you target? How much money?"

Karen sighed. "Well, I did not kill Eugene. And I never blackmailed anyone. I was not involved, except I was on the dating apps looking for guys. Married men with good jobs. I would look them up on the web to make sure they had money."

"And Jonathan had money?"

"All those preachers do. Church money," she said. Canet said nothing, staring at his hands and occasionally holding his breath.

"Was there anyone else recently?" Murphy asked.

"Yes. Some guy claimed to be the son of a Mohawk Chief. But I looked him up. No such Chief. What a loser," Karen said.

"Did you tell Eugene?"

"Yes. He went to meet him, anyway. He told me he was going to turn it into a fight video. So you see, it was not me. You need to look at Jonathan and that other guy, Charlie something," Karen said.

"Is the app on your phone? Can you give me the username and password so I can see the photo of the other guy?" Murphy asked.

"The app is called MonsterDick. The user ID is Ubap1, and the password is 11111," Karen said.

"Just say 'no comment'," he implored. This meant his firm had to set up a strict Chinese Wall, a formal process to ensure no information about the case was passed to anyone representing Haidt. Even after a new lawyer was hired, it would be complex. He let out an enormous sigh. He hoped Haidt would pay the bill.

Murphy laughed. "It's a little late for that. You have told us a lot of things, Karen. We need time to check them out. I am going to ask that you stay here for a little while longer. Recording paused." And with that, Murphy and Girard stepped out. They met Parker and Hamilton coming out of the observation room.

"Okay, let's head back to the atelier. Michael, call Mitch. We have a lot of IT forensic information to get through."

"Mitch, it's Michael from Homicide. Can you come up? We need some help to access an app on Karen's phone. And we need an update on what you have found on laptops and cameras."

"Are we sure, one hundred percent, that the phones are not in the house?" Murphy asked.

"Frankly, they could be anywhere. We have them pinging off a cell tower near the home, but they could be anywhere in the vicinity," Parker said.

"Damn. How did we get so convinced they were in her home? Is there another way to track them?"

"It depends on the apps, if the--"

"Hey there," Mitch said as she strode into the room. She was wearing a pair of latex gloves and carrying Karen's phone. "What are we looking for?"

"A dating app she and Eugene used. It's called MonsterDick, which frankly sounds like a really good name for a gay dating app. Anyway, the user ID is Ubap1, and the password is 11111," Murphy said.

Mitch browsed the phone, found the dating app, and signed in with Ubap1. She browsed through the app. "Thought so. Most of these are chest and dick photos. No faces. It will take time to figure out who is--"

"Stop. Go back," Girard said. "That one." He had stopped at a photograph of Charlie Belanger.

"Let's see. Charlie. Twenty-three. Son of Chief Samuel Belanger, Mohawks of the Lake Wakawaka."

Hamilton laughed. "Lake Wakawaka. That's a fake."

"How do you know that?" Parker asked.

Hamilton shrugged. "Why wouldn't I?"

"There are thousands of lakes," Parker said.

"There are less than 1,700," Hamilton said. "Do you not read up on local history? Kidding, kidding, I do not know. Let me look it up."

"Okay. We found Charlie," Murphy interrupted. "Can you find Jonathan Haidt?"

"That's him, right?" Mitch said, pointing to a photograph on the link board. "He's got his own folder on Eugene's laptop. Let me show you." She sat down at a desk, logged into the computer, and accessed a copy of the laptop's hard drive. When everyone gathered around her, she protested. "Whoa whoa. This is all home made porn. I can show you, but maybe you just want me to find a clear shot of his face?"

"If you have a clear image of his face that in some way ties him to Eugene, I want to see that. In the meantime, we now have Haidt as a blackmail victim. How thorough was our check on his alibi for the time of the murder?" Murphy asked.

"I checked with two people from the church who said he was at the church giving a sermon, and then stayed to provide Bible study," Parker said.

"Just two? Did they seem reliable?"

"Sure. Plus, he has actually posted the study on the Haidt website. This guy films almost everything he does," Parker said.

"I bet he doesn't put this on his website," Mitch joked. Everyone turned to see an image of Haidt's face twisted in sexual ecstasy, with Eugene clearly visible behind him.

"He was being blackmailed, and he can account for his whereabouts at the time of the murder. He could have hired someone."

"How are the forensics coming along?" Girard asked.

"The Forensic Unit has confirmed they have a female DNA profile from the t-shirt found on Eugene's face. Eugene's was on there, and no one else. There is his DNA on the pants, and they said that was it. No other DNA," Hamilton said.

"Hmm. Charlie said he kneed him in the face," Murphy said.

"I can get them to recheck the knee areas. But you aren't always going to find DNA," Girard said.

"Yes, please, do that. Remind me of the postmortem results?"

"He was slightly intoxicated. Died from blunt force trauma, likely from hitting his head on the rock. Found where he was killed. No defensive wounds, no signs of other DNA on the body."

Murphy sighed and looked at the link board. She really wanted Haidt to be a murderer, but it was clear he was not. It seemed less likely that Karen was the killer, and more likely Charlie was. The female DNA on the t-shirt could be a red herring. "Mitch, can you exactly locate either Eugene's or Charlie's phones? The cell tower says it's pinging right there. Right by

Karen's home. If it's at Karen's home, can we locate it exactly?" Murphy tapped on a red dot on the link board map.

"Did they have a Find My Phone app? Or a Google or Apple account?"

"Don't know. Is that the only way?"

"It's the easiest and most accurate," Mitch said. "Is that the tower? That tower has about a three kilometre radius. The next tower is here, right? Just about three kilometres away. So the phone could be anywhere in that radius. You are lucky. Some towers have a radius of over one hundred square kilometres."

"You know, if Eugene was blackmailing men in the community, it could have been any of them," Hamilton said.

"I know. Or any of their wives or girlfriends. We have the female DNA profile, and if it doesn't match Karen, it will be next to useless," Murphy grumbled.

"It might be useful once we know who to compare it against," Girard added.

"Mitch, can you do facial recognition on all the faces in all the videos? Maybe we can develop some kind of list of victims," Parker said.

"Easier than that. He named all the folders. Let...me...there you go!" The printer hummed.

"Just like that?" Murphy asked as she looked at the papers.

"Sure. Select all, right click, copy as path, paste, print," Mitch said. "He had their names as folder names."

"Wow. I did not know. Cleo, give this list a scan. See if anyone stands out. Okay. Back to Karen. Despite everything, do we have any physical evidence that puts her at the crime scene? GPS on her truck?"

"No boss, the truck did not leave the house," Parker said.

"GPS on the phone?"

"The Google Timeline shows she was at home," Mitch said.

Murphy did not know what the Google Timeline was, but if it said she was at home, it was not evidence that she was at Lac Sainte-Marine. "Okay. And we currently have zero evidence that she was involved in blackmail. Except the confession. Ahhh. Okay, Cleo, put together a package of what we know about the blackmail. Include all the names," she said as she handed over the papers. "Include Eugene's financials, Karen's. Track down what you can without notifying any potential victim. Karen said the blackmail has been going on for five years. That is before she met him."

"His father is in prison for cheque fraud. Maybe it was a father and son thing?" Hamilton asked.

"Not exactly a wholesome father and son bonding experience, but get details on that fraud and any other charges related to finances. Prepare a file for NSPD Major Crimes, Staff Sergeant Phillips. We need to talk to Haidt."

"Boss, we have dozens of other names here. Are we targeting him?" Girard asked.

"We have dozens of possible blackmail victims, and one whom we have reason to believe actually is a blackmail victim. Based on information provided by Karen. We do not think he committed the murder, but understanding how he and Eugene communicated about the payoff is vital. We did not see multiple payments received in Eugene's bank account, so there must be another way," Murphy said. "Unfortunately, Haidt could give us that vital information."

"Boss," Girard said as he sat down. "This could ruin Haidt's career. His life."

"That's the threat of blackmail, right? That is why some people pay. But, and let's not forget this, nothing Haidt did is criminal. He is the victim. And yes, I know victims do not always like to come forward, but we aren't prosecuting that crime. This is not about the blackmail, it is about murder.

If he can tell us something about how Eugene worked, then we might find the killer," Murphy said. "Having consensual adult sex with the same gender is not illegal in this country. It certainly has not ruined my life and career. If it ruins his, that's on him."

"You aren't wrong. I support you on this. I just want to make sure you are ready for the fallout," Girard said.

"Ready. We have to talk to Haidt. He might deny it until we play the video. Ha! Okay, maybe that's a little malicious. We can show him that photo Mitch printed first. Then play the video if he denies it."

"What about Karen?"

"She can go home. We have no evidence she was involved in criminal activity. No evidence yet. Michael, let her go, please."

CHAPTER TWENTY-FOUR

C anet walked into the parking lot and called his law partner, Pierre Binoche. "They have released Karen Baptiste without charge. I told her to find a new lawyer. Jonathan was being blackmailed."

"What? Why? Why didn't we know?" Binoche asked.

"Gay sex."

"This is not the first time someone has made that allegation," Binoche said.

"This is the first time it is tied to a murder. They have video."

"Oh no. Not good."

"Really not good," Canet said. "They will want to talk to him about Eugene's death," Canet said.

"Okay, let's control this. I will call Harvey Silverman. He can bring Jonathan in on our terms," Binoche said.

Murphy had notified both Shevchenko and Valencia before calling to ask Haidt to come in. Both warned her about protesters and physical attacks by his followers. Murphy did not care. He and his followers had already attacked her, her friends, her town, her people. She needed to talk with him to find out if, perhaps, he had hired someone to kill Eugene. Or perhaps he sent one of his crazies.

Murphy and her team sat in the atelier, throwing out theories. The suspect pool had grown exponentially. Haidt could have had a follower kill Eugene. Jessica Haidt could have done it. Crystal Bradford's alibi comprised nothing but text messages. Charlie Belanger was still in the frame. And anyone of the long list of other blackmail victims, and their wives and partners.

Murphy stared at the board, frustrated by what she was not seeing. "Do we have an exact location of the phone yet?"

"No. I have no Google account information for either Eugene or Charlie," Mitch said.

"And do we have any news on who gave Eugene the cashier's cheques?"

"Yes, his grandmother. The cheque said 'Merry Christmas' in the memo field," Hamilton said.

"Wow, nice gift grandma," Parker said.

"How is she getting that kind of money?" Murphy asked. "Someone dig up her financials. Maybe Eugene was blackm--" Murphy's phone rang. "This is DI Murphy," she said as she answered the phone.

"DI Murphy, nice to talk to you," said Silverman. Harvey Silverman was a well known and well respected criminal lawyer. Murphy was grateful he had never handled a homicide: his success rate for having charges reduced it dropped all together was high. "It is Harvey Silverman. I represent Jonathan Haidt. I understand you would like to speak with him."

"Yes, I have information that he might be able to help us with our investigation," Murphy said.

"Into Eugene Baptiste? Why?"

"He sought marriage counselling. I would like to have a better idea of the marriage."

"That is protected information, detective."

"No, it is not. As you well know, Ontario does not presume religious communications to be privileged. The Wigmore Criteria for confidentiality is essential to the maintenance of the relation between the parties. Eugene is deceased, there is no relationship anymore," Murphy said.

Silverman sighed. "Not many people understand the Wigmore Criteria."

"I'm Catholic. I know all about the Seal of Confession, from all sides."

Silverman laughed. "Fair enough. Jonathan will be there in an hour."

The entire team stood in the lobby of headquarters, looking out the window. Haidt had posted a message on his website that he was heading to NSPD headquarters to help with a homicide investigation. There were three reporters from mainstream media and a representative from Canadian Christian Liberties. Everyone was waiting for Haidt.

On the hour, Haidt and his lawyer arrived, parked and stood on the steps.

"Off the record, I hate this man," Murphy said.

"On the record, I hate this man," Girard said.

Murphy ensured her cross was hanging on the outside of her shirt. It would barely be noticed by anyone except Haidt. Haidt turned to resorts and smiled. Cameras raised up, and the reporters began asking their questions. Why are you here? Are you going to be arrested? What are the charges? Are you a murder suspect?

Murphy waited patiently while Haidt addressed the media, but he was wary. Finally, she put a smile on, walked outside, and said, "Mr. Haidt is here as a concerned, law-abiding citizen. He is assisting our investigation into the death of Mr. Eugene Baptiste. This investigation is in its early stages and a team of detectives is working to establish exactly what has happened. It is too early to comment on the exact nature of the incident."

As expected, Haidt vehemently protested, declaring his innocence. "The Northshore Police department has ulterior motives!" he shouted.

His lawyer asked him to be quiet. Silverman cleared his throat, waited for all the cameras to be on him, and spoke. "The allegations are based entirely on hearsay and falsehoods. Mr. Haidt rejected a woman's advances, and this is her revenge. She is a liar and a harlot. Mr. Haidt denies any allegations of assault, abuse, violence or homicide. He is a peaceful man of God."

Murphy tried hard not to laugh. She had to hand it to Haidt. He hired a good lawyer. "What are the allegations?" a reporter shouted.

"There are no allegations. He is not alleged to have done anything criminal," Murphy said. "I think Mr. Silverman misspoke. Sir, would you come with us, please," she said. Silverman murmured in Haidt's ear.

Haidt dramatically turned to the cameras. "I stand before you, a shattered man, robbed of justice! The accusations laid upon me are a grotesque perversion of truth. As a man of God, I have dedicated my life to righteousness and compassion. Yet the chains of deceit bind me, trying to crush my spirit. I am not so weak! I have the strength of the Lord in my soul. I will implore my faithful followers to rise in protest against this heinous miscarriage of justice! Let our voices echo like thunder, demanding truth and vindication. We will not be silenced! We will fight until the light of justice pierces through this darkness and restores my name to its rightful place! They are fools!

Murphy wanted to clap at his speech, but thought better of it. She wondered if the RCMP Anti-terrorism unit was watching. "Matthew 5:22. 'But I say to you that everyone who is angry with his brother will be liable to judgment; whoever insults his brother will be liable to the council; and whoever says, 'You fool! ' will be liable to the hell of fire.'"

"Don't you dare quote scripture to me," Haidt spat.

Haidt looked around and saw the cameras he had forgotten about in his rage. He knew that if this ever went to trial—and he was certain it would not—the footage of the Reverend cursing might sway the jury against him. He held his tongue.

In the station, the detectives brought Haidt into the elevator. Murphy was glad it was only one floor. She could smell Haidt's mouthwash and cheap body spray. It made her gag.

Haidt and Silverman were escorted into Interview Room Two. Silverman wanted a few moments alone with his client. Before leaving them, Murphy asked if they needed food or water. Both declined. Silverman advised Haidt to say 'no comment' to all but the basic questions. If he was in doubt, 'no comment'.

"You are being awfully nice to Haidt," Girard noted.

"So no one can say I treated him with prejudice," she said. "He is a victim."

"You say that with a straight face," Hamilton joked.

Everyone was ready. Murphy was eager, alive, thrilled to talk to Haidt. She would not be as rude and aggressive as she wanted to be, but she had a chance to humiliate him. Girard and Murphy walked into the interview room carrying a laptop and a file.

Parker, Hamilton, and Mitch gathered in the observation room, whispering excitedly, although there was no way Haidt could hear. They wanted to see the interview; they had to see the interview. One look at his face was enough to see that he was still confident, arrogant, sure. This was going to be satisfying. Parker started recording.

Murphy gave the standard opening. She specified the date and the people in the room. Then she sat in silence, waiting. It became more uncomfortable with every minute.

It was not the first time Murphy sat in silence in this room. It was not the first time Murphy sat quiet and still, waiting for the evil to pass by. She hid from imaginary and real gunmen as a child. She was an expert in silence. So far as her life permitted, anyway. Her life now was rarely quiet. But she enjoyed the silence.

Haidt, however, did not. He did not understand. Why was she was silent? He was full of fire. Ready to fight. But she sat there. Silently. Sitting there. He looked at Silverman. Silverman shrugged. Silverman looked at Girard. Girard shrugged.

They waited.

In the observation room, everyone shifted. They sought comfort and, unable to find it, shifted again.

"Wh--"

Hamilton held up a finger to silence Mitch. They waited.

Waited.

Waited.

Slowly, Haidt's face went from pink to red to purple as anger grew in him. He twitched a little and glared at Silverman. Haidt was beside himself, clenching and unclenching his fists. He breathed in deeply and let it out noisily. "What the hell is this? Am I here to answer questions? Let's get this over with."

"Oh, I'm sorry. I just wanted to give you a few minutes to calm yourself," Murphy said, feigning innocence. "Most people are so nervous about coming to a police station. I just wanted to give you a moment to compose yourself."

"It doesn't take ten minutes for me to compose myself," snapped Haidt.

"That was less than three minutes, but we will start. As a reminder, this is being recorded." Murphy enjoyed going through every piece of evidence against someone, watching them squirm and lie. But she had to play it differently with Haidt. There was no way she would do anything Silverman could criticize. Being in the room with Haidt made Murphy's stomach churn. She needed this, the community needed this.

"Are you comfortable, Mr. Haidt? Do you require water or food?"

He slammed his fists down on the table, and Silverman put his hands on Haidt's. "Detective Inspector Murphy, you have already asked that and we have already declined. Can you please get on with your questions?"

"Mr. Haidt, can you please tell me if and how you knew the deceased, Mr. Eugene Baptiste?" Murphy said.

"No comment."

"Mr. Haidt, we have spoken with Karen Baptiste who said you provided marital counselling. Mr. Silverman and I have already discussed it." She was delighted to see Haidt's glare.

"No comment."

"I understand you ministered to Eugene. You provided spiritual counselling. Or am I wrong? Do you provide spiritual or marriage counselling? Your website said you do."

"No comment," Haidt replied.

Murphy's phone buzzed. Cleo sent a text. 'One woman on Eugene's list.' Murphy's brow furrowed. "Excuse me."

Murphy left the room while Girard announced her absence.

"Cleo, what have you got for me?"

"Boss, there are fifty-four names in this list of folders. One is a woman. Evangeline Badeaux. Her folder had no videos, just encrypted PDF files. Mitch is working on decrypting them."

"Yes, and...?"

"Evangeline Badeaux is a French Canadian widow. There is not much in English. One husband drowned in the bathtub, the other fell in the shower. She went on trial for manslaughter for bathtub guy and was found not guilty." Hamilton said.

Murphy stared at her. "Yes, and...?"

"She was born in 1955, and had one daughter, Paula. I am uncertain, because the records are in French, but I think Evangeline Badeaux's current married name is Baptiste."

"Wh... Eugene was blackmailing his grandmother? About... A husband?"

"Maybe. I have contacted Language Services to request a French translator. I have Mitch searching records in Quebec and Ontario for more details," Hamilton said. "It might be nothing, but it might be something big."

"Shiiiit. Okay, keep going. Great. Find out more about Eugene's mother. Um... If it looks good, build a profile on Evie. Tomorrow is garbage day. Go to Evie's house and see if she had put out her garbage and pick it up. For DNA. Excellent work Cleo!"

Psyched, Murphy headed back to the Interview Room. "Okay, let me get right to the point. I do not believe you were involved with the death of Mr. Baptiste. I believe you were a victim of Mr. Baptiste." Murphy smoothly opened and turned the laptop toward Haidt. She tapped the Enter key, and the video of Haidt giving Eugene a blow job began.

Haidt slammed the laptop closed. "Lies! It's a fake!"

"For a lot of people, truth takes a back seat to perception—what truly counts is what people believe to be true. As a detective, the real truth is more important than what people believe. If you want people to believe this is fake, that's not my concern. My concern is, it is true. And he was blackmailing you. His wife told us he was blackmailing you. I want to know how. How was he blackmailing you?"

Haidt threw his head had back and let out a guttural scream. It was loud and forlorn and raw. "Bastard"

"Jonathan, Jonathan," Silverman said as he gripped his client's hands. He wanted Haidt to stop. "Jonathan, get control of yourself."

Haidt slammed his fists down on the table. "I lost control. One time."

"Many times," Murphy said.

"There are nine videos," Girard said.

"You are the victim." Murphy almost choked as she said the words. "I only need to know the process of blackmail."

Haidt's shoulders slumped. "He said he would show my wife if I did not give him $1,000. I gave him $1,000. Then it was $5,000, then $20,000. I had to dip into the Church funds. It would never stop. But I did not harm him."

"I do not think you did. How did you pay him?"

"He sent me messages on... A dating app."

"MonsterDick?"

Haidt turned bright red. "An app. He told me to drive to Bigwind Lake Provincial Park. There is a rest area. An older woman, dark hair, in a gold car, was waiting to take the money."

Murphy whispered to Girard, who exited from the room. "It was a gold four door, wasn't it?"

"Yes. A Lantern. I do not know who the woman was. But she was the one I had to pay every time."

Girard walked back in to the room and gave Murphy a piece of paper. She looked at it, then slid it face up toward Haidt. "Her?"

"Yes. Who is she?"

"Her name does not matter. You paid her cash?"

"Yes."

"Because Eugene was blackmailing you over some sex tapes?"

"Yes."

"Has anyone been in touch with you since Eugene died?"

"No."

"Okay, thank you for your cooperation, Mr. Haidt. Mr. Silverman. You are free to go."

Haidt panicked. "What about the videos? Are you going to release them?"

"Mr. Haidt! I am deeply offended that you think the NSPD, or I personally, would release sex tapes," Murphy said. Haidt let out a big breath, relieved. "They will come out at trial. This concludes the int--"

"Stop! No! I'm sure we can work something out," Haidt said.

"Jonathan, shut up. He did not mean that, detective," Silverman said.

"I understand. Gay sex tapes can be stressful. I mean, you were willing to pay to keep them quiet."

"They are not part of the murder, though," Silverman said.

"Maybe, maybe not. We will not release these unless it is part of the trial. But I do not know who has copies."

Haidt retched. Hot vomit flew across the table, splashing Girard. He shouted and backed away, but was too late. Red brown liquid splattered on his shirt.

"You can arrest them, can't you?" Silverman asked as he handed a handkerchief to Haidt.

"I am creating a file on the blackmail aspect for pursuit by Major Crimes," Murphy said. "We are done now. This room stinks."

Murphy escorted Haidt and Silverman out while Girard changed his clothes. Parker had a sweaty t-shirt from his morning run into the office. Disgusting, but not as disgusting as vomit. Girard accepted the offer.

Outside, reporters gathered quickly around Haidt and Silverman, who scurried silently to their car and fled.

In the atelier, Murphy was excited. "I cannot believe you caught this so quickly, Cleo!" she shouted.

"Score one for human eyes," Hamilton said.

"Absolutely. We would have potentially missed this if we relied too much on technology. Sorry Mitch." Murphy grabbed a marker and slammed it onto the map on the link board. The red splotch sat just over one kilometre away from Karen Baptiste's house.

"Evelyn fucking Baptiste. Okay. Let's get her. I want warrants and production orders. We need her finances, vehicle and property owner-ship information, social media presence, cell records, employment records. That retreat she runs. I want her business records. Cell phone location is primary. I want search warrants for the damn phone," Murphy said.

She could not believe this was another elderly murderer. Murphy had arrested Cornelius Price for murder less than three months ago, and he was in his eighties.

She ruminated over the conversation she had with Evie. Evie had almost immediately turned the conversation to the fight videos and blamed Eu-gene's wife. She appeared to live in near poverty but gave her grandson $120,000 for Christmas for one year, possibly more. She mentioned her daughter Paula, and that she was a widow.

"Give me information about the two dead husbands and the dead daughter."

"Is she a Black Widow?" Parker asked.

"Even more interesting, she could be a Family Annihilator," Hamilton said.

"This is going to take a while, isn't it?" Murphy asked.

"Yes, boss. Almost everything is closed for the evening," Girard said.

Murphy laughed. "Okay. Get done what you can, then go home. We will be back at it tomorrow."

Everyone promptly talked excitedly about the possibility of catching a female serial killer. "Female serial killers are as rare as a Red Revenue Small One Dollar stamp," Hamilton said.

"As rare as a mint Pikachu Illustrator card," said Parker.

"As rare as a quiet weekend," said Girard.

"Yeah, I got nothing," Murphy joked.

CHAPTER TWENTY-FIVE

Murphy tramped out the door and into the forest behind her home. She and the team had spent a week getting documentary evidence. They had worked with the Quebec government, the Sûreté du Québec and local Quebecois police departments. And of course the NSPD Interagency Liaison. Phone companies and banks had all provided information, but it was difficult to track. They had the help of a forensic accountant from the Canada Revenue Agency. It was one of the most administratively complex murders she had ever worked on. They were keeping the RCMP, OPP and CRA updated.

Murphy had spent restless nights thinking of arresting a serial killer. While she might only investigate one murder, she and her team could open the possibility of the murder of her daughter; it was within the NSPD jurisdiction.

She walked for a few minutes and then stopped. Murphy laid down on the brown leaf-covered forest floor. She put her hands behind her head and gazed up. The early morning breeze skipped through the tops of the trees, leaves fell, birds sang. The ground sloped gently away from her, away from the house. It headed quietly toward a rarely used dirt road. There was an old wooden bridge, wide enough for one car to pass at a time over the deep, fast stream. She had heard once there was good fishing there, if you were patient.

She spread her arms out and tried to make a dirt angel. She failed, and it did not matter. Murphy got up and quickly checked herself for ticks. "Those bastards," she murmured. She brushed off a beetle and looked around. It was quiet here. No, it wasn't. It was just a different noise. Different from the town. Different from the highway. Different from the house.

Her home would soon welcome another life, and she hated the idea. She knew, without having to hear it, that Del wanted Bob to move in. It would probably save his life, but Murphy hated the idea of another person in the house. Girard's comment the previous day at work, about his weekend, made her think. He lived in a house, with his mother and grandparents in a granny flat out back.

Murphy imagined having a stone cottage out here. Small, rustic. Maybe a wood-burning stove. A couple of parking spots, a paved driveway to make winter arrivals easier. She could visit the house for beers and bbq in the summer. She could learn how to fish the river and clean her catch. Maybe she could watch the leaves change in autumn and the snow fall in winter. And she could get up, go to work, catch killers and come home again to the quiet cottage.

She made her way back to the house, clothing damp from the dew on the ground. Once inside, she looked at herself in the mirror. She picked a leaf out of her cast and smiled. The team has worked hard. Now, it was time to catch a murderer.

Everyone was in the atelier, preparing to present their work. There was great anticipation in the air. Everyone wanted this project to come to fruition, to have a solid case against the murderer. Parker began. "Evelyn Baptiste, aka Evangeline Badeaux. Sixty-eight. She currently lives at 8925 Highway 3," Parker said. "She lives one and a half kilometres from the Baptiste home. She uses the same cell tower the phones were pinging off." Parker walked up to the link board and added Evie's drivers' license photograph.

"Eugene's and Charlie's phones are no longer active. Charlie's stopped pinging on Friday. Eugene's stopped on Monday," Mitch added. She was becoming a regular fixture in the atelier.

"She owns four properties other than the one on Highway 3: two in Toronto and two in Ottawa. Worth millions," Hamilton said. She had looked on the Ontario Land Registration System. "And she owns a gold four door Trurok Lantern," Hamilton said. Property listings and vehicle registration made their way on to the board.

"Her son-in-law, Alexander Baptiste, was arrested this year for cheque fraud. Mitch checked the trial transcripts," Parker said. "He got on the stand and said Evie was an accessory, but she was never charged."

"The translation of the trial transcript for the murder of Claude Wambergue, bathtub man, will take a month to arrive. Then it will go to Language Services. He died in Annecy, Quebec," Girard said. "Her first husband, Victor Badeaux, died forty years ago. Hit his head while in the shower. They ruled it accidental."

"Dr. Chen has forwarded the postmortem report on Paula Baptiste. She drowned in Dundar Lake six years ago. It was not deemed suspicious, but Dr. Chen will take another look," Hamilton said.

"She loves her water deaths, doesn't she?" Murphy noted.

"Evie banks with Royal. She has one personal and two business accounts: $1.5 million $3 million, and $7 million. I have transactions for one year for each account. She is making cash deposits through ATMS multiple times a week. Between $80,000 to $120,000 per month, in total," Girard said. Mitch let out a low whistle. "She is paying tax. Ostensibly, this is probably cash from her couple's retreat."

"Canada Revenue has been surveilling her for almost a week. Their investigator will tie any visitors to income," Hamilton said. "That's not for our investigation, but they have agreed to notify us if there is anything suspicious."

"So she is making at least one million dollars a year, mostly in cash. Which we think are blackmail payments. But she gives her grandson only $120,000 a year? I could see why he would be angry if he found out," Murphy said. "What about her business? Could it be legit at some level?"

"It has an Internet presence, but the reviews..." Mitch laughed. "Allegations that she filmed the couples having sex, then posted it to PornHub."

"For money?" Murphy asked.

"Yes, I think so," Mitch said.

"Any other social media?"

"Nothing under either name. We cannot find so much as a mention in Karen's Shout Du Jour account. Nothing on Haidt's website," Mitch said.

"Employment?"

"She seems to always have been independently wealthy. No employment outside her couple's retreat," Hamilton said.

"The pièce de résistance? Cell phones?"

Parker jumped up. "Ping ping ping, to Lac Sainte-Marine. Then ping ping ping, home. This is the same cell tower that shows Eugene's and Charlie's phones. The timing is perfect on the Thursday he died."

"I have arranged all the warrants and for her and her home. We could not get them for her other properties, as there is no indication they have anything to do with Eugene's death," Murphy said.

***

Murphy sat opposite Evie. She was confident that, unlike Haidt, Evie would not vomit. Murphy measured her up. Evie was conventionally feminine. Her hair was high and smelled strongly of hairspray. She wore sensible make-up: a bit of blush, a bit of concealer, a bit of lipstick. She had on a simple blouse and pants with white runners. It was hard to believe this woman might have annihilated her family over the years.

Yet somehow, she lacked the typical range of emotional intensities a wife, mother, and grandmother would usually have. She was the kind a woman who wanted no drama, no comedy, no tragedy, no passion. Evie made no connection with other human beings beyond her own needs. She was one dimensional, almost completely empty.

Murphy handed Evie a large-text version of her rights. "Can you read that?"

"Yes, why? Is this some kind of test?" Evie asked dismissively.

"No. I am going to read it out loud. You can read along." Murphy read out the rights of an arrested person and offered to let Evie use the telephone to contact a lawyer. She declined, saying she had no reason for a lawyer. She had done nothing wrong. Murphy introduced herself and stated the time and date. Girard also introduced himself. The interview was being video recorded.

"I met you both earlier," Evie said.

"That's right. We told you, we are police officers."

"Yes."

Murphy noticed she had a flat affect. She was drawn and emotionless. Evie had been through an interrogation before, but unfortunately, Murphy still did not have English transcripts. She did not know what worked or did not work for the first murder charges against Evie.

"You have a cell phone, right?"

"Yes, you took it."

"Do you ever lend your phone out to people? Like let a stranger use it? Or give it to a friend for the day?" Murphy asked. She was flipping through some papers in a folder, looking up occasionally at Evie.

"No. I don't like other people's germs. I lent my phone out once a few years ago. There was a gross oily film from the person's face. Never again."

"I hear you on that one," Girard said.

"When did your grandson Eugene start living with you?" Murphy asked.

"Seven or eight years ago. He and his mother moved in. But it got cramped pretty quickly."

"Right, Paula lived with you. And what happened to her?" Murphy asked.

"Drowned."

"But you kept Eugene with you."

"Yes. He was good. Did what he was told. Then Karen arrived. Put ideas into Eugene's head," Evie said. "Did you speak with her?" Evie felt like every word she spoke was falling from her lips, like they would just keep falling and gather on the floor.

"Yes, we did. She gave us some very interesting information. She said Eugene was blackmailing men. We have some of their names," Murphy said. She kept her demeanour low and steady. She wanted nothing accusatory in her voice. "Did you see Eugene much after he moved out?"

"No. You'd think your grandson could visit since he lived just down the street, but no. I only saw him, maybe once a month. For dinner. Him and that woman," Evie said.

"In your home?"

"No. Restaurants. Once he moved out, he never stepped foot in my house again. Not him. Not his wife."

"Did you go to their place to visit?"

"She can't cook."

"Maybe for tea?"

Evie scoffed. "Never set foot in that place."

"Okay. When was the last time you saw Eugene?" Murphy asked. Murphy wondered if Evie preferred people to come to her. Like the couples she filmed fucking. Were they the people she cared about? Her true family? Likely, they were just money and entertainment.

"Maybe a week before he died. Maybe two. I'm not sure."

"Maybe a week. Okay. He was found at Lac Sainte-Marine. Do you know the place?"

"No. Never heard of it."

"So you have never been?"

Evie finally moved: she shook her head slightly. "Never."

"Okay. Did you support Eugene and Karen financially? Give them gifts of money, maybe help out a bit?"

"Yes. Once a year, I would give them $120,000. Ungrateful. They did not care."

"Where did you go to give them money?" Murphy asked. Evie had said they never set foot in her home after leaving, and she never went to their place. She hoped to catch Evie in a lie.

"Goddamn Tim Hortons. I hated every minute of it. Both Eugene and Karen would do whatever they wanted. Film themselves, take selfies. They would do whatever they wanted. They never talked to me. Never asked me how I was, or if I needed help. Brats. He was a damn brat."

"They did not thank you for the money?"

"No. Not even in those stupid viral video things they did. Not once."

"You gave them a lot of money. How do you get that much money?"

"Here and there. The retreat. The couple's retreat. I pay my taxes, you know. It is all legit," Evie said.

"When did you last see Eugene?"

"About a week before he died."

"Evie, did you know cell phones track where you go? Every place you go? And we can call that up on a map to see where you were on what day at what time," Murphy said.

"Goddamn police state."

"You were with Eugene when he died, weren't you? Evie? The cell phone tells us."

"Goddamn surveillance state."

"What happened? What happened with Eugene, Evie?"

"He slipped."

"Okay. He slipped."

"I didn't want him getting hurt."

"But he got hurt, Evie. He got hurt bad."

"I don't think I was there."

"Be honest with me Evie. About everything. I do not want to keep going over and over this with you. I feel you are finally doing the right thing. You have got to be honest with me about everything. While we have been in here, you know people are going through your house," Murphy said.

"Goddamn police state."

"Not just police, Evie. Canada Revenue is going through your books, your taxes, looking for undeclared cash in your home. The RCMP knows about the blackmail."

"Blackmail."

"We know about the blackmail, Evie. I know how you used Eugene to blackmail men. I know you got a lot more money than Eugene realized. Did he figure it out? Be honest."

"He was too damn stupid. That boy thought I was a goddamn beginner. He underestimated me," Evie said. The ugliness of her life was opening up before her, and she did not want to look into the chasm.

"No, he did not. He knew, actually. He knew about Paula. He knew about Claude. He knew about Victor," Murphy said.

"Never heard of them."

"Evie. You are lying. Paula was your daughter. Drowned. Claude was your husband. Drowned. Victor was your husband. Hit his head in the shower. Do you know how I know? Eugene had a folder with your name on it. Evangeline Badeaux."

"Death is never that far from my thoughts." Evie slumped forward, her face in her hands. She did not want to talk anymore. She knew her words were piling up on the floor, to be swept up by the detectives and sorted out like a puzzle.

"It is over, Evie. The blackmail and the deaths and the money. We know about it all. You had millions, Evie. You had valuable real estate holdings. Why did you have to keep going?"

"I still have decades of life ahead of me," Evie said. "I needed the money. There are all kinds of things that can go wrong in your life."

"You needed millions?"

"Two million dollars will barely buy a house in Toronto. A shit house. Four or five will get you something nice, in a nice neighbourhood. I do not have all that much."

"And Eugene was dipping into that pot of money?"

"It was not about the money so much. It was about hating that little shit. I hated his mother. I hated his father. I hated his wife. I hated him. So. Much."

"Why did you hate him?"

"To be honest, he would not grow up. He would throw things, have these tantrums. Adults should not act like babies. No tantrums. No acting out. No hitting people. That's what children do."

"Did you see him hit that man at Lac Sainte-Marine?"

"A knee right in the face. For no reason. I had to talk to him."

"Did you know the man?"

"No. It was his next target. Why would you hit your next target? That ruins the game. I just had enough of his bullshit, you know?"

"What happened?"

"He kneed that guy in the face. You are only getting money if they suck your dick. You aren't getting any money from someone you bashed in the face. Eugene ruined a perfectly good mark for a stupid fight video. They bring in one, maybe two hundred dollars. Not tens of thousands. I got so mad I started yelling at him. He ruined it when the guy ran. Thousand of dollars, gone, just like that." She was a far cry from the modest woman they had met earlier. Her acting skills were excellent and probably saved her during her first murder trial.

"So you pushed him?"

"There is a time and a place for everything."

"So you pushed him?" Murphy asked.

"I never touched him. He slipped. And you can't prove otherwise."

"He hit his head. It seems like after he hit his head, you waited around. What were you waiting for?"

Evie remained silent. She tried unsuccessfully to stifle a yawn.

"You waited until he passed, and then you covered his face. Did you call for help? Did you call 911? Did you check for a pulse?"

"Stupid. I needed to know if he was dead. I thought I could see the t-shirt rise and fall with his breath."

"You covered his face to see his breath?"

"Yes."

"Did you call 911?"

"Yes." Evie wondered when this would be over. She wanted it to be over. She wanted a nap.

"From Lac Sainte-Marine?"

"No. I went to find a pay phone. My cell phone had no service."

"Yes, it did. That's how we know you were there. It pinged off a cell tower. That means you had service. So you checked to make sure that he was dead. Then you went to find a pay phone."

"He slipped."

"Do you know why you didn't call right away, Evie? I think I know. He was a fuckup. You got to where you were pulling your hair out, trying to get him to do the job right. You were frustrated."

"I did not know what else to do. He slipped and fell and hit his head. I called 911 just like you are supposed to."

"Be honest."

"I am."

"You delayed calling 911."

"I never said I called right away, just that I called." She yawned again. This was exhausting.

"Did you think that eventually after everybody died off, Victor and Claude and Paula and Eugene, they all died in similar ways. All with water. Did you think we might show up to talk to you? Or were you pretty confident?"

"I did not think I would get caught. And even if you showed up, after Claude, I knew I could get off. Even Alexander's testimony on cheque fraud did not touch me. But I have double jeopardy."

"Autrefois acquit."

"Whatever. Eugene slipped and fell on his own and you cannot prove otherwise. You cannot charge me with murder."

"I can. Criminal negligence causing death is culpable homicide. Subsection 222(5)(b) of the Criminal Code of Canada covers it. You watched him die instead of helping in even the smallest way. You made sure he was dead before you left his body."

"Bullshit police state. I want some water now."

"It's right there. Get it yourself," Murphy replied. She knew she would get nothing more from Evie. She was always going to deny pushing him, deny killing him. Murphy signalled for a uniformed officer and then she and Girard left the room.

CHAPTER TWENTY-SIX

E veryone gathered in the atelier. There was a palpable excitement as everyone discussed the evidence and possible charges. Supt. Shevchenko had arranged for representatives from multiple police divisions and government agencies to attend.

"As you all know, Evangeline Baptiste has been arrested for the murder of her grandson, Eugene Baptiste. We expect multiple charges raising from the investigation by DI Murphy and her team. Murphy?"

"Thank you sir. Parker? Please begin."

"Yes, boss. A blue knapsack was found in a closet In Evie's home. Inside was a video camera and two cell phones. They confirmed the one phone that still had power appeared to belong to Eugene Baptiste. They will update us on the other items later," Parker said. He spoke quickly, knowing everyone was eager to have their say.

"I will probably be involved in that," Mitch said. She was delighted to have found more work worthy of her IT skills.

"Boss, they have done a preliminary DNA on the buccal swab we took when she arrived. It matches the touch DNA on the t-shirt," Hamilton said. Parker held up his hand and Hamilton gave him a high five.

"We found bank statements for accounts we were previously unaware of," said Aravind Joshi from Canada Revenue. "We will continue pursuing the financial aspects. Great job everyone." The usually staid man gave two thumbs up and a smile.

"Absolutely. If she somehow slips out of the murder charge, you can keep her in prison," Murphy said.

"We will be pursuing her for extortion," Henry Phillips said. He and the Major Crimes team were eager to get involved in what was going to be a case of some renown. There were already rumours circulating about the names of the men on the list.

"Will you consider Karen Baptiste in that investigation?"

"Yes. She said she was involved in finding the victims," Phillips said. "We will go after everyone we can, every instance we can." The investigation might justify additional staff for Major Crimes. It would also lead to an increased solve rate percentage.

"And we will have another look into the death of Paula Baptiste. People, we have a lot of work ahead of us. A year's worth, at least. I have to thank all of you for your help with this," Murphy said.

She applauded, and everyone in the room joined in. There were shouts of 'great job' and 'can't wait.' It took twenty minutes for people to stop chatting, theorizing and analyzing. Visitors began filing out.

Supt. Shevchenko spoke with Chief Valencia. Murphy spoke with the Media Relations people to provide information for a press release. The Chief would speak briefly at a press conference that night.

When only the team and Mitch remained in the office, Murphy suggested a late dinner. It was worthy of celebrating.

"Oh, can we go to Kamado's? Can we go there?" Parker asked. "They have such great burgers," he said. "Can we go to Kamado's?"

"Michael, you sound like a six-year-old who wants to get ice cream," Murphy joked.

"They sell ice cream there. Made on site. It's so good. Has everyone tried Kamados?"

"Yes," Girard said, "My family and I go maybe once a month."

"Not me, never tried it," Hamilton said.

"It's world famous," Mitch said.

"Oh, you are in for such a treat. The burgers are soooo good," Parker said. "Geez, I think I'm drooling already. They have a great mushroom burger you will love, Cleo."

"Okay. If anyone needs a ride, you can come with me. Let's meet there," Murphy said.

In fifteen minutes, they were standing in the long outdoor line for Kamado's. Kamado was an iconic hamburger-shaped building, where, on a long weekend during the summer, they served hundreds of people a day. They had a large parking lot to accommodate the increased traffic during the summer. The spacious back yard had outdoor seating and a play area for children. There was a foodie influencers tent where people could take photos, shoot videos and livestream their meals.

"Yeah, I don't get that," Girard said, eyeing the tent. "I mean, the food here is good, but I don't know if it's that good. Like, to eat it on the internet? Who would watch that?" Parker, Mitch, and Hamilton laughed. "What? Have you guys watched online eating?"

"Not me," Murphy said.

"It can be food reviews, or a cooking show. There are cooking shows on television. This isn't much different," Hamilton said.

"Unless it's mukbang, and then it's like porn," Mitch added. That made both Parker and Hamilton burst out laughing while Girard and Murphy exchanged confused looks.

The line moved along quickly. Murphy ordered the sirloin burger without fries while Parker had the sirloin burger with fries and onion rings. Girard and Mitch ordered elk burgers and Hamilton opted for a Portobello mushroom burger with extra mustard. Sitting at a picnic table away from the influencer tent, the team ate. Some yearned for beer and wine rather than the iced lemonade in their glasses. "An ice-cold Moosehead," Parker said.

"A glass of Rombauer zin. Mmm, fruits with clove and white pepper," Hamilton said. "Perfection."

"No no," Girard said. "A club soda with a twist of lemon. They should serve that here. It is simple and classy."

"Same " Mitch said.

"I'll take all of them," Murphy laughed.

They ate and talked about their food. The Portobello mushroom burger, slathered in Worcestershire mayo and crackly slaw, was succulent. Hamilton held up the burger to show where the juice had slowly dripped out of the mushroom and into the bun. She wiped her chin for emphasis. The sirloin burgers swelled with toppings. Manchego, wood ear mushrooms, green chiles, caramelized onions and ketchup chutney oozed out from between the buns with every bite. Havarti cheese seeped out from under the bun of the elk burgers. House-made maple bacon jam, arugula and crispy onion rings completed the symphony. When Mitch slowly bit down into her burger, the onion rings crunched loudly.

With hunger satisfied and the last of the tangy lemonade gone, the team headed out. Hamilton left first, revving her motorcycle and speeding out onto the highway. Girard took Mitch and Parker, since they all lived north of Kamado's. Murphy lived south. After everyone left, she got into her Brawler and left.

Murphy headed to St. Mary's Catholic church to think, perhaps talk with the priest. Both homicides had strong religious influences thanks to Haidt, as did the riot, and she found it unnerving. It was fake faith, and she needed something real. It saddened her that none of the established churches came out against the preacher's hateful actions.

Murphy walked up the marble staircase to the main entrance: two massive wooden doors with black wrought iron handles, hinges and latches. Even though one door was open, they heightened the sense of the power and permanence of the church. She stood at the threshold, looking in.

Dark wooden pews stood row upon row like soldiers in the wars of the soul. The stain glass windows afforded little light inside, but Murphy could make out the Stations of the Cross along both walls. She knew them by heart. The design on the marble floor enticed the churchgoers in. It took Murphy's eye to where all the attention was to be given. The massive altar was made of white marble and featured a sculpture of two angels carrying the bloody body of Christ. Above it was inscribed *ego sum via et veritas et vita.*

Murphy's heart was pounding madly, and she felt sick. She both loved and hated being here, but soon she turned away. Just inside was the donation box, in case you missed the basket passed around during the service, and didn't scan the QR donation code stickers to the pew. Murphy reached up and unclasped her gold cross. She dropped it in the box. After walking back down the steps uneasily, she drove off. She did not look back. The knot in her stomach untied itself and her jaw unclenched.

Murphy pulled over, took out her personal phone, and dialled. She had faith, just not in the church.

"I'd really like to see you tonight."